ANOTHER
WORLD'S KRONICLES
NOMADIC WARRIORS

To Jewel
I would Like
To thank you for
the Show of Support

ANOTHER WORLD'S KRONICLES NOMADIC WARRIORS

THE AGE OF GIANTS
BOOK I

D. R. SIMPSON

To order additional copies of this book, contact:
Xlibris
1-888-795-4274
www.Xlibris.com
Orders@Xlibris.com
767531

DEDICATION

In dedication to my mother, Julia M, Simpson a God-fearing Christian woman and lover of Christ whom at the age of ninety has provided that light for me to follow as she continued to show me unwavering love and support. This has been an inspiration for me my entire life, and all of my endeavors, encouraging me to follow my dreams. She is responsible for me in being the man that I have become. First as a D.C. firefighter and now as a published author and writer. She is someone that is always in my corner and I just want to say, Thank you "I love you"! Mom for always being there and for all you have done.

ACKNOWLEDGEMENTS

Over the years from the pages of my imagination I was not only able to translate my vision through my illustrations and designs but also with the creation of the figurines specifically made for this book which helped to bring this story to life. This helped inspired me to also turn them into a literary expression from my mind.

I would also like to thank my wife, children, family and friends for encouraging me to display my drawings and designs for this my first literary work that make up the cover as well as any and all drawings that are displayed in the interior of this novel. Also I would like to acknowledge Xlibris, for the editing, organization, marketing and the distribution of this book.

CONTENTS

PROLOGUE

IT WAS WRITTEN that in the beginning, God created the heavens and the earth and all living creatures that dwelled upon it. There he created man in his own image, where he was to have dominion over all that lived. But there was another world—a distant one not yet spoken of. Like earth, it, too, was teeming with life and was home to mankind. But unlike earth, man's role was not so clearly defined. These are their stories and their tales. This is *Another World's Chronicles*.

On the far side of the universe, in the spiral galaxy Alexius, lay the planet Tyrus, the realm of the Living Light. It was a strange and mysterious world, a vast and untamed home to both fierce and mighty creatures where some were beyond the realm of imagination.

Among them was man, who was constantly struggling to find his place in this savage world. Divided, man remained in constant warfare. Dwarfed by many of these creatures that surrounded him, his numbers began to dwindle, leaving him vulnerable to these powerful creatures that sought to prey on him.

There were also other manlike species living throughout the land. Some living beside him in peace, while others were barbaric and brutish, constantly seeking to dominate him, driving him farther into the wilds. Facing annihilation and overwhelming odds, man began to band together, putting differences aside.

It was during this time that man learned their strength were in their numbers, and they began building trust, which was absent in the beginning. Together they fashioned armor and weapons, honing their skills and effectively using them. Now capable of dominating these great beasts, man's numbers once again began to grow, carving out their place among these creatures.

The rise of man had now begun. As they began to blossom, they built a mighty civilization, driving these great beasts into the wilds and the remote places. Even the manlike brutes that once dominated man were driven beyond the boundaries of civilization.

No longer huddled together in small tribes, man now ruled the land. Over the centuries, they built great cities throughout the land, finally becoming united. This was their time—the golden age of man on Tyrus.

While man flourished, there was another struggle about to unfold between the forces of the realm of the Living Light and that of the realm of the Darkness. Unknown to all were four angelic-like beings called the Elders of the Living Light.

Draped in white robes, having faces without features, and having an aurora of light illuminating around each with the reminiscence of a star in its full glory, these immortals were charged by God to protect the realm of the Living Light.

Also given to them was a scepter of immense power called the scepter of the light. Forged from the essence of stars, it was a golden staff with a circle on its end, radiating energy at its center with the brightness of a star. Within it contained the most powerful force in the universe capable of opening and closing portals to other dimensions and capable of desolating anything within its path.

Its power was so great only an immortal with the power of the light within them could wield this unstoppable force. Never were these elders to interfere with the natural order of life, but they were to guard against supernatural forces from a darker dimension called the realm of the Darkness. Each elder sat in his or her temple and meditated atop the highest mountains on Tyrus named the Mighty Brims.

Both isolated and remote, these four snowcapped ranges aligned the four corners of the planet, resembling waves rising from the depth of the ocean. Its peaks curled into the clouds, giving the appearance of cresting waves breaking along an ocean shore.

When struck by the light of the twin suns, its rocky terrain gradually turned into blue the closer the sun came to its peaks. Towering high above all other mountains, there wasn't a place on the planet where the Mighty Brims could not be seen.

Ruling the dark realm were four shadowy figures having the appearance of hooded shadows, each having flaming eyes of different colors that pierced the darkness, like flickering flames. They desired to cross over into the light, transforming this world to the likeness of their own. Relentlessly they searched until they finally found a way.

CHAPTER 1

Of Smoke, Fire, and Giants

P LOWING THROUGH UNTILLED fields, two ram-headed steeds—with their curved horns pointing downward, separating the tall grass—were guided by their riders as they pressed at full speed toward the fortress city of Dioria, the king's city and capital of the Westland Kingdom. Behind them, a raging inferno of smoke and flame engulfed the landscape, destroying everything in its path.

Both were driven by fear and desperation, pushing their steeds to the measure of their limits. As fast as their legs could carry them, they gave a warning to every villager in their path, shouting, "Drop all that you are carrying! Flee for your lives! Death lies at our heels! Time is fleeting!"

High atop the city walls stood King Odarr of the Westland Kingdom, donning his armor alongside his archers aligning the fortress walls as they stood ready, awaiting his orders.

Also beside him stood his most trusted commander and confidant, General Ultur. They watched in the distance as the countryside was being turned into an inferno with heat so intense it was like looking into a fueled furnace. This was more than just a fire that they were preparing for; it was what had fueled it.

Hundreds poured into the city gates from the countryside for protection as the two riders rapidly approached the gates, leaving a trail of dust behind them. With what the king and his army were witnessing, a report was not needed. What fueled the fire had now come into fruition.

Distorted by the heat rising from the ground, eight creatures made of smoke and flames, equaling the height of the city's fifty-foot walls, steadily approached. Their shape and features were like warriors wrapped in an armor of blackened smoke from their head to legs, which resembled pillars of fire swirling together.

Ultur turned to the king and said, "What manner of demons do we face, and from whence did they come?"

"Only God knows the answer," the king replied. "I pray that our walls will protect us."

Everyone who was there witnessing these events unfold could not help but tremble at the sight of what was moving toward them.

From the bravest of warriors to the weakest, even the king himself, no one had ever seen creatures such as these. Fear moved through the ranks of all the warriors, along with those they were sworn to protect.

With the stench of sulfur filling the air, it intensified the closer they got to the city. When they roared, their voice was like thunder shaking the foundation of buildings well within the city itself. The smoke surrounding them was so thick that nothing could be seen beyond them as it filtered between the cracks and crevasses of the most hidden and secure places within the city of Dioria.

Many scurried to find whatever they could to cover their faces, filtering the foul smell that left everyone gasping for what little air there was that remained breathable. Their steps were steady, long, and gaping with each move closer toward the city fortress, releasing heat so intense they set structures aflame, even those that were far beyond their reach.

With arms resembling swords made of fire, they swept them forward, clearing a path and laying waste to everything that stood in their way. The two riders finally reached the city, making their way through the panicking crowds until they reached the steps to where the king awaited.

Unable to wait any longer, King Odarr looked at the gatekeeper with a heavy heart and shouted, "Close the gate! We can wait no longer or we all shall perish, for those creatures are now upon us. We must leave those that have yet to enter to their fate and those behind the walls to theirs."

With the closing of the gates, screams and cries of those left outside became muffled. Some even attempted to squeeze through the gates as they were closing before being crushed by them. Many were left scratching and attempting to scale the walls in a futile attempt to get in.

They were left with no other option but to run in another direction, but it was now too late. The fire was now upon them all. Those who were trapped outside the walls between the flame and stone were incinerated.

Now but moments away from the outer wall, the heat generated by these creatures was so intense soldiers hid behind shields, stone walls, and whatever they could to protect themselves from the heat. Finally reaching the king, with Ultur standing at his side, the riders began to tell him all that they had seen. Beyond what was obvious, they had more to reveal to him.

One of the riders began to speak. With sweat pouring down his face, he began to tell the king, "There was another peril that lay beyond the flames—" Before he could finish his words, the fiery creatures simultaneously roared.

It was so loud it shook the foundation of the city walls, causing many that held their position to fall, including the two messengers standing in front of both the king and his commander.

While attempting to speak, a crack streamed along the walkway, separating the two men from the king, causing that portion of the wall where they stood to crumble beneath their feet, sending them, along with the others, tumbling to their deaths.

Had his general not grabbed hold of the king, he would have joined them in death. Odarr then turned to his bowmen and shouted, "Release your arrows and stones from their bows and slings!"

At that moment, hundreds of arrows were released, along with boulders of all shapes and sizes. But their arrows burst in flames in midflight and turned into ashes, blowing in the wind, before reaching any of the creatures. Stones were liquefied, regardless of size, upon contact.

Whatever these creatures were, they were not of this world. No longer able to hold their position, King Odarr turned to Ultur and said, "We must give way."

Following the king's command, Ultur turned and shouted, "Leave the wall, and join the ranks of those that stand ready within the courtyard!"

Without hesitation, those who remained abandoned their post, following the king's command. Unsure of what was to follow, they began to fall within ranks as they stood ready. It was their hope that the walls would hold, but they didn't have to wait long for that answer. That time was now over. The creatures were now standing within reach of the walls.

One after the other, each of these smoked warriors took their place along the outer walls. Rearing back their fiery swords, they let out another roar and struck the wall simultaneously, which exploded on contact and sent stones shooting like stars. Sending them with such force, the stones penetrated stone buildings that were in the farthest parts of the city, killing rows of men that stood ready to defend their homeland.

The sheer force of the concussion collapsed many of the buildings, killing hundreds in the process. Those who were slow to leave their post were killed instantly. Hundreds lay dead under the rubble, while others were deafened by the blast.

With the walls now laid to waste, the only barrier between these fiery creatures and the Westland army was the rubble of a once-mighty wall of stone.

The king stood firm, along with his general by his side, and raised his sword, shouting, "Prepare for glory, and defend that which you love to the last! For God has a place for each of us if we shall fall with grace."

Though fear ran rapid through their ranks, each warrior prepared for the worst. And though the outcome appeared to be inevitable, they found comfort in the words of their king. Following their king's example, each warrior raised their swords high in the air and roared like savages ready to die in defense. To their surprise, each of these creatures turned into lit cinders of ash and smoke as they dissolved harmlessly, vanishing into thin air.

The smoke left in their wake was so dark it blacked out the rays of the dual suns above them. The people could barely see their hands, which were a few inches from their faces. Nearly all gagged and puked, trying to catch their breath.

Despite this, they held their ground, not knowing whether it was over or if these creatures would reappear. As the smoke dissipated, the king slowly stepped forward, along with several of his men who surrounded him.

Cautiously they moved toward the wall, stepping over the bodies of many of the soldiers killed by the debris that was scattered around them. All remained quiet while the wind slowly began to pick up, relieving them from the heat, smoke, and dust that was strangling them.

When the air began to clear, it revealed all the death and destruction left by these creatures.

The questions that now remained were what they were and why they came. Ultur looked at the king and asked why. Odarr had no answer; he could only ponder while hearing moans and lamentations from those who were injured and from those who had lost their loved ones in return.

As the king stood in silence, contemplating what had happened and why, Ultur's expression changed, sensing that something was wrong, and he asked, "Did you hear a sound?"

The king looked at him and replied, "No, I heard nothing."

The ground then began to tremble as Ultur said, "Look at the ground." At that moment, a pebble began dancing across the ground, in tune with the thumping sound that ensued it. The king then replied, "Yes, I feel it, as well as the rumbling of a distant storm."

Looking toward the sky, General Ultur said, "Beyond the fading smoke, the skies are clear." Everyone was now confused by what was happening. Each one looked around and wondered what was the source.

The dust had now settled and the smoke had cleared when someone shouted, "Look beyond the rubble!"

Odarr then shouted, "Stand ready!" Looking in disbelief, he said, "What manner of army is this?"

General Ultur then shouted, "Giants!"

Fast approaching was an army of thousands, each standing over nine feet tall with their war beast being a foot taller. As the smoke lifted, it revealed the true horror of what they faced.

Liboroxes they were called, having teeth like that of a lion, tusks like that of a boar, and horns like that of ox. Their bodies resembled two of the beasts, equipped with claws to the front and with hooves to the rear. They had a ravenous appetite to go along with their appearances.

Their riders were wielding huge axes and swords. Their bowmen shot arrows resembling spears. They were massive with reddish-brown skin and heavy black whiskers covering the sides of their face and chin.

They had an underbite, revealing two sharp upward teeth and a mouth that could swallow a man's head whole. These hairy beastmen were of a race of nomadic giants called Troguares. This was man's first encounter with creatures such as these. No one had ever seen the likes of them before, and many would never live to see any again.

They came from beyond the unknown lands of the Western Brims, and soon they would make their intentions known. As they approached, their slow advance turned into full stride. Heavily armored, these giants shook the ground, along with deafening roars that unnerved the Westland army, while they braced themselves for their attack.

Confused by the first assault, King Odarr and his army had little time to make themselves ready. The giants were led by a powerful wizard warrior named Obizar. He was the Troguare king.

Master of the dark arts, he was ruthless, with a fire that burned inside him for conquest that could not be quenched. He had summoned the smoked warriors to go before his army, wreaking havoc and fear on whomever they faced.

Pouring into a city no longer protected by its fortified walls, the Troguare army engaged the Westland forces. Wielding his weapon of choice called a mal-lace, an expandable rod with spiked balls on both end, Obizar threw himself into the charging Westland warriors, sweeping them away as if they were weeds needing to be cleared.

He was smashing the men's skulls like one would crush a melon, with their blood splattering in all directions. One after the other, he battered his enemies, sweeping them aside while his war beast pounced on their prey, like a cat would pounce on a mouse, consuming all that they could along the way.

Never before had an army of men faced an army such as this. Unprepared and outmatched, the battle was a slaughter from the start. Despite the odds, a few fought with valor and were able to kill with great efficiency, but they were too few. King Odarr was one of those who fought with such skill.

"Behind you, my king!" Ultur shouted while fighting alongside him, warning him of a charging liborox that was unmounted by its master. As it charged and leaped for the kill with the king in his sight, the king quickly rolled under it as it passed over him, and the enemy quickly chose a second target—General Ultur.

Taking a second bound, with one swipe it struck the general on his chest, knocking him onto the ground on his face and stunning him for a moment. Ultur regained himself and stumbled to his feet with his sword in his hand.

King Odarr shouted, "Ultur!" But it was too late. The beast had recovered from its first failed attempt and pounced on him, sinking its fangs into Ultur's neck and shoulder, but not before the general was able to impale his sword into the underside of its huge skull and up under its throat as both fell lifeless to the ground.

With the battle raging, the Troguare warriors, with their axes and swords, swept away three and four of the Westland warriors with a single swing. They were cutting them in half with little effort while fangs and claws ripped through armor and flesh as if they were naked.

The screams filled the city as giants had their way with their human foes. While many of the men were being ripped apart, others were fed upon.

Men fought with all they had to defend their women, their children, and all they possessed. But that served as little comfort, for they were no match. The battle was intense but brief. They fought house to house, from courtyard to courtyard, with the same results—men being no match—until finally, only a few remained, one being the king himself.

Standing their among the few remaining who could still fight, Obizar sat atop his liborox, grinning and looking down at Odarr, who was surrounded by six of his men who were ready to protect him to the death. The battle was all but over before the giant wizard led his growling beast to where the king stood.

With a deep, gravelly voice, Obizar looked Odarr in the eye and said, "You must be the king of these humans."

"That I am. Who are you, and why did you come here? It was you that brought those demons to our doorstep!" Odarr defiantly shouted.

"Very perceptive," Obizar smirked, dismounting his beast. He then said brashly, "I am Obizar. They that you see serve me, as you all will. I came for what is mine."

"Yours?" Odarr responded.

Obizar quickly replied, "Yes, mine! This world will belong to me, and I shall lay claim on all of it, starting with this kingdom, piece by piece."

Odarr then said, "Neither I nor my people shall bow to you!"

Obizar responded, "Then you will all die." Obizar then walked toward the king with his mal-lace in his hand. A few steps away, he faced Odarr and those who protected their king. Towering over them as if they were small children, with his weapon held close to his side, he was now close to them. While the men guarding the king raised their swords, preparing to defend their king, Obizar's warriors began moving in to kill them all.

"Stop! I have no need of aid for insects such as these." Obizar shouted, halting the advance of his warriors. "This matter I shall handle alone." He casually stepped forward. Immediately, those guarding the king formed a barrier of swords and armor between him and the giant wizard.

With a smile, Obizar said, "After you are dead, I shall feed your corpses to the liboroxes and enslave the rest." With his mal-lace down on his side, he continued toward them when Odarr's guards went on the attack.

Twirling his mal-lace like it was a baton and with little effort, he killed two of the defenders, overpowering their defenses with a powerful blow. He embedded his mal-lace into the skull of one of the king's defenders, breaking the man's sword as he tried to deflect the giant's assault.

Despite his great size, he was fleet of foot and simply evaded and outmaneuvered the other, crushing yet another skull. Then lifting the man off his feet and into the air by the throat, Obizar discarded him to the side, as if he was waste.

The king then ordered the rest of his soldiers to back down and then said to them while he stared Obizar in the eyes, "I shall fight him myself and send him to his place."

Obizar then broke out in laughter. "Come forth and die, little king, so that I may wear your skull as a trophy around my neck."

"You will try!" Odarr shouted. "Come forth, giant!" Obizar smiled as the king took his stance, moving forward with his sword high over his head as he charged toward the giant king with all the skills he possessed, giving everything he had. But it was barely enough.

Though powerful as a sorcerer, Obizar was also a skilled warrior. He let Odarr go on the attack until the king made a fatal mistake. Overextending his thrust, this allowed the giant king to sidestep him. Then with a powerful downward thrust, and with the full power of his stroke behind him, he struck King Odarr with such force it caved in the backplate of his armor, breaking the king's back, paralyzing him.

The king slumped over a crumbled piece of wall that had fallen. Obizar then placed his mal-lace back on his hip, drawing his sword. While Odarr lay helpless and barely able to breathe, Obizar walked casually over to him. Not saying a word, he raised his sword and separated King Odarr's head from his body.

Then with his sword, he impaled Odarr's head with it. Standing there before the Westland survivors and his own army, he lifted Odarr's head in the air for all to see and then said, "This is the first of many kings I shall wear as a trophy around my neck." Like an apple, he began peeling the flesh and hair from its skull before gouging out the eyes. He then ran a string of beads through it, making it into a necklace before placing it around his neck still dripping with blood.

After the fall of the Westland city of Dioria, along with their king, Obizar stood before the Troguare army and all that was left of the city's inhabitants. With his sword on his right side and his mal-lace on his left, both covered with blood, Obizar stood victorious with his commanders standing in formation before him, and he began to speak, "Today is the dawn of a new age—our age. We shall carve this world into our image, that of the Troguare, and all shall bow before us. The Troguare name shall be feared by all that hears it."

In the midst of making his declaration, one of his commanders interrupted him while he spoke, jesting, "None but a fool's fool would dare such ignorance," followed by his own laughter.

Obizar ceased to speak, immediately ordering his commander to step forth, while the rest remained silent and disciplined. Obizar then stepped forward—having both hands behind his back—looked the commander in the eye, smiled, and then asked calmly for him to repeat his words.

As the commander began to speak, in the middle of his sentence, Obizar pulled his mal-lace from his side and split the commander's skull, splattering brain matter and blood on himself and those standing in front of him before the commander dropped lifeless where he stood.

Afterward, Obizar stepped over the lifeless body that lay in a puddle of blood mixed with brains. Abruptly, he then said, "This is a reminder to all that none shall speak unless commanded to do so. My words, my laws, my thoughts are absolute. To disobey, regardless of status, the price to be paid will be that of my choosing. Today I chose to be merciful in giving a quick death, but I promise you this, I will not always be so merciful. The next time, it shall be slow and suffering."

After speaking those words, there was no response and no acknowledgment, not even a grunt, only silence, fearing the consequence. Continuing his speech this time without interruption, Obizar moved beyond his commanders and stood before hundreds of his captives that were unfortunate enough to survive, for life as a Troguare slave was hard and unforgiving and most difficult to survive.

Forced to keep their eyes to the ground in the presence of these giants, Obizar spoke to them, saying, "Every town, every village, I shall take. Your lands, your possessions, even your worthless lives shall be mine to do with as I choose. All that you have built, I shall turn to ash and rubble only to be replaced by the standards that I shall set. By the sweat of your labor will this be accomplished." After his speech, Obizar then turned and ordered his guards to feed the body of the commander he had slain to the commander's own liborox. This was a reminder to all of his ruthlessness. He dismissed them all only after they had witnessed this gruesome sight, which was the price of disobedience.

After the beast had its fill, he then ordered it to be slain and then ordered them both to be burned. With their king dead and the Westland forces all but destroyed, the once mighty kingdom was no more.

Obizar then led his army, numbering in the tens of thousands, across what remained of the kingdom, facing little resistance and setting everything aflame in their path.

They hunted down those who attempted to escape, enslaving them while killing any that resisted. From beyond the unknowns of the Western Brims, they came sweeping across the lands that were once the Westland Kingdom. Obizar's rampage didn't stop at its borders. His goal was far beyond the boundaries of this one kingdom. He was to lay claim on all of Tyrus.

CHAPTER 2

The Rise of Obizar

A S HE DID against the city of Dioria and its forces, time and time again, Obizar used the power of his dark magic repeatedly, calling upon these warriors of smoke and flames to go before his army, destroying fortress after fortress and raining terror upon the kingdoms of men and all their inhabitants. Obizar's ruthlessness was on full display, butchering everyone and everything in his path.

The use of such sorcery was not without cost. Calling upon these entities slowly drained him of his ability to control these forces. No longer willing to take that risk knowing that one day he would truly need it, Obizar chose to use Troguare might instead, which proved to harbor the same menacing effect.

The mere sight of these savage giants on their war beasts created panic and fear as men threw down their arms and surrender before them. Those who chose to flee were run down and butchered. But the true might of this army lay not only in their great size or the liborox that they rode but in their great numbers. Unlike men, they were united as one force, not divided into many separate kingdoms.

Word quickly spread across to far-off lands. Many prayed and cried out to God to deliver them, but their prayers went unheard, causing many to flee into the wilderness to an uncertain fate. There were those who did stand while attempting to hold their ground. Battles were both fierce and brutal, but it was the blood of men, not giants, that flowed like a river throughout the land.

All attempts to repel the Troguare army were futile, for no army was able to overcome the Troguare onslaught. It wasn't long before Obizar had seized all the lands ruled by humans until he reached the great Wasteland Desert, which seemed as endless as the ocean and vastly unknown.

Just as his lands were unknown to the conquered, these were unknown to all. As the desert was barren and unyielding, Obizar was left to ponder what lay beyond its boundaries. So he turned his attention back to the conquered lands and began to settle them.

With the labor of human slave, he began erecting cities, replacing those that he had burned to nonexistence. The Troguares had begun giving up their nomadic lifestyle, a life they did little to prepare for, and started living like that of stationary people.

They were a race that was accustomed to taking from others, and there was a time they even took from their own. With no skills in tending flocks and growing food, they also lacked the skills to build structures. They now depended on their human slaves to carry out their labor. For humans, life under Troguare rule was bleak, hopeless, and cruel.

Men worked relentlessly from dawn to dusk. Days were long and unyielding, and the fate of women were far worse. With Troguare females being unpleasant to look upon, even Troguare males found them repulsive, with their only purpose that of reproduction and the rearing of their young. But Troguare males found human women most appealing to the eyes.

Humans and giants were unable to reproduce, so women were taken away to serve the sexual pleasures of Troguare males, who did to them whatever they so desired, with most women unable to survive the experience of their brutal acts. The human plight didn't end there; it would become far worse.

It took a lot to fill the belly of a giant. When food became scarce, they began to look at humans as a food source and began to develop a taste for human flesh. As food sources became more limited, the flesh of men became more and more prevalent. This led to the beginning of harvest camps, which were human slaughterhouses, that sprang up in every Troguare city and large encampment.

When a slave was no longer useful—being too old, too weak, or too injured to work—they were sent to these camps for consumption. Over time, some humans were bred for that sole purpose, while small children served as pets for the cruel Troguare youths, making survival difficult for them.

For those humans fortunate enough to reach adulthood, males were sent to labor camps, while females were in danger of being used for pleasure. While cities were built by the hands of slaves, temples also arose wherever the giants laid claim.

The lands of the Western Brims to the unknown boundaries of the great Wasteland Desert were now under Obizar's rule. What lay beyond its boundaries remained a constant thorn in his mind.

After all he had accomplished, Obizar remained unsatisfied, for this was not enough. His spirit remained restless. He stood at the edge of the unknown, at the burning sands of the Wasteland Desert, only to wonder what lay beyond it.

Later that evening, within his chamber where he worked his darkest spells, Obizar stood alone before a fire burning in a pit. With his eyes closed, the sorcerer began to chat a spell in a language unknown to the ears of anyone.

While chanting, the fire began to burn with greater intensity but was absent of heat. With a wave of his hand, the smoke above the fire began to spiral horizontally as a portal began opening into the realm of Darkness that appeared over the flames.

Obizar then dropped to one knee with his palms facing upward. Slowly appearing within it, a shadowed figure with flaming blue eyes came forth out of the shadows, followed by another with flaming yellow eyes. Then another with eyes of red flames appeared until, finally, all gave way to the last of these beings with eyes that burned with a greater intensity than all the others, the one whose eyes burned white with fire.

He moved forward, standing prominently among the others. They were the Dark Ones, absolute rulers of the dark dimension. Once all were present, Obizar spoke, "Masters of the darkness, I am yours to command!"

With those words, the one whose eyes burned white and the brightest began to speak with the sound of a hissing serpent. Commanding their darkest disciple to rise, it asked, "Why have you summoned us? Have you found that which we seek that we may be free to roam this world once more?"

Obizar spoke humbly, "No, master, I have not. My sight beyond my natural view has yet to return to me. I summoned you because I seek an answer. Before me is the vastness of an endless ocean of sands, for it has stalled my advance. I fear the uncertainty of blindly venturing into the unknown sands, risking being lost and perishing within it. Therefore, I seek an answer to this natural riddle."

The Dark One whose eyes burned yellow stepped forth and said, "Ours eyes are clouded beyond this portal that separates our worlds.

But this we can foresee. Your destiny lies beyond this unknown, and you have within you the power to set forth eyes that are not your own to go before you. Use what you have within your power, and you shall receive the answers that you seek."

After speaking those words, each of the Dark Ones fell silent and then slipped back into the darkness one after the other until nothing remained but a lifeless black void. Obizar then rose to his feet, contemplating the meaning of the dark lord's words. Then with a wave of his hand, the portal disappeared.

The next morning, he summoned twelve of his fiercest warriors. Among them was Abithar, the leader and the greatest warrior. As they stood before the Troguare king, with his heavy voice, he began to speak, "You are the best in what you do. That is why you were chosen. You have never failed me. Go and bring me back a report of all that you see beyond the sands if anything exists at all beyond it or if there are any occupied lands that remain unseen and unnoticed to any that may dwell there. And kill any that lay eyes upon you. I want there to be no knowledge of our existence when the storm of our wrath rains down on all that stand in our path. For I shall not rest until this world is ours. Fail me not, for if you do, you know the price of failure."

"Yes, my lord. We shall return to you with the answers that you seek, my lord," Abithar replied. Acknowledging their master's command and knowing the giant king was true to his words, they turned and went forth as commanded into the desert, not knowing what they might find or if they would ever return.

Obizar stood and watched as his warriors rode off into the desert. Standing beside him was Rolo, his ranking commander. He looked at Obizar and said, "What if they fail to return, my lord?

"Then I shall send as many as required until I acquire the answers that I seek." Silently, Rolo bowed to the king and went his way as Obizar held his place until his warriors faded from sight.

CHAPTER 3

The Land of the Talishar

FOR SIX MONTHS, twelve giant figures braved the unrelenting desert heat and biting sands on the backs of their beasts. Sandstorms seemed to appear out of nowhere, while the sands tore away at their flesh. It was a land that appeared lifeless and as alien as the moons above.

The deeper they journeyed through the harsh desert, the more alien the world around them seemed. It was both rocky and arid, while in other places, it was engulfed with the softest of sands. With dunes resembling mountains, everything was either tan or gray, absent of green.

There was no vegetation or signs of any water to be found. If any existed, none of them knew where to find it. There was nothing around them they could use to mark their trail for a return. The winds and sands wiped away all evidence they would attempt to leave.

Beyond its edges was a sea of dunes with sands, remnant of an endless ocean. Following the stars at night and navigating the placement of the suns by day, they kept their course straight, keeping to solid ground and only traveling along the edges of where solid ground and soft sand would meet.

Staying their course, this prevented them from traveling in circles while ensuring a route in which they could return when that time came. This was a journey that only the strongest or hardiest could endure, whether man or beast. They pressed forward by the strength of will, motivated by fear of their master and the consequences of failure.

In the distance, they spotted what appeared to be structures rising up from the sand. After months of braving these harsh lands, their eyes and their senses had played tricks on their minds many times. In the beginning, they believed it to be an illusion caused by the heat of the desert.

They no longer placed trust on their own eyes, though each saw the same thing. As they came closer, it was evident that it was what it appeared to be—a city in ruins that had been reclaimed by the desert long ago.

Moving closer, they saw none of the previous occupants, only lesser creatures seeking refuge from the scorching heat of the two suns. Slowly and quietly they passed through before finding the first remains of those who had previously dwelled there.

Obscure figures that once had life, their strange bodies petrified over time as if they were broken statues. All were either young or having the appearance of being females clinging to their young with either their heads cut off and separated from their bodies or their torsos cut in half.

Being Troguares, there was nothing in their nature to show any compassion or concern, only a curiosity of what may have occurred and who caused their fate. The fate of these inhabitants had also proved the existence of other civilizations that might lie somewhere beyond the lands in which they had left behind.

With that evidence, they now had to push to find them, keeping in thought what they had witnessed thus far, until they finally reached the limits of this forgotten civilization. The question in their minds was what lay beyond what the eyes could see.

If there was once a civilization here, then there might be others beyond if they continued pressing on. After a few more hours, they came across lands even stranger than any they had left behind.

Out of the ground rose strange formations, hundreds of curved stones rising forty feet in the air, worn smooth by the harshness of wind and sand over time. Curved in all directions, they resembled claws belonging to a mammoth beast ready to emerge from the desert floor to devour them all.

Scattered among these stone formations were hundreds of sinkholes—some enormous in size—ranging from nearly one hundred feet across to as small as ten feet. It was as if they were passageways leading to something that they had yet to see. Even these seasoned and fearless warriors had become wary of the unknown. While they moved slowly and quietly forward, they were harvesting great suspicion.

With each step, they had a sense that they were not alone. Abithar would halt the others occasionally to survey their surroundings, with their weapons ready for anything they considered a threat. They saw nothing around them but blowing sands and winds that bit their rough, hairy faces.

Even their war beasts were uneasy. Snarling and growling, they were even hesitant at times, sniffing the ground and moving their heads from side to side, gathering any scent that may have been in the air. One of the giants lagged behind the others to relieve himself and noticed a sudden movement in the corner of his eye.

A ripple in the sand had caught his attention. He then shouted to the others that he saw something as he drew his battle ax. The others then turned to investigate, drawing their weapons while fervently looking around before focusing on the spot that their comrade had thought he had seen something, but there was nothing.

Satisfied that there was nothing, they began to believe that the desert heat had begun playing tricks on their minds. Dismissing the thought that something may have been out there, they calmed, and even their beasts began to settle.

Moving forward, they weaved through the strange gauntlet of holes that were in their path. Finally making through it, they named this place the Land of Holes. Their journey into this harsh place had now begun to take its toll on them all. Exhausted and on the verge of collapse, just before nightfall, they saw their first sign of life other than the occasional creatures scurrying along the desert floor.

It appeared to be vegetation in the distance, an island of green that stretched across an endless horizon, like the shoreline of an ocean. Cautiously they moved toward it, with the question of whether it was real on their minds. Was it a mirage, or was the heat playing more tricks with their minds again?

They weren't sure, but they didn't have much choice. They had gone too far and had nothing left even if they wanted to return. Shortly after nightfall, what they thought they saw was confirmed. With barely enough energy remaining in their bodies, they arrived on the grassy shores of what would be the western edge of the great Talishar Empire.

Under the cover of night, they sought refuge, careful to avoid any prying eyes they might come across in this strange, new land. Looking around, they saw a patch of forest in the distance across a sea of grass and what appeared to be a stream of water flowing through it.

Not sure if there were others around and to keep their presence a secret, they didn't want to chance starting a fire. They waited until dawn to familiarize themselves with everything around them before taking such liberties.

After a few days of rest to replenish their strength, they did as their king commanded. They set forth to do the task at hand. They fanned out in twelve separate directions to gather all the information that they could find. One remained on Talishar lands, while others ventured out beyond the Talishar borders to see if any other civilizations existed, agreeing to return to their meeting place at the rise of the twelfth phase of the trimoons, which aligned the center skies once every thirty days.

These lands were vast and beautiful, whose boundaries seemed endless, home to a powerful race of humanoids known as Furriers—a fur-based variety of manlike species with most being barbaric and savage. The Talishars were unlike any that bore that name.

They were one of a few such species that preferred living a peaceful existence with humans without conflict. Having short velvetlike fur and being pale blue in color, they were heavily muscular with catlike features. Standing at least six feet eight on average and weighing well over three hundred pounds, their muscles rippled with their every movement. They were physically superior in strength, stamina, and speed to any other humanoid.

They were led by their king, Norval the Great, both wise and just. Under his reign, peace flourished and prevailed over these great lands that seemed to span out endlessly. Great and powerful armies had fallen in attempts to possess their lands. Those who made the attempt learned quickly, testing their blades.

Hidden in the forest, the Troguare scouts concealed themselves behind an assortment of terrain. Forests, woodlands, or along rocky hills, each of these giants silently observed all movements through the view of their looking glass, which magnified the Talishars' daily activities from afar, in eight locations throughout the land while carefully avoiding patrols, ready to kill if necessary.

The scout that remained was astonished by the magnificence of the Talishar cities that he saw. Not a race that would be sensitive to such things he was, nevertheless, impressed and taken by the beauty and the design of their walls that were laced in precious stones and trimmed with gold and brilliant metals.

Each of the Troguare spies took note of the great bounties of gold and silver that commerced daily in what appeared to be a loosely guarded community. Hundreds of travelers of all types, both humans and humanoids, frequented their lands and markets daily without incident, whether trading goods or simply passing through. But it was their defenses that held the Troguare's real interest.

Despite the range of movement extended to all that visited these lands, it was out of fear of their king that they followed Obizar's command to the letter. Because of their size and violent nature of both themselves and their beasts, they would have been a sight not easily forgotten and etched in the minds of many, so they remained hidden, only to move about under the obscurity of night.

At night, they traveled about on foot after muzzling and securing their war beasts in remote areas to prevent discovery, only to return shortly before dawn. Once both suns set, this gave them freedom to roam about, giving them better access and a closer view as they constantly sought out weaknesses and vulnerabilities in the defenses. They still had to be selective in their movements. The Talishar's vision was far superior to that of an ordinary human's. Their catlike traits gave them excellent night vision.

For weeks, the Troguares stalked the lands of the Talishar undetected, as they went about their daily lives, studying everything that they held with importance. The lightly guarded cities and dwellings, even the king's city of Tajheire, appeared to lack sufficient protection for a fortress city with walls and barriers. Each of the cites these giants came across were small replicas of the king's palace, and like the great city, all were surrounded by white stoned walls laced with crystals and beautiful gardens. None but the city of Kromere appeared to provide adequate protection against an invading army, making their defenses appear easy to overcome. From every city, village, or town, all roadways and paths led to the great city of Tajheire, with farmlands and open plains surrounding them all. What was also most surprising to the Troguares was how lightly guarded their borders appeared to be.

With everything to lose, the Talishar people went about their daily lives, showing little concern of the possibility of being invaded. Their forces appeared unorganized, with their warriors spread thin across its vastly open lands.

This led the Troguares to believe that they were vulnerable and, in their eyes, to invade en masse would leave them without time to mobilize quickly, giving them reasons to believe conquest would be as easy as it always had been for them.

The things that captured their interest the most were how the Talishars trained and what weapon they used, which was called a swovel. Heavy and awkward, the swovel was a weapon only wielded by a Talishar warrior. Also known as the spinning ax, it had rotating blades on both ends, mounted on a shaft, with swordlike blades at the end of each of these rotating blades.

Having a wooden shaft forming the base, it came with a three-inch gap separating the two overlaying wood coverings. Once snapped together, it activated a mechanism that started the blades to spin with a force that could cut through armor, bone, and flesh, as if it were the thinnest of cloth. From their youth, Talishar were trained to use a vast assortment of weaponry. But the swovel was the weapon of choice, and they were one with it.

As children, they were taught to design their own, making it as much of them as if it was another limb. All Talishars carried the swovel they designed. Another weapon they used was the foreblade. Attached to their forearm, it extended the length of it and beyond. Their skills and their agility, coupled with their fluid movement, made them precise in their motions and twice as deadly. But not even that was enough to discourage any thoughts of these lands being taken without any difficulties.

It was now the twelfth cycle of the alignment. For a year, the Troguares miraculously remained undetected while gathering whatever knowledge they could acquire before returning to the agreed place on the agreed time. The Troguares arrived to the place they first arrived one after the other. With much to share, they set their sights on the six-month trek back across the unforgiving sands and their arduous journey home.

CHAPTER 4

The Anticipated Arrival

IT HAD BEEN two years since Obizar sent his scouts into the great desert abyss. He was weary and impatiently waiting for their return until, finally, his patience came to an end. Believing the first twelve to be lost, he called another twelve to take their place to carry out the task.

He was determined to get an answer regardless of how many giants failed to return. Standing on the desert's edge, twelve new warriors were ready to carry out their master's command and to begin their journey when the sound of a Troguare trumpet rang out from behind a cloud of dust from out in the desert.

Suddenly, a soldier cried out, "My lord, look from the desert. They have returned." Steadily approaching amid the blowing sands and wavering heat, twelve figures appeared in the distance. As they approached, Obizar waited anxiously for their report.

Finally, they stood before their king as they gave a salute. With their fist pressed firmly against their chest and heads bowed, they waited patiently for permission to speak.

Worn down and weakened from the harsh journey, Obizar showed little concern at their condition as he looked at each and shouted, "Your report!"

Abithar stepped forth, and with his head bowed, he began to speak, "Master, for six months we journeyed across the great wasteland with unyielding heat that scorched the ground everywhere, unforgiving sands biting our faces with every step. It is a barren, lifeless place with only the most insignificant of creatures roaming about, with cities that were abandoned long ago. But beyond the desert lies lands with far greater kingdoms than any that we have ever seen, kingdoms filled with riches that dwarfed any that we have taken—gold, silver, emeralds—beyond comparison. And all will be yours for the taking, for we have found none that could challenge us except one.

"As you commanded, once we arrived, we concealed ourselves from all eyes that dwelled there, remaining hidden before spreading abroad, seeking the knowledge you so desired. What we found were lands occupied by weak humans that were divided, squabbling among themselves, constantly at war with one other—all but one.

"There are a powerful people known as the Talishar. Their borders lie at the edge of the wastelands. A people that are not divided, free of the chaos who ruled the lands beyond their borders. Theirs is a land that is richer than any we have seen. But not even they could withstand you, my lord. Though they are skilled fighters, we have the advantage in numbers. And if we defeat them, there will be nothing that can stand in our way."

Obizar smiled for the first time in two years since his last conquest. Immediately he summoned his commanders and his warriors and then issued a decree.

He would leave a third of his massive army and a complement of commanders to govern the lands he had taken in his absence. The rest he gathered at the edge of the wasteland, along with provisions they would need, which included females and their young, as he prepared to lead them, along with his army, across the barren desert toward what he believed would be his destiny.

It was a perilous journey to the lands he had planned to lay claim upon. Standing before them, Obizar addressed his army, saying, "Beyond these sands lies our destiny. We will take everything in our path and lay waste to everything in our wake, for this is our world to claim. And we will reshape it into our image. Nothing will cause us to stray from our path, for this world I shall take. Every hill, every mountain, all shall bow to me and the Troguare nation." After speaking those words, the roar of his army was carried with the wind for miles. He then turned, raising his arm in the air, giving the command to march forward as they stepped forth into the great wastelands in their quest to conquer the world.

CHAPTER 5

A Journey Back in Time—
Talishar Border Wars

THIRTY YEARS EARLIER, the king's city of Tajheire was
the heart of the Talishar nation. With walls towering over
fifty feet above the trees and gardens below and with a palace that rose
even higher, it was a realm of birth, breeding warriors whose skills were
superior.

Despite this, they remained on constant alert. Pressing its borders
were two barbaric civilizations that posed a constant threat with the
desire to possess their lands and destroy their kingdom. To the west
was a race of sand-like shape-shifters known as Sanulites, led by King
Soya, who made their home beneath the sands of the barren lands of
the Wasteland Desert.

While to the north, beyond the tree line within the Northern
Mountains, lived seven clans of a rocklike race of semigiants known as
the Kraggans, who were led by a powerful ruler named Kromus.

Both had a deep desire to destroy the Talishar and take their lands
as their own. In times past, each of these races made separate but futile
attempts to lay claim to the Talishar Empire, only to be repelled at every
turn. Wary of constant defeat, each retreated back to their place, biding
their time until the right moment would arise once more. And that time
had now come around once again.

Within the Talishar Kingdom, its people mourned the death of
their ruler, King Torrad, who had succumbed to illness. In his place,
his young son, Prince Norval (his only son), had inherited the throne.
Barely seventeen, the young king was both wise and brave and advanced
well beyond his years.

Like all Talishar people, he was taught from the time he was able to
walk to wield both foreblade and swovel. As a youth, he demonstrated

greater ability than any of his age. During this time, his father had already begun to teach him the art of war and strategy.

It was a talent in which he excelled both in understanding and skills. As he grew, his skills with both foreblade and swovel grew with him. There was no one in all the land that could match his abilities. His talents of being both a leader and a warrior would soon be called upon. Talishar lands were the richest and more fertile of any that were known.

It stretched hundreds of miles and was filled with countless lakes, rivers, and forests. Like its western border that led to the Wasteland Desert, its eastern border was even more mysterious, for it hovered along the coast of the great unknown oceans and what lay beyond its coast.

To the north, fading high up into the clouds, lay the Northern Mountains. Like its western borders, the Talishar kept a watchful eye for the threats that had plagued them for nearly a century. Deep within its rocky caverns, the ruler of the Kraggan clans, Kromus, had summoned the seven clans together.

Having grown weary of confinement within the caves, he called for the gathering of all the Kraggan clans. Standing before him in what appeared to be an endless cavern lit by walls of phosphorus stones, his people awaited his words.

With skin like the texture of the granite walls of the caves they inhabited, these semigiants, each nearly eight feet tall, blended perfectly with their surroundings, hiding their numbers and making them appear nearly invisible within its shadows.

Kromus, like his kind, was large, dark, and gray with eyes resembling black crystals as he stood high upon a ledge, overlooking them. With a deep, bellowing voice, reminiscent of the sound of thunder, he began to speak, "The time has come once again that we leave this rocky prison and set our sights to the warmth of the plains below that was stolen from us by those treacherous, furry scum.

"Since that time, we have suffered a life within these abysmal caves for far too long. For generations upon generations, our kind has desired to reclaim what was once ours and return to the lower altitudes and into the warmth of the open plains to a more gentle climate, only to suffer defeat at the hands of the Talishar.

"But opportunity has now presented itself once more, but this time, we shall not fail. It is our time to claim our destiny and take what has been denied to us for far too long. The Talishar filth has become weak after the death of our longtime enemy Torrad.

"After his demise, they have crowned a new king—his son. This is a weakness that we shall not pass upon. A kingdom is only as strong as he that leads them, and they are now led by a boy. I have devised a plan and have sent an envoy to the west to arrange a meeting with the Sanulite shape-shifters of the Wasteland Desert, who also share our disdain for the Talishar and who share the same desire to claim these lands as their own. Together our chances will increase fourfold with the belief that we may divide their lands between us. There is no better time than now to unite our forces and destroy our enemy once and for all and lay claim to our destiny."

Standing beside him was Brotos, whose power was second only to Kromus himself. Leaning forward, whispering into what appeared to be his ear, he said, "You wish to make a pact with those worthless puddles of puke for a land that is rightfully ours and ours alone?" Kromus looked over at him, not saying a word, only smiling, which spoke as loud as any word that could be spoken. Knowing the nature of the Kraggan people, there was yet another plan that was hidden beneath his words— it was a pact he had no intentions to honor once the Talishar had been vanquished. In that instance, Brotos understood clearly, smiling back at his king with that unspoken message.

Meanwhile, far to the west within the Wasteland Desert lay the Sanulite city of Mordune. Sitting on his throne, Soya, the Sanulite king, had also received word of the death of the Talishar king. For centuries, like the Kraggans to the north, the Sanulites had made many attempts to destroy the Talishar people and possess their lands, only to be defeated at every turn.

Behind Soya stood his most trusted commander and confidant, the shifter named Slyth. Shifting his face to his rear without turning, he now faced Slyth, and with a hissing voice, he began to speak, "The time has come once more that we turn our attention toward Talishar lands. Their king is dead, and they are now being led by an inexperienced boy. There can be no better time than now to strike. They cannot be more vulnerable than they are now."

Slyth then replied with a similar hiss, "Master, there are risks, for even with a boy leading them, they are still a most formidable foe."

"Perhaps," Soya replied, "but it is a risk I am willing to explore."

"Is it?" Slyth asked and then said, "Master, you know the nature of our kind, for if you fail, you will be in danger of rebellion. Our people judge our king by his strength, and we have failed three times in our attempt, only to be defeated by the Talishar and driven back into our realm. If we are defeated once more, it will be uncertain how our people will receive it."

Soya stood quietly and pondered Slyth's words, then he replied, "I shall contemplate all that we have discussed for a time, then I shall make my decision."

After a seven-day journey down the treacherous slopes of the Northern Mountains, through the thick of the forest, until sometime during the night, three Kraggan warriors finally arrived at the edge of the sandy Wasteland Desert.

They brought with them a proposal of great importance. They stood silently and motionless for nearly an hour before one of the three unstrapped a large stone mallet. With three powerful swings with the stone weapon, he smashed it into the edge of the bank where sand and solid ground met.

D. R. SIMPSON

Striking the ground with such force, a shock wave was felt for great distances as they waited for a response. Shortly afterward, the sand began to ripple, like a pebble cast into a still pool, gradually getting larger and larger until the sand began to rise, taking shape and transforming into twelve sand-like warriors with obscure features until they configured into an identifiable form.

With one being Soya's most trusted commander, Slyth, they faced the powerful stone figures. As Slyth spoke, it was the sound that resembled a hissing serpent. He asked, "Why have you come to us, stone creature? What business do you have with us beyond that of your death?"

At that moment, the warrior, whose name was Brolhar, wielding the stone mallet stepped forth and said, "We have not come here to do battle with the likes of you, creature. We bring a message from our king, Kromus, a proposal of alliance against that of our common foe—the Talishar."

Slyth replied with a hissing voice, "An alliance! Why should we make an alliance with ones such as—"

Brolhar then interrupted, "For decades, both your people and ours have made many attempts to defeat the Talishar, only to be driven back in defeat. With the death of their king, his young son now holds the mantle as king and will now lead them.

"Never before have we united our forces. They would not expect nor would they be prepared to face us both at once. With their defeat, my king offers that we would then divide their land in half, claiming it as our own."

Slyth then replied, "Why should we divide what we can claim ourselves?"

After those words was a pause and then followed by silence before Brolhar spoke again, "We have not come to debate but only to relay this message from our king. Kromus desires a meeting with that of your king within the valley of the Stoned Forest. In ten days, if your king so chooses to come, our king, Kromus, will be there waiting for your arrival. At that time, we shall begin to discuss strategy."

With those words, both became silent, then Slyth hissed at the gray semigiants and said, "I shall relay your words to my king, and in ten days, you shall have your answer. Our presence or absence will be the answer that you seek."

Afterward, the Sanulites dissolved back into the sand before drifting away with the wind. Like stone pillars, the Kraggan warriors stood and watched until they disappeared from sight. Brolhar then looked at his companions before turning and going their way.

Not far away, hiding within the tall grass, a Talishar scout was watching their every move. After both the Kraggans and Sanulites parted ways, he mounted his steed and headed back to the king's city of Tajheire to inform his king.

Back in the city, King Norval stood atop the palace walls, his eyes fixed to the west, on the horizon. In the distance, his Talishar scout was heading toward the palace gates, leaving a trail of dust in his wake.

The king's eyes were fixed on the scout as he approached while he wondered about the urgency that pressed the rider toward the city's gates before a soft hand resting on his shoulder broke his concentration. With a slight turn of his head, his peripheral vision caused the source to come into view. Norval smiled and said, "There is but one with such a touch, having the sweet fragrance of honey and roses filling the air. No one but my beautiful wife could have such an effect."

With those words, Pricillica, the queen, replied, "I missed the warmth of your body before my eyes even opened, confirming that you had left my side before I could reach out to you." She placed her arm around his waist and then her head on his shoulder. They shared the view of the approaching rider.

Before the rider entered the gate, she asked, "What could be so urgent?"

Norval looked at her and said, "I shall soon find out. There is already much on my mind. I shall soon know what else will be added to it." Staring into his wife's eyes, he then said, "My love, there are many things I have to address." Before he could speak another word, the scout was quickly approached the steps that led to where the king was waiting. Norval then leaned forward and kissed her, then he said, "I must go." He looked down at the warrior making his way up the stairway. The queen then quietly left his side, allowing him to receive the message that was meant for the ears of the king.

After making his way up to where the king was waiting, the young warrior bowed his head, pressed his fist firmly against his chest, acknowledging the new king, and then said, "My lord!" as he awaited the king's response.

"You may speak," Norval replied.

The warrior then spoke, "Along the borders of the wasteland, three Kraggan warriors, along with a dozen Sanulites, engaged in a meeting of some sort. I lay hidden in the tall grass a short distance away, undetected. Though I was close, it was difficult to understand all that they were saying. But there were words I did hear and understood. There will be a meeting held in ten days' time between the kings of the Sanulites and the Kraggans within the Stoned Forest. The meeting will take place at its center core where there's an open space.

"Not much more could I understand what was said between them. After their exchange of words, each turned and went their own way. Forgive me, my lord, that I have failed to deliver all that was discussed between them."

Norval then reached out and touched the warrior on his shoulder and replied, "No need for forgiveness. You've done well. Now go and rest yourself." Acknowledging his king, he bowed while clutching his fist against his chest before taking a step backward and walking away.

Norval then returned to his thoughts while overlooking the wall as he slowly began pacing back and forth. The news of the gathering did not surprise him but only confirmed the thoughts that was buried in his mind, which were deeply vexing him. He was still grieving the death of his father, and now he had received the news of a gathering between the Talishar's two most hated enemies.

The unexpected death of his father was barely enough for him to bear, but now this. He was unable to hide his feelings, as he wore them on his face like a cloak in summer. Pacing back and forth, once again, he had yet another visitor. This time it was Theor, his chief commander, adviser, and friend, a post Theor had also held in the service of his father.

After saluting his king, he addressed Norval, saying, "My lord."

Trying to suppress his true feelings, Norval quickly tried hiding it behind a smile. "Greetings, my friend, what brings you to me so early in the morning? Shouldn't you be enjoying it with your lovely wife, snugged tight in your chambers instead of pacing this wall with me?" Norval replied, speaking in jest.

Theor laughed and replied, "If my king is troubled, so shall I. You have been in mourning since your father died. You have been wearing it on your shoulders since that grievous day. It is something you cannot hide behind, my lord."

"Which is what?" Norval asked.

Pausing, Theor replied, "A smile. I do not fault you, for your father was a great man, a great warrior, and a great king. And he was also a great friend."

Finding comfort in the words of his friend, Norval smiled, then he replied, "That he was, and you had served him with honor. My father had always spoken highly of you, and with his life, he trusted you. But he was also an even greater father, for he taught me all that he could before illness robbed him of his life."

Theor then replied, "Yes, but I sense it's more than just the death of your father that troubles you."

The king then said, "You are perceptive in your observations, and you're correct, for I believe our enemies will take this time to test our resolve. The death of my father is well-known, for spies are always present even from afar. I received word this morning from one of our scouts patrolling the western borders. He told me of a meeting at the edge of the sand between the Kraggans and the Sanulites.

"Being as I am, a young king, this will always strike the interest of an enemy, questioning both my resolve and my experience, along with a certain arrogance that usually accompanies the throne. I believe our old enemies, the Kraggans and the Sanulites, will take this time to attack us but with a different strategy than before, one of an alliance."

Theor replied, "In all our history, they have never unified their forces against us. The Kraggans are not even unified among themselves. They remain in constant warfare among one another despite having one ruler, while the Sanulites remain wandering about in the desert, no more than a collection of bandits raiding unsuspecting travelers. Even their attacks on our borders never amounted to any more than a dust storm before we sent them back into the sands."

Norval looked over at his white-haired commander and said, "My father taught me many things concerning war as well as life, but the one constant that had always remained fermented in my mind and heart was to always expect the unexpected, for both war and life yield the same constants. I sense they will take this moment to attempt something like this, believing my youth will hurt us."

"What will you have me do, my lord?" Theor asked.

Norval then replied, "I was told there would be a second gathering between the two. One that will take place ten days from now within the Stoned Forest. One that I believe will hold the answer to the unanswered question that is hovering before us. Therefore, I shall not wait on that answer. Go prepare the people for war, for I believe it is once again knocking at our doorsteps, and we shall not be left sleeping if they come calling.

"Double our patrols along both the western and northern borders and beyond. If there is to be a meeting in ten days in our honor, we shall not disappoint. We shall join them, an unseen, unheard guest aloft in the shadows where we shall remain. Instruct our warriors to track all movements and remain hidden. Do not attack or engage them regardless of the odds. I have other plans in store for our two friends. We shall give them something that will be remembered as long as breath remains within us."

"And what will that be, my lord?" Theor asked.

The king responded, "I shall reveal my thoughts once their plans are confirmed. Go, we must act quickly. There isn't a lot of time."

"Yes, my lord, I shall," Theor replied, acknowledging the king before turning and going his way to carry out his instructions.

Afterward, the king returned to his chamber to be with his wife, where she lay across the sheets, waiting patiently for his return. Following the king's command, the Talishar patrols tirelessly patrolled both the western and northern borders, looking for signs of any movements.

CHAPTER 6

A Reluctant Alliance— the Enemy of My Enemy

DAYS BEFORE THE gathering, Talishar patrols observed movements along the desert's borders. An envoy of Sanulites, along with Soya, their king, moved along the edges of the forest on the western borders of Talishar lands until entering the forest toward the northwest. They left a trail of sand in their wake that shone as if it was a beacon of light in the night sky, lighting the trail as they moved along through the trees and foliage.

As Talishar scouts lay hidden along the trails. As their king commanded, they watched and waited as about thirty shape-shifting warriors passed by them. Meanwhile to the north, there was also movement. Thirty or more Kraggan warriors were equally as easy to track, lumbering noisily with heavy steps while crashing through the forest like a plow. They also were being led by their king and leader of the seven clans, King Kromus. In anticipation of the gathering, the Talishar scouts were already in place at the location that was agreed upon by their unsuspecting enemies.

Hidden high up in the trees and among the heavy forest and pillars of stones that were intertwined together, which gave the forest its name, like a cat waiting on its prey at a water hole, the scouts were perfectly camouflaged, motionless and silent. For hours they waited until just after the second sun had set and the cool of the evening began to settle in when an abrupt sound of trees crashing about could be heard in the distance.

It was the Kraggans who were the first to arrive, finding their place among the rugged terrain with the king of the seven clans, King Kromus, and his commander, Brotos, flanked closely beside him as he and his warriors stood silently and motionlessly behind them.

Patiently they awaited as hours passed for what they had hoped would be the arrival of the Sanulite warriors and their king, Soya. Their arrival would perceivably answer the question that Kromus had sought. Shortly after midnight, a swift swirling wind suddenly began to blow as the swirl began to take shape into more identifiable forms, that of Sanulite soldiers.

They were about thirty in number. And at the forefront was Soya, the Sanulite king, along with Slyth, his commander, by his side. Gliding forth as if riding the wind, they moved slowly toward the center of the clearing away from the tree line. And with every sliding step forward, they transformed what was once green into the texture of light-tinted sand.

Shifting his face to the rear of what was the back of his head, Soya gave out a hiss only the Sanulites could understood, commanding his warriors not to follow but to hold their ground before shifting his face forward once again to face the Kraggans, who were standing on the opposite side of the clearing. At that moment, Kromus and his commander came forward to meet the Sanulite king and Slyth at the center of the clearing.

Kromus smiled at the Sanulite king and said, "Greetings, king of the sands! I was beginning to think you were not going to show up. I am happy that you decided to join us."

Soya then replied, "You may dispense with the pleasantries, Kraggan! I have not made any such decision."

Kromus responded, "We assumed that you had made your decision after taking such a tenacious journey so far away from the blistering sands of your home."

"Your assumption was an error. I have yet to come to such a conclusion."

Kromus then asked, "If a decision was not made, then why have you come?"

Soya responded, "Curiosity! Curiosity!"

Kromus repeated, "Yes, curiosity."

Soya then continued, "What do you have to offer us that is rightfully ours to claim, stone king?

Kromus replied quickly as tension began to grow and as emotions began to escalate. Kromus stared into what was, at that moment, Soya's face with cold black crystal eyes, repeating Soya's words, "What is yours?"

Kromus replied aggressively, with a voice that rumbled like thunder, addressing the words launched at him by the Sanulite king, "Before you ever crawled out of those wormholes of the sandy depths of the desert, my people had already laid claim to these lands before they were driven out by those Talishar thieves that stole them from us in the very beginning, driving us atop the mountains deep within the cold cavern depths. If there is a claim to be made, it is solely our right to claim it."

Soya then replied, "But you were too weak to keep it. Therefore, it's no longer yours to claim. A prize we shall not relinquish, we do not share your depth of weakness." Soya spoke with an unrelenting arrogance.

Kromus simply smiled and said, "I am willing to put our frivolous squabble and debate aside and focus on the present while relinquishing the claims of the past, which would be to our mutual advantage. For a war between us would pay the same dividends of that of our mutual enemy. If we agree to share, something that those furry creatures refuse to do, there will be more than enough for the both of us."

"Share!" Soya replied. "This is a concept the Sanulite people are not familiar with, and by our observations, neither are the Kraggans."

Kromus then chuckled and said, "Now is the time for both of us to change our ways or forever be denied of that which should rightfully be ours at the hands of our mutual enemy."

Soya then said, "I am listening."

Kromus continued, "For decades, both our people have attempted to take Talishar lands, only to be driven back and humiliated at the hands of those furry vermin. What would lead you to believe the same will not happen again to you, shifter?"

"They have a boy as their king," the Sanulite king responded. "One that is full of arrogance but lacking the experience, which will make them weak. With it, the odds will now have shifted in our favor."

"They may have a boy leading them, but neither his commanders nor their warriors are lacking in that area," Kromus replied. He then posed the question, "Why should either of us take such an unnecessary risk when we can unite our forces and destroy them in one sweep and divide both the spoils as well as their lands between us? We have an advantage—the element of surprise—for they would never expect an attack by both of our forces at the same time.

"Never before has this happened. They believe each of us to be both weak and divided, constantly bickering among ourselves. And our history will prove them correct, which is why we must find a middle ground and attack as one force, something they would never expect. That is why I believe they will fall." Soya listened closely and, in a subtle way, began to take interest in Kromus's words, hissing out the word *continue.*

Kromus, with his hands behind his back while grasping his wrist, began to pace and circle around both Soya and Slyth, as they shifted their faces to follow his movements while they listened. With his eyes fixed on the Sanulite leaders, he continued his speech. Pausing just for a moment, he continued to express his thoughts, "I see an opportunity that is before us, one we must not hesitate to take and one that may not ever come again. So I say once more, let us put our differences aside, for the time is right, king of the sands. There is more than enough to split between us while destroying the Talishar forever in the process. Let us not pass on this chance or fight among ourselves while our real enemy is ours for the taking."

Soya then smiled and said, "Now you have my full attention as well as my interest. What is the plan that you propose?"

Kromus then stopped in his tracks and smiled, looking over to the Sanulite king, and then he said, "On the first trimoon after the death of a Talishar king, a great celebration is held in honor of the new king in the king's city of Tajheire Though we have never ventured to where the city lies, many travelers have paid with their lives in revealing its location to us, along with the many lights that light the night skies. It is during this time of celebration that they will be the most vulnerable—the time in which they officially crown their boy king.

"For three days, they will celebrate with song and dance. Believing that we are too weak to threaten them, they will then relax their borders, all the while indulging themselves like drunken vagabonds—overconfident and relaxed. The last thing they would expect is an attack by both our people at once.

"They will journey from all four corners of the kingdom to celebrate, and while they are all together, after three days of drunkenness, they will be vulnerable like never before."

Enthusiastically Kromus spoke, "My plan is twofold, which entails attacks on two fronts—both day and night. After the full rise under the dual suns at their height, you attack first with the full Sanulite might, drawing their attention under the blazing heat, an element in which you thrive, draining them of their strength, while at night, under the cover of darkness, is an element in which we thrive.

"Those of the Talishar that remain will be drained while licking their wounds. While attempting to recover, we shall fall upon them like a flood, confusing and overwhelming them, along with their young king and his forces. Exhausted and worn down from the heat and battle, a full night attack from the Kraggans while exhausted would then finish them off."

In that instance, Slyth looked into the Kraggan king's eyes and said defiantly, "You must take us for fools. We draw the full force of the Talishar blades, and you, in turn, launch your attack while both forces are exhausted and vulnerable from combat when they'll be less resistance for you and your army to come in and destroy the remainder of both, and then you claim the prize for yourselves."

Soya then looked at the Kraggan king, but before he could reinforce his commander's thoughts, Brotos, Kromus's commander, shouted with his thundering voice, "You dare speak to the ruler of the seven clans in such a manner. For such insolence, we shall separate your head from that in which you call a body and send you back to the dust from whence you crawled out of."

Immediately Slyth responded, "You filthy pile of walking rubble, you dare challenge us? It is a mistake you won't have the chance to repeat." In that instance, the Sanulite warriors instantly began shifting their limbs into weapons as they prepared to attack, while the Kraggan forces prepared to do the same as they drew their arms of stone and rock.

Kromus looked over to his commander and shouted for silence, then he ordered his warriors to stand down. Turning to Soya, he said, "Forgive the outbreak of my malcontent commander. He can be quite anxious at times. My apologies." Silence then filled the air, before Soya hissed, calming his forces.

"If you find my strategy unagreeable, what do you propose, great king of the sands? Kromus said while making a bowing gesture with his palms open and slowly waving his arms apart.

Soya replied, "On the eve of the setting of the second sun, the first night of the trimoons, we begin our march together. We attack together but on two fronts under the cover of darkness, splitting their forces with the full might of our two armies attacking simultaneously. We have always attacked under the warmth of the sun, which is advantageous to us but has yet to relinquish any dividends in our favor. But we are not limited to that in which the sun provides to strengthen us nor does the cool of night hamper us.

"Under the stars, they will not expect an attack from us. And by the time they realize we are upon them, it will be too late. We would then overwhelm them and end this once and for all." As the two rulers stood before each other in momentary silence, Kromus broke it with a ground-shaking laugh. King Soya, along with his followers, stood silently and without expression, waiting for whatever words that would follow next.

They didn't have to wait long before getting an answer. As Kromus ceased his laughter, he smiled and spoke loud enough for all to hear. With a single word, he shouted, "Agreed!". Immediately, all tensions began to calm. King Soya shifted his faced toward his warriors, giving a hiss that all understood—that they had reached an agreement.

Kromus then said, "The Mautaur Valley in which the Atarus River flows is the dividing points of all Talishar lands, and the city of Tajheire lies at its center. We shall unite our forces at the mouth of the valley and split our two armies.

"From the east, the Kraggans shall draw them from the city walls, while from the south, you and your army engage them from the rear. Together we shall then bear down on them with our combined might until they exist no more. Once we accomplish this, everything to the north will be ours, while all that is below shall be yours, as we split everything eastward until we reach the great endless ocean."

"I issue a warning that both our people must heed to. If this barrier is crossed by either of our people, there will be no treaty or discussion. There will be nothing but war and annihilation."

Kromus then said to the Sanulite king, "Agreed!"

Soya moved forward, as if riding the wind, until he was but a breath away from the Kraggan king, looking him in his black crystal eyes and said without the satire of the Kraggan leader and without expression, "We have an agreement, and if broken, we will destroy you all."

Kromus responded with equal force and intensity, "It shall not be us who shall perish. But we shall not have to worry, for this treaty will not be broken by either of us." Both sides remained silent with clear understanding of each other's thoughts.

With those words, an uneasy pact was formed between the two. But it was clear that neither trusted the other, for they had only found a medium between the two of them. Soya then said, "There are only twenty days left before the trimoons will rise again. Therefore, we have little time to waste. There shall be no further contact between us between now and then, for all is now set. And we shall come together in force, attacking without mercy and destroying every male, every female, every child. We shall burn the memory of the Talishar from the face of Tyrus forever until the name fades into oblivion."

"The torch shall be their final destiny," Kromus smiled and said as he nodded in agreement. At that moment, Soya, along with Slyth, shifted their bodies toward their warriors and slowly moved away. The Kraggan king and his commander, Brotos, stood at the center with their eyes fixed on the two of them while they moved slowly away.

Soya shifted his face toward Slyth and hissed in a language only that of the people of the sands could understand and said, "Once the Talishar are no more, we shall dispense with the Kraggans as well." This was a gesture that Slyth found to be pleasing, as he smiled just before reaching their comrades. They dispensed into clouds of dust before drifting into the darkness of the Stoned Forest.

After he was certain the Sanulites were gone, Kromus looked over to Brotos and said, "His strategy, I could not have planned out any better." Once again he began smiling and then continued, "They are the arrogant fools that I have perceived them to be. For the cool of night plays into what our strength has now come to be. After we left that world we once knew, it now plays well to our advantage."

Abruptly with a commanding voice and no longer wearing a smile, Kromus, with a glaring stare, then said to Brotos, "Once the Talishar has been vanquished, we shall then turn our attention to the Sanulite shifters and destroy them all as well, turning them into worthless mounds of sand only to be trodden beneath our feet before being dispensed into the four winds."

Immediately after those words, he paused and then continued his thoughts and said, "Just as they have faded into the darkness, also shall they fade from memory, along with that of the Talishar." After hearing those words, a smile crept across Brotos's face as he nodded in agreement, showing his satisfaction in hearing them.

Before they returned to their forces, they, too, went on their way into the darkness. Mingled among the stone pillars and trees, the six Talishar spies that had lain hidden among sixty of their enemies had fulfilled their mission, as their king had commanded.

Now with their ears filled with all the knowledge that was needed, serving as both eyes and ears of the Talishar king, they left their hiding places to return with the plans of their enemies mapped in detail. For days, the six pressed forth with great urgency.

The future of the Talishar depended upon what they had to say to their king. Before their return, life in the city of Tajheire went on as before, seemingly oblivious to the danger that had begun to mount beyond its borders. It was no more than an illusion, for it had been rumored throughout the kingdom that the threat of war was looming, and all stood ready.

The Talishar were a warrior race and had always stood ready to defend their homelands if the need ever arose. Though life went on as usual, soon all that would change in an instant. Everyone knew that danger was now lurking along its borders.

CHAPTER 7

Joy and Pain

ON THE ROADWAY leading to the city lay the great marketplace. Not far from the gates that led within its walls was where people from all over the kingdom and travelers from far-off lands would come to buy and sell merchandise from great distances.

The great multitudes of Talishar people went about their daily lives, buying and selling goods—from fragrances to livestock and animal skins, along with the finest of stones that could be found anywhere within the kingdom. All was normal, even the sight of the king and queen strolling alongside the multitudes of people along the crowded streets accompanied by four of the king's guards.

It was common among Talishar royalty to mingle among their people. As they walked along casually, they looked over everything that was being sold. Norval and Pricillica casually conversed. Pricillica looked at the king with her emerald-green eyes and said to him, "My husband, once again you drift away in thought. It has become far more frequent these days, more than any time before. The events that have begun to build around us have taken you to a place I cannot follow unless you share them with me, my love."

A smile began to expand across Noval's face. He then replied, "Yes, you are very perceptive. I cannot go but so far from you without you drawing me back, whether it is in this world or that which lies in a corner of my mind. I am beginning to realize that you know me better than I know myself, and you are correct.

"Yes, I have been preoccupied with the events that are leading us to war and the things I must do. That is, to end all threats that loom over the future of our people. The act of war is the easy part. It's the final conclusion that I ponder. The uniting of our most dangerous enemies and what they are planning vexes me deeply, and the actions I must take will determine not only our future but that of our children and children's children as well."

The queen then responded, saying, "So much on the shoulders of a king so young, so early in the reign of a king. But this moment in time will define what you will be as a leader and as a king."

As they walked, Pricillica continued to express her thoughts, saying, "Even as darkness looms over the horizon, you hold your head as high as any that has come before you. Our people see this and are willing to follow you as they did with your father before you."

Norval stood there in silence with a sense of awe and exuberance, for he saw not just a companion but a strong queen whose wisdom was also beyond her years. Seeing the strength that was inside her, Norval saw a woman that was full of wisdom. And just as young as he, it was at that moment he knew that his bond with his queen was stronger than he ever could imagine.

As the king stood and listened to every word she spoke, she continued on, saying, "In a few weeks, the kingdom will officially honor you as our new king. I always have honored you as both my husband and my king, something I shall do while breath remains inside me."

After a moment, she paused to gather her thoughts, then with a smile, she said, "And now you are the father of our child." Briefly Norval looked away then suddenly turned his head back to her and looked into Pricillica's eyes, as if stunned. But before he could respond, she smiled and said, "Yes, my lord, you are going to be a father," before she casually turned her head as she looked away from him, placing her attention on the items that were being sold around them.

Norval was speechless but only for a moment before he reached out, taking hold of her shoulders as he gently turned Pricillica toward him, looking into her eyes as he asked the question with a reserved and relaxed voice, "Did you say that I am to be a father? That we are to have a child?" Unable to hold back, even the tone in his voice quickly turned from reserved emotions to that of exuberance and adulation before stopping in front of a vendor. He drew her close, holding her firmly around her waist. For that moment, the powerful and muscular king did not want to let her go as joy reached the deepest depth of his heart. He kissed her passionately as onlookers began to clap.

At that moment, he didn't care if he was a king or that they were in public for all to see. Showing such a display of caring was uncommon for ones who held such stature. Norval was to be a father, and nothing in the world at that moment even mattered before the reality of everything came back into focus.

"You must not be walking," Norval said with a voice of concern. He then shouted to one of his guards, commanding him to bring one of his steeds to him. But she quickly stopped the guard and said to her husband, "No need to worry, my love. I am fine."

"But you must not exert yourself," Norval then replied, his voice calm and relaxing.

"No, it's all right. It is good for our child that I move about as I do daily. Besides, it's not yet my time." Norval slowly began to calm himself. As Norval released her from his powerful arms, she turned to the merchant, an elderly woman with long flowing white hair, who was standing nearby when the king received the news. Hearing the news, she became quite eager to give whatever she had as a gift to her queen.

Though she didn't have much, it was as if it was she that was to be a mother. She humbly bowed her head toward them, addressing Pricillica, "My queen, anything that you wish that I own is yours to have, my lady, as a gift. Though I do not have much, I will give you anything that I have."

Pricillica looked over to her with a smile, one that had not left her face since revealing to the king that he was soon to become a father. She responded, "It would be an honor to accept anything you are willing to offer, but that would not be necessary. Your loyalty to the kingdom and to our people is all that is required. This would more than suffice." As the king stood silently looking on, he was still lost in the moment. Still lost for words of the news that he was to be a father. Pricillica then asked, "What a strange-looking fruit. What is it?

"It is called an adorba, found in the far lands to the south, having the sweetest nectar of any that you will ever taste." After taking a bite, the taste was so sweet she squinted, then she purred a pleasurable sound in delight. "Ummmm! Taste this, my lord, its flavor is exquisite" she said as she handed it over to him to take a bite.

He slowly sank his fangs into it, looking over at her with a smile and nodded to her in agreement. Looking back over to the merchant, Pricillica then said, "I'll take all of them."

"Yes, my queen, anything you ask is yours. No payment required."

Norval responded with a smile, "Even a king must pay their own weight, for commerce benefits us all, from the lowest to the greatest."

"And that is the wisdom that rules our lands," a voice spoke out from behind him. "It is true he has an aurora of greatness that surrounds him." The king turned and saw it was the patriarch of one of the four great families of the Talishar called Elites and the parents of Pricillica.

Her father was Tybrus, and her mother, Juniella. They had journeyed from their home in the southernmost corner of the kingdom to the king's city of Tajheire in preparation for the inaugural celebration to the new Talishar king on the next trimoon alignment.

"Father, Mother, you didn't send word that you were coming," Pricillica cried out, as she ran over to embrace her father first and then her mother.

Her mother, Juniella, then replied, "We came a little earlier than planned. We wanted to surprise you."

Norval then replied, "I am very pleased to see you once again, Mother." He walked over and embraced her. He then extended his hand to Tybrus, as they grasped each other's forearm firmly, acknowledging each other as brothers. Tybrus bowed his head to acknowledge Norval's kingship. "It pleases me to see you both, as always," Norval said.

"It is an honor to be here once again, this time to honor my new son as our newest and youngest king. We will all miss the greatness of your father. Those who knew him best mourned him the most and will honor him always, and I am sure you will do the same."

With gratitude, Norval replied, "Your presence brings double joy to this day." Pricillica's mother and father looked on in anticipation of what that could be, what words that would follow. Norval looked at them both and then said with exuberance and pride, "I am to be a father."

With those words, Tybrus and Juniella were pleased to hear that they were to become grandparents. Juniella extended her arms to embrace her daughter. Pricillica came to her, placing her head on her mother's breast and smiled at her, as they allowed the love they had for each other to be placed on display.

Tybrus then said, "Those words indeed filled my heart with joy." But before he could finish his thought, the warning trumpet sounded. Everyone immediately looked over toward the gates of the city as the king stood there, adorned in his silver-blue armor. A few hundred yards away, as he watched, were the six warriors that he had sent to patrol the outer boundaries of the northern borders and the western gateways of the Wasteland Desert.

Riding feverously toward him, he waited anxiously for what he had already anticipated. Quickly they dismounted their steeds, then all kneeled to one knee, while the lead rider approached him. King Norval then gave the command to rise and said, "You may speak."

"All is as you perceived, my lord. On the night of the next trimoon, the day that we honor you as our new king, they shall unite their forces and attack. They believe that we will be drunken in celebration and unprepared, making us vulnerable, thinking that they can then annihilate us in one massive attack.

"They are to gather at the mouth of the Mautaur Valley, then begin their march before surrounding the city when they believe they can catch us all at once. Having the advantage in numbers, along with being led by a young and inexperienced king leading us, they believe we will be easily defeated, my lord."

After hearing those words, Norval looked at his father-in-law, Tybrus; then his wife; and her mother without saying a word. Then he looked over to the open gates and then back at the message bearers and said, "Go to Theor, and gather the rest of our commanders. Inform them that we shall meet in the war chamber within the hour. Tell them the time has come and that war is once again upon our gates." Acknowledging their king, they rode off in separate ways to deliver the message. Norval then turned to the queen and said, "There isn't much time, and I have much to prepare." He leaned forward to kiss her on her lips. "I have to go."

Pricillica then replied, saying, "I shall return to the palace and wait for you." Norval smiled at her and then looked over at his father-in-law, Tybrus, and said, "Join us for our council of war." He then made a gesture for one of his guards to bring him his steed, which he then mounted, and rode off with Tybrus alongside him, accompanied by two of his guards.

Pricillica watched them ride off before she herself returned to the palace with two of her own guards escorting her. Within the hour after the command was given, the Talishar generals and commanders had begun arriving to find the king there already waiting, sitting on his throne.

CHAPTER 8

A Declaration of War

A S THE OTHERS began arriving, whispers had already begun in anticipation of what was already rumored throughout the kingdom and what they had all expected to hear—that war was imminent. Norval heard all that was needed, a confirmation, so that he could deliver his strategy.

Finally, after all were accounted for, King Norval rose to his feet with Theor standing close by him, along with his father-in-law, Tybrus. All anxiously awaited to hear what Norval had to say. Looking around the chamber at everyone that had gathered there, he then began to speak, "You have all heard the rumors that have been whispered in our ears of our greatest enemies that lie beyond the boundaries of our borders. As all of you know, for generations, to the north, the Kraggans led by Kromus, the king of the seven clans, have tested our might, believing that we took from them something that was never theirs from the beginning.

"To the west, the Sanulites of the desert sands led by their king, Soya, have tested our resolve, believing that our lands were also theirs, boasting wild claims that were never true. It has now been confirmed what I have expected all along—that they assume that I, being a young king, am arrogant, brash, and too inexperienced to lead an army, a weakness in which they believe will make us easy to defeat."

A random voice among those who had gathered shouted, "Let them believe what they will. We shall send them back to the gutters in which they spawned."

This brought a smile to the king's face, as he continued on, "A pact has now been made, and now they will unite. With an arrogance of their own, they believe they will both overwhelm and destroy us and claim our lands as their ultimate prize. But we are Talishar of the plains. No matter the shape they shift, no matter the power of their form, each has fallen before our swovels as well as our swords."

While Norval continued to share his thoughts, he began to walk among his men, speaking with such passion and fury that he began to ignite the flames of fury of all those who were gathered there, with each of their oval ears focused on his every word.

All raised their swovels, their swords, and whatever weaponry they had brought high in the air as they began to chant their young king's name again and again, "Norval!, Norval! Norval!" Though unproven, for each that were assembled there, they saw his father, King Torrad, in him, with the same fire, the same resemblance of greatness, the strength, and the dignity that his father before him had displayed.

The roar of his warriors supporting his every word only fueled the fire and passion of the young king as he continued to speak, saying, "Since I was a lad, my father, your king, had trained me in the ways of a warrior, finding finding both strengths and weaknesses of my enemies as well as myself. In the process, I learned that humility is what makes us strong. With those lessons, he taught me well. Our enemies, the Kraggans and that of the Sanulites, were the first that he had me to study as well as how to defeat them."

Theor stood boldly before the king, agreeing with his every word before offering words of his own. As he began to speak, he said, "I have fought both of these enemies, as have many that stand here among us."

Theor looked around at his comrades and his king, who gave Theor the nod to continue, giving him his time to share his thoughts. Theor knew of all the warriors that were present. He was, by far, the one with the most experience.

With equal fire in his voice that matched the king's, Theor spoke boldly, saying, "I have engaged both of our enemies that now plot against us. The Kraggans are large and powerful, but they are slow and cumbersome, making them easy for us to outmaneuver. We have proven with each encounter to be more than their equal in strength while we hold an advantage in both speed and agility. In each encounter, we have always driven them back into the mountains, humiliating them.

"But the Sanulites have proven to be far more challenging. Where they lack in brute force, they more than make that up for in their flexibility, able to strike in any position, taking any form, shifting any part of their body into a weapon. Therefore, all blows have to be precise. Stabbing them will only displace the sand, rendering the strike useless, for they will reorganize the sand in its place. What makes these foul creatures most deadly is the foul-smelling slime that they release from the bowels, regurgitating it from their bellies, dissolving flesh into sludge on contact. To kill them, one must have to get close, separating their heads from their sand-like bodies or cutting them in two while avoiding their regurgitation, which is deadlier than any weapon." All watched intensely as they listened, absorbing every word that Theor spoke.

As he turned to the king, it was obvious that Norval's focus had become more intense. All expressions had left his face, while tension quickly began to swell, evoked at the very thought of his enemies. He then looked at everyone and began to give his narrative, saying, "Both the Kraggans and the Sanulites share the same weakness—water—but with a different result on each."

With that, many looked over at one another, pondering the thought. For no one who was in the king's presence had ever engaged either foe under such conditions, not even Theor, the eldest of all the warriors that was there. He repeated the words of the king, appearing to be in wonder, "Water, my lord?"

The young king nodded to him, returning the reply, then repeated himself, "Yes, water." And then he began to tell a tale that his father had shared with him, "My father once told me of one of his adventures he had not shared with anyone. When he was a young lad, about nine, he had wandered far from the protection of the camp while he traveled westward with his father to a far-off land to establish trade with a distant kingdom. He had come across a strange patch of land with a substance that resembled sand, but it was different.

"He was too young to be left alone in such a dangerous world but with a combined boldness that drove him to venture too close to this strange clump of soil. Then it began to take shape. It was a Sanulite shifter. As it began to form, he stood there like a stone statue, amazed as it rose above him and began to move toward him. With a small swovel in his hand, one crafted by him, as with all who are taught, from the time he could walk, he stood before his giant foe, ready to engage the shifter. Being that he was too young and no match for it, it knocked him to the ground.

"Quickly he knew that it was more than he could handle and had no chance to defeat it. He began to flee as fast as his young legs could carry him. When he started to run, it released the foul slime from its belly, grazing him slightly on his arm, causing his flesh to burn and blister. My father was lucky that day. But he learned his first lesson, and he found that he could not escape his pursuer. Believing that his time had come to an end, with his pursuer at his heels, he leaped over a small stream of water.

"Falling to the ground, holding his swovel upward, believing his time was over, with a last-chance effort to protect himself, he saw that the sand warrior was almost on top of him. But he wondered why it seemed frozen as it stood on the bank near the edge of the stream. The Sanulite was held solid as it caught up in the pursuit as well as the moment and hadn't realized it was standing in the shallows. It was too late as he realized that the one thing it feared the most was water.

"As the moisture rapidly crept up its body, turning it into sludge, it could not shift. It released a hissing sound, as if in agony. All the while, it was attempting to release the substance from its belly to kill my father but could not. The water had binded its stomach. Now unable to release its fluids, it placed the creature in extreme pain.

"Seeing that it was vulnerable and helpless, it was then that my father walked over and separated its head from its body. But he never told a soul, for he was too prideful, too ashamed to tell that he had fled from an enemy despite his youth.

"Another time a second lesson was learned when, he once engaged two Kraggan warriors in battle alone. As a teen, once again he found himself in a place where he should not have been and was told never to venture alone. Once again, being a teen, along with being stubborn, despite being the son of a king, he was still searching to find his true self. After disobeying the king's order, he traveled along the northern ridge of the mountain slopes to the north.

"Curiosity had driven him beyond Talishar boundaries into dangerous and hostile lands. It was then he was ambushed by the two stone warriors at the edge of a mountain pool of shallow water. Though young, with his speed fueled by arrogance, he held off his opponents but still lacked the experience to sustain a long battle with such seasoned foes. As the fight carried on into the water, the two semigiants began to sink deeper and deeper into the soft, muddy silt bed under the murky water as their weight and bulk held them fast and without leverage, allowing my father to smash through his opponents' defenses, killing them both. Another valuable lesson was learned on that day, as well as a valuable secret that he kept until he shared it, but only with me. And now I am sharing with you.

"It is this weakness that I plan to exploit." After his speech, he found himself where he had first begun to address them. Directly back in front of all his commanders, he continued his speech, only pausing for a brief moment to gather his thoughts. He then began to tell them of his strategy as his focus became intense once more. "In the past, we would drive them both back to where they came the moment they stepped onto our soil, but I have a different plan!" he shouted. "This time, I shall invite them to the ceremony to partake in celebration with us."

Theor then asked, "You would offer our enemies an invitation? The Kraggans and the Sanulites, the ones that hope to destroy us?"

"Yes," Norval replied, "those very ones."

Theor then said, "My lord, but that is madness, an invitation they would gladly accept—to be at our very heart and stab us through it." After those words, the council chamber began to fill with murmurs and rumblings.

Norval then said, "Yes, it echoes with the sound of madness, but it will not be the invitation that any of you perceive nor will it be one that is expressed to them through words. It will be one with a more obscure nature. We will invite them in by allowing them to advance unobstructed. To lead them to believe what they are already believing—that we are both unaware and unprepared. Therefore, the invitation is a free entry into our homeland. But it will be a path that we will set for them to follow.

"It will come far short of the city they hope to visit, sack, and pillage. It is known that neither the Sanulites nor Kraggans have ever set foot in or near that of the king's city. Only by word of mouth of travelers that were unfortunate enough to be captured and tortured, relinquishing whatever information that they had until finally being killed."

One among the council then asked, "How are we to lead them onto this set path?"

Norval replied, "At night we will light up the night skies on the days leading up to the ceremony with torches and fire, as many that can be gathered until we turn night into day. We shall brighten the sky until the city outshines the great moons, but it is not Tajheire whose light will outshine the stars but that of a false city of Tajheire we shall build away from here. But it will be only a shell."

"What shall that be, my king?" Theor asked.

"Trenches!" the king responded. "We will dig hundreds of shallow trenches and shallow pits throughout the valley's path that we will lay for them to march into. We will lead them to believe that it will give them the advantage they seek while remaining undetected. We will also align both the walls and the bottom of these pits and trenches with assurpetine oil, which will lay dormant and harmless until mixed with water, then it will cause both liquids to mesh and take on the same qualities as it will then adhere to any substance, becoming a mucky substance, flammable as well as volatile.

"We will then dig hundreds of canals that will feed these trenches from the Atarus River. We will carve the hollows out of the trees we cut down and direct the river water through them, concealing them along the way.

"When the Kraggans and Sanulites hear the sounds of song and dance, I believe they will then release their entire force, believing they will annihilate us in one massive strike. They will believe that we will be consumed in celebration in my honor, as we will give them that illusion using trumpets and horns to magnify the sounds through the night.

"They will believe us to be a kingdom of drunkards, unprepared for battle, while we celebrate the crowning of my new kingship, never expecting an attack, let alone a war. They will think that there will be little resistance, no obstacle following a trail that we shall leave for them to follow, allowing them to believe the gateway to the empire is open and will be theirs for the taking.

"Once they reach the center slope of the valley where all sides are even flat at their lowest point, I will send the signal to release the water, bogging them down. I will give the signal for our archers to light their arrows with fire and then release them into the air onto the oil-based trenches, consuming them within the flames, offering little escape.

"By this time, they will have realized that it is them that have walked into a trap. At that point, we shall come down upon them in force, come down like the very waters that have trapped them both. It is then that they can join in on the celebration as our honored guests until none of them remain alive."

But there was yet another question asked to their king, as another of his commanders stepped forth, giving a salute, then saying, "Sire, I thought only separation of head and torso would kill those such as the

Sanulites. Also the thickness of the Kraggan's stonelike hides would offer them some protection against the flames."

Norval looked at him and smiled, then he replied, "It would be impractical to charge into battle with flaming swords and swovels. Therefore, I omitted it from my words. As strange as they may be, they are still living creatures and can be consumed by the flames. The thickness of Kraggan hides or the shifting of Sanulite bodies never hindered our swords. Therefore, both can die by other means, flames included. We will use everything at our disposal to achieve victory with the least amount of effort."

All were amazed and dazzled by the prowess of one so young. Even Theor, who was the eldest and the most experienced of all the warriors that had assembled in the chamber, was beyond impressed. It was then that all were certain that they had a king that they could follow.

After his speech, the young king stood silently. Once again as they all did until a random voice out of the midst of generals and commanders broke the silence. They began chanting the king's name once again, calling out, "Norval! Norval! Norval! Norval!"

As everyone erupted, calling out the king's name, he then looked around at each of his commanders and generals before continuing to speak, "I've grown weary of tales of these intruders pressing our borders, along with them being driven back, only to return generation after generation. I intend on ending this madness once and for all."

Theor then looked over to his king, sensing the weight of the next group of words that would follow.

"Both the Kraggans and the Sanulites will be anxious, even reckless, and that's what I'm counting on. With our northern forces lying in wait, camouflaged among the open grassy fields, we will also keep an equal force well within the cover of the forest, as we watch them pass, while we remain hidden, making any chance of escape impossible for either of them. Those that may filter through in retreat will have to take that same path to return to their home, and it is there we will finish the rest of them.

"We shall extinguish any of their lingering hopes of escape, but it shall not end there. We shall invade both the desert sands of the Sanulites, as well as the caverns of the Kraggans, and kill everything that lives there—females as well as their offsprings. When it's all done, neither shall remain on the face of Tyrus. I have sent word to my commanders that guard the outer boundaries of the empire, relaying to them my plan and what they must do."

He then turned to those in attendance and said, "Under the cover of night, we must begin immediately. We have little time and much work to do." Then he looked across at them and said, "From this day until the next moon alignments, no one shall be allowed to enter or leave the boundaries of our kingdom, for we must guard against any possibilities of our plans being revealed to our enemies. Now go, we haven't much time."

At that instance, they all stood—not saying another word—saluted their king and went about doing the king's business. Theor was the last to leave, looking over at the king without either sharing another word, but it was evident in the eyes of Theor that even he was impressed with the savvy of the young king before he, too, went his own way.

CHAPTER 9

The Preparation

ALONG THE PERIMETERS of the great Mautaur Valley, Norval ordered additional patrols to the north and to the west to guard against any spying eyes that may have been sent from those of the mountains and those of the Sanulites. The Talishar worked feverously from sunset to sunrise as thousands worked relentlessly without a break to complete the task at hand, careful to cover their work to prevent detection from any spy that may have slipped through the gauntlet of watchful eyes that were set upon to prevent it from happening.

For miles, trenched canals were built like veins leading from the heart, fed by the Atarus River. Along with it were a series of small tributaries and waterways that were littered around the valley, all leading to the large shallow trenches the Talishar had built.

They covered nearly the entire valley, which were held back by floodgates that were built at the entrance of the canals to hold back the water till the signal was given to release it. At night they worked with an acute vision that allowed them to see where others could not.

Only the Kraggans possessed nearly equal ability, but they kept watchful eyes upon their borders for any and all movements. With only the light of the stars and the giant moons as light to guide them through the night, they finally had everything in place and complete. Finally, they were ready, and their trap was now set a little more than a week before their enemies planned invasion.

Neither the Sanulites nor the Kraggans had a clue what the young king had in store for them. After receiving word that the work had been complete, Norval summoned his people. Thousands gathered just outside the great fortress wall. Standing on a loft high above them, King Norval, with his queen, Pricillica, by his side, looked down at the multitudes of people, each trained from their youth with the art of war.

As they stood anxiously awaiting the words of their king, they chanted frantically the king's name over and over again, honoring their young king until the sound became almost deafening.

Having already addressed his commanders and expressed his plans, it was now time to fully address the people about what they had to prepare for. What he was about to say was no secret. For months, all had been aware of the approaching danger. It was now time to make it official.

Raising his arms overhead to calm the crowd, the chants slowly began to die down until all was quiet. Standing tall and strong, the muscular figure reminiscent of Talishar males with pale blue, peach-like fur covering his body, the king began to speak, saying, "People of the Talishar! War is once again at our door. Our enemies have once again desired to try their hand in annihilating us from the face of this world. But they are in grave error in their assessment of who we are. We are a people bred for war. Though peaceful at heart, we stand ready to defend our homes, our families, and our kingdom. We are unequal in might and ability. Any that dare to attempt to destroy us will mirror that fate and without mercy.

"For we are Talishar, warriors from birth, and we neither fear nor bow to no one. And that is what the Kraggans and Sanulites will soon learn, a lesson I plan not to repeat. For they have become allies, partners in destruction, a fate they will both share for the error they will soon make.

"I have grown tired of the constant threats and annoyances, and I shall take the fight to their doorsteps. For once we destroy their armies, we shall trample upon their lair and destroy the very essence of life in which they dwell. Not a female, not a child, not anything, only the memory that they ever exist will remain until it, too, fades in the vastness of time.

"This was the very fate that they had planned for us—to wipe us clear from this world. But it will not be us that will fade from memory, for we are Talishar. No army can withstand either our blades, our swovels, or our will."

Once again the crowd erupted, chanting the name of Norval, as Pricillica stood back, watching her husband with prideful eyes. Once again he raised his arms to quiet the crowd, then he said to all with the thunderous voice of a roaring lion, "It is now time for each of us to prepare for war. Arm yourselves, and pray that God will favor us and empower our swovel to vanquish our enemies forever. That time is now upon us. Now go and make yourselves ready, for in three days, we will begin our march and set the trap for the vermin that now threatens our very existence."

After hearing the words of their king, all went their way to prepare themselves. Norval had already sent word to the outer boundaries, to those who guarded both the west and the north, to withdraw their forces. Moving them inward as planned, he was opening the door, allowing their enemies to enter their lands while a second force was sent to both regions to spread out beyond Talishar borders.

They were careful to remain hidden, which would allow their enemies to pass by unabated. After the gathering, they returned to their homes before leaving for war, never truly knowing if they would return again to be with their wives and their children and not knowing what the future might hold before donning their armor and sharpening their blades.

Back at the palace, Norval walked down the hallway, along with Theor, as the king shared his personal thoughts with him. Looking over at his commander, Norval said, "The time has come to present the invitations to our honored guests. I will split the bulk of our army that is here waiting for my command in two parts. As the Sanulites come in from the west of the Mautaur Valley, you shall come up from the south, then circle west around behind them.

"They will not suspect or anticipate our actions. While you march to attack the Sanulites' rear, I take my forces north, outflanking the Kraggans, circling behind them. With reinforcements already in place to help finish what we will have begun soon after they join the celebration, we shall have an even greater surprise waiting for them both. Are our forces within the decoy in place?"

"Yes, my lord," Theor responded.

"Excellent!" Norval responded. "I want the sounds of music to rival that of the true event. The greater the sound of celebration, of songs, and of laughter, the happier we shall appear. With no thought what so, not even an inkling of suspect that they would be the ones who are under siege, making the celebration even grander.

Theor looked over at Norval, astonished with the knowledge he had displayed, as well as his talents and savvy. He then said, "You are destined to be a great king, for your thoughts are far beyond your age and experience, and I am honored to have you as my king."

Norval replied, "No, it is I that honors you, for you have been a loyal servant of the Talishar, fought many battles to preserve our ways, and proved to be the most trusted at my father's side. And to know you stand here at mine, there is no better warrior or friend that could be by my side."

Giving his salute to the king, Theor said, "It is time that I to go to prepare myself for the task ahead." He turned and walked away, while Norval continued on to go to his chambers.

Waiting for her husband in the royal chambers, Pricillica had adorned herself in an attire that could seduce an entire army. Standing over six feet, she was tall and eloquent, tall even for that of a Talishar female whose stature had long been renowned and one of note.

She was born in one of the four great Talishar families called the Elites. These were high-ranking families of noble bloodlines among the Talishar people. Both honored and respected, they were established from the early days of the Talishar Kingdom. Norval had fallen in love and married Pricillica nearly a year before the death of his father. She wore what amounted to a thin red body veil, exposing all, as she had plans this night for her husband, her king, her lover.

The evening before he would leave to lead his warriors to battle, he retreated to his chambers for the night to find the queen waiting and the room was adorned with flowers, along with sweet-smelling herbs with a fragrance that would set the mood for any man of Talishar descent.

As he entered the chamber, she greeted him with a kiss before he walked over to the balcony and stood silently, looking to the west in the direction he would march. Undeterred by his wife's preparation, his mind was still heavy in thought, and she understood the weight of the burden that was lying on his shoulders.

In three days, his enemies would begin to launch what they believed would be their surprise attack. With his strategy already planned and waiting to be carried out, he was taking the time to allow them to sink into his head.

The queen walked up to him and stood beside him, resting her head on his shoulders, while she wrapped her left arm around his waist. With her hair drawn back into a tail, she then said to her husband, "I see that you're heavy in your thoughts. Share them with me."

He looked over to her, giving a half smile, then he answered what his men had already known. He repeated the words he had shared earlier, but this time, they were delivered more passionately and more personally to her, "Our two most dangerous enemies have pressed our borders for the last time. No more. I remember being the height of my father's knee when the Kraggans last attacked us. Years before that, it was the Sanulites. I remember clinging close to my mother the day they were driven back, which was the day that my mother died, like my father, of illness. It was the only time I saw my father weep, for he loved my mother more than life itself.

"After she died, he took me into the throne room and sat me on his knee and said, 'One day you shall be king, and on that day, your enemies will come once again to destroy not only you but all that we are. For you are very young as I am old, even for that of being a father, and if something were to happen to me suddenly and you were propelled to the throne, they will perceive your inexperience as well as your youth as a weakness and will attempt to destroy you.'

"Then he put me down from off his knee and stood before me and said, 'From this day, I shall teach you what you must learn to be king—how to think like your enemies, how to strategize and go beyond yourself—so that you will become more formidable than any could ever dream. For it is the mind that makes the strategy, the heart that leads the people, not the swovel or the foreblade but this'—he held his swovel in front of me—'will enforce your will.'

"From that day, my lessons had begun, and it was that day I began to learn what it meant to be king and how to rule as one." As Pricillica stood close and quietly, only listening, Norval paused and said, "This time, they believe they truly can defeat us outright and destroy us in the process."

She then replied, "You, like your father and his father's father before him, will guard and protect our people the same as all that came before them."

"Yes! That is true," Norval responded. Then he looked deep into her eyes with such intensity she could feel it. It was as if a weight was placed on top of her, and he said, "Unlike those that have led before me, this time I intend to do much more. On my father's name, I shall rid us from these threats forever, though what I've decided to do may seem cruel and callous. There may come a day when they may very well succeed, and I shall see to it that the day never comes."

He then leaned down and kissed his wife, kissing her with such passion and intensity that he was oblivious to the world around him before closing the drapes, as he backed her up into the bed while removing the hair band, allowing her hair to flow freely. And there they remained until dawn.

The king rose early, leaving his queen in a deep sleep from a night of heavy passion. Donning his armor, he left his quarters to meet with his commanders before addressing the entire force. Standing before his armies, the large muscular king had his long hair drawn back behind his oval ears and was garbed in his gold-plated armor.

His abdomen was exposed, showing his rigid, well-defined stomach, with his swovel draped across his back, a sword on his hip, and daggers strapped to both thighs while his foreblade aligned with his forearm.

This was the attire of a Talishar warrior regardless of status, each being equally deadly as the other. With his thoughts sharp and direct, he stood before his army, then he began to address them, "Our enemies believe us to be weak because of me. They believe because of my age, I will make mistakes—mistakes they believe that will bring us defeat. They will come, and when they do, they will come with their entire force in the attempt to overwhelm us, make us break rank, and flee like cowards. I intend to end these constant struggles that we have endured through the generations.

"Every time they test us, we drive them back again and again and again. I have grown weary of this. I intend to end the wars with our enemies forever. Unlike times past, we will lure them into our bosom and welcome them in with open arms. We shall allow them to join in on the celebration, then lay them to rest forever. If they flee, we will follow them were they hide and destroy them there. We will have peace—peace that will last for generations to come.

"Make yourselves ready, for we are Talishar! Nothing or no one can defeat us, for we are one!" Norval turned to Theor, interlocking forearms, which was equal to a handshake.

"May God be with you, my lord," Theor said to the king.

Norval then replied, "May God be with us all." With the ending of those words, the king mounted his powerful large black ramsteeds—fleet of foot, built for the open plains. It was a valued tool used in battle, ramming an enemy with great force, unbalancing them. Following these words, the king was applauded with cheers. The people of Talishar were enamored with their young king, chanting his name with great fervor by both warriors and laymen alike.

All those who were there watched them ride off to defend their kingdom. With twenty thousand warriors in place, awaiting their king's arrival, Norval began his journey to join them, anticipating a combined force that was twice that of the Talishar.

CHAPTER 10

The Mautaur Valley, the Trap, and a Time for Reckoning

A S THE TALISHAR king marched to the north of the Mautaur Valley, to the south, Theor and his forces marched to join the twenty thousand Talishar in place, like their northern counterparts. While the Talishar began placing their plan in motion, the Sanulites and Kraggans began to prepare their warriors to march.

In the sand fortress of Mordune, known as the city of sand, the king of the Sanulites, Soya, also stood before his army of shape-shifters. Ready and prepared, he and his people were reaping in confidence. So sure were they of the outcome of what they believed would be their final conflict and long-awaited victory of their vaunted and unsuspecting foe.

In a low hissing voice that carried on the wind like the desert breeze, the obscure leader began to speak to his warlords and his warriors, "For the first time in generations, after many campaigns and failures, we will have an opportunity to have our way against our hated enemy. We will unleash our entire force upon their soil with the aid of our stone-faced allies, destroying them while laying waste to the green before turning it into sand, making what was theirs into what will soon be ours. If those lumbering fools of stone do their part according to plan, the war will be brief, and we will kill every Talishar left standing.

"After their defeat and we have secured the land agreed upon under that meaningless treaty with the Kraggan king, we will then turn our attention on them, turning their worthless hides into rubble."

All stood silent until Soya finished speaking, then with an eerie sound in the way of Sanulites, the air was filled with the sound like that of hissing snakes. But unknown to one another, each of them shared the same thoughts.

High up in the Northern Mountains, deep within its caverns, the king of the seven clans, the Kraggan ruler, Kromus, stood before nearly fifty thousand of his warriors, who were eager and ready to pour down from the mountains, like an avalanche, to crush every Talishar they faced.

With a renewed sense of confidence, this was the first time they believed they had a true chance of victory. This wouldn't be a series of raids but an all-out attack, taking the lands agreed upon with the Sanulites.

But the Kraggan king, like his Sanulite ally, had something else in mind. He then began to speak to his stone warriors. With a voice so strong and intense, his thunderous voice shook small stones from the cavern walls, he said, "Soon we shall lay our wrath upon those furry vermin of the Talishar, a surprise long in coming. But we will not stop there. After we are done with them, we turn our attention on the Sanulites with equal fury, treading over then wiping their crushed bodies from under our feet as well, taking it all. The Sanulites pose no threat to us. Their fowl muck has no effect on us. They are too weak to defeat us."

Three days had now passed since Norval left the city of Tajheire. Finally, he, along with his twenty thousand warriors, arrived at the north of the Mautaur Valley, quickly spreading out to reinforce those forces that were already hidden in place.

Upon their arrival, he was greeted by Zorrax, commander of his northern forces. As Norval dismounted his steed, Zorrax stood before him and said, "Greetings, my lord. We are most honored by your presence and stand ready and waiting for your command, my lord."

Norval then replied, "Tomorrow at sunset, the armies of both Kraggans and the Sanulites will cross our borders. For three days, the illusion of a celebration has been ongoing, lighting the night skies with the sounds of songs and grandeur as it is carried along the winds well across Talishar borders to that of the Kraggan lands."

For three days, both Kraggan and Sanulite armies had begun their march. To the north, the Kraggan army came down from atop their mountain kingdom, while to the west, the Sanulite forces approached from their desert home. Each only taking pause as they awaited the nightfall before crossing into Talishar lands.

Neither army wanted to risk detection before arriving at the appointed place with such a large force. But what they didn't know was that they were already being watched by skilled and concealed warriors. Following Norval's command in the north, the Talishar allowed the Kraggan army to pass by them, undeterred and unabated, through the thick forest, which offered the perfect cover for the large Talishar force stalking them while they remained undetected under the heavy thickets and foliage.

While to the west, with a terrain so varied and so vast it offered various places to hide, even an army could find refuge and conceal itself without being detected. With an array of hills, tall grasses, and trees, the Talishar exploited all these areas leading up to the great arid desert. A mighty people renowned for their frontal and direct assault, they were also expert stealth fighters with a reputation of having catlike abilities that most of their adversaries had long forgotten.

Pressing forward, the Sanulites continued their march. It would be hours before they would reach the mouth of the Mautaur Valley on the time agreed upon. With King Soya leading his army, Slyth looked at Soya and said with a hiss, "This is too easy. We have come across no patrols, no people, not even random movement. Even the villages and towns have been vacant. Does it not seem strange? Something about this is not right. Maybe we should wait. Maybe this is all a trap."

The king looked at Slyth with only the briefest of pause and replied with an even deeper hiss, "The time of our waiting is at its end. We have waited long enough already. We will arrive at the appointed place at the appointed time, and I will allow nothing to hinder us. Together with our unwanted ally, we will finish this once and for all and claim what is rightfully ours."

With that, Soya dismissed the thought that Slyth's assumption might have had merit. Then he finished his thought, saying to him, "You worry too much. If they had an idea we were coming, they would have faced us long before us venturing this far within their lands."

Reluctantly Slyth replied, "Yes, my master." And with those words, they didn't continue speaking any further on the subject.

Meanwhile to the north, the king of the seven clans, Kromus, shared similar words with his top commander, Brotos, mirroring that of King Soya and his general. Well within their march, Brotos, too, had become skeptical with the ease in which they had journeyed so deeply into Talishar lands without any obstruction. Though they were careful in their movements, it all seemed too easy. Like the Sanulites, they, too, had encountered empty villages and towns. Unknown to both armies, the Talishar people had also withdrawn from view, relinquishing the comforts of their home as they held to their king's plan, allowing their enemies to pass.

They were a kingdom of warriors. All that could hold a weapon stood ready in the event that they, too, could be called upon to fight if need be. Kromus elected not to put the torch to any village or town they came across, fearing that smoke and fire might alert unwanted eyes and would alert Talishar forces, thus spoiling their surprise. Instead he kept his forces constantly moving.

Kromus was confident that the Talishars were clueless of their plans, for he believed that the Talishar had not an inkling of the events that were to unfold. He had little doubt that the absence of the Talishar was because this was occurring within the three days of celebration and the Talishar had all journeyed to the king's city to honor their king. With that thought in mind, he showed very little concern.

As they continued on, Brotos turned to Kromus and said, "Our path is far too easy, for there has been very little movement of any kind since entering these lands. We have seen nothing of their people. It is as if we were being given an invitation to the very heart of their lands."

Kromus looked at him with an arrogant smile and said in a heavy, gravelly voice, "I am certain they haven't a clue, or we would've met in battle once we crossed into their lands." Brotos looked at his king, offering no reply after hearing his thoughts. His only reply was a silent compliance as he nodded his head in agreement while all remained silent as they continued on.

Hours had passed, and finally, each of these great armies arrived at the mouth of the Mautaur Valley as agreed upon. Face-to-face, the two armies met each other under the cover of night—the stonelike Kraggans on one side and the sand-like shape-shifters on the other. As the two rulers faced each other, Kromus said to Soya, "The time has finally come that, together, we will eliminate our greatest enemy forever. Together we shall make them pay for the grief and injustice they caused us through the ages, one they will truly regret." Soya stood quietly, listening to the stone king carry on with his speech until finally interrupting him and saying, hissing like a serpent, "Enough talk! It is time that we end this and claim what is ours. Once this is done, we will divide the spoils as agreed upon. Remember our treaty, Kraggan, or you and your people will share their fate."

Shrewd and deceptive, Kromus smiled and replied, "As you have stated, enough words. Let us begin. When we reach their precious city, we kill them all, an invitation they unwittingly extended."

Soya then shifted his face toward his own army. He opened his mouth with a width that seemed to cover his entire face but did not speak a single word, only a long pronounced hiss that vibrated through their ranks that signaled to his army that it was time to move forward.

At that same instance, Kromus turned to face his forces, raising his arm into the air, also giving them the signal to begin their march. Thousands of Kraggan warriors walked side by side with that of the Sanulite shifters as they both moved forward together with one goal in mind, and that was to destroy their mutual enemy.

The Kraggan army rumbled on alongside that of the Sanulites, who were taking the forms of humans with the texture of sand, with their arms formed as weapons. They were focused with one purpose: to kill every Talishar they faced—man, woman, or child. There should be no survivors. As their forces pressed forward, unknown to them, Norval and his army began to close the door of escape behind them.

Torches were lit, with hundreds of warriors hidden behind the false gates of the great replica city, giving the illusion that it was occupied by those who had journeyed both far and near to be in attendance, while they sounded out the sounds of celebration as it rang out through the night, carried atop the night winds. Trumpets sounded as laughter filled the air. It was as if it truly was happening.

Every torch was lit while large piles of wood delivered a glow that was received like a beacon under the starlit sky. It was like an open invitation to join the celebration with an army of drunkards celebrating the reign of the new boy king.

What Norval had prepared was an exact replica of the outward city fortress of Tajheire—wood painted to appear as stone that was built by the tireless efforts, with nonstop hours both day and night, of determined people in a very short time. Coupled with the darkness of the night, it appeared to be flawless, but it was no more than an oversized decoy created to perfection. Meanwhile, the two armies followed the path given off by the illusion of this false city. Both the Kraggan and Sanulite armies slowly moved into the trap that was within the center of the valley.

Finally, they had gone beyond the edges of the hundreds of trenches that were dug and concealed. The Talishar army patiently lay in position, waiting for the king to give the signal to spring the trap.

Warriors spread about every hundred meters or so as they waited on Norval to give the silent signal that had already been set up to move along the ranks in the directions of the floodgates that were manned by those charged with opening them, releasing the waters.

Warriors stood ready at the highest points, overlooking the valley floor below. Norval was at a perfect vantage point as the great moons allowed enough light for the catlike vision of the Talishar to see the enemies' every move.

Standing beside Norval was his bowman, waiting to light a fire to dip the tip of his arrow in once the order was given to light it. The closer the enemy came to the false city, the greater the sounds of laughter, and the music had become more prevalent, even joyful.

The anxiety mounted as both the Kraggans and the Sanulites got closer. The anticipation allowed the adrenaline to flow through the veins of the two allies as they moved closer in anticipation of battle that would end their conflict with the Talishar once and for all.

Anxious and thirsting for revenge, they picked up their pace while recklessly advancing. Once both armies were in place, Norval then gave the signal to release the waters. Quickly it flowed down the hill through the canals as the trenches and pits quickly filled. He then looked at his bowmen as they waited for the waters to flow before nodding his head, giving them the signal to release thousands of their arrows into the air, finding their mark in the valley below.

With the release of the water, the Kraggans and the Sanulites continued to advance. They were still oblivious to the events that had occurred until, suddenly, Slyth stopped and then looked down at his feet, realizing that he had begun to sink into the soil. It had been gradual and subtle as his lower body began to bind, absorbing the waters and becoming stuck.

He was the first to notice, but he was not alone. Both armies had also begun to become trapped. Slyth then looked at his king, Soya, and said, "It's a trap! We must retreat." Soya looked back and opened his mouth as wide as he could, giving the order to retreat, but it was too late.

Alongside the Sanulites, the Kraggans had also become trapped, but it was at a much-faster rate as their heavy bodies began to sink more rapidly. Kromus, now knee-deep, reached down into the mucky water, twisting his finger in it. Then he brought it to his nose to smell it and then quickly looked over to Brotos as both exchanged eye contact.

Both immediately knew what the substance was. Kromus looked around and roared the order to retreat, then he looked up as a flicker of light caught his attention. The sky was lit by thousands of flaming arrows that began to rain onto them.

At that moment, Kromus and the others knew it was too late. As the ground began to burst into flames, along with the two armies that were trapped in them, they became consumed by the flames and explosions. The sounds of an eerie agony from these strange creatures filled the valley as a few managed to find a more solid base away from the flames.

The Talishar had already surrounded the advancing armies and simply waited until they were completely entrapped before readying for their attack to conclude this conflict. It was then that Norval gave the command to attack as his forces. Along with those led by Theor, they rained down on their enemies.

Leading the charge, Norval and his forces, along with Theor and his, ran through their ranks, slaughtering everything that was not consumed by the flames. Even while burning alive, both the Kraggan and Sanulite forces attempted to put up a fight. But it was useless, as the swift and deadly Talishars were too agile for hindered warrior, avoiding their fleeting blows as sword and swovels met. The stone blades, though interlaced with metal, were still no match for the blade of the Talishar swovel. Most exploded on contact.

Even the Sanulites who had managed to free themselves from the flaming muck found it difficult to find their target with blades from their limbs and the acid from their bowels, as Talishar after Talishar evaded their attempts, only to find their mark in separating the heads and the torsos of the Sanulites.

Miraculously, both the Kraggan and the Sanulite kings had managed to escape the muck, but Brotos and Slyth weren't quite as fortunate. Brotos had partially freed himself, only to lose his head by the swift blow of a Talishar warrior. Brotos had briefly engaged as he lunged awkwardly toward the Talishar with his rock ax missing badly while partially in flames.

His opponent had dealt the final blow and ended it, sidestepping his attempt before taking his head as he fell slowly back into the flames. Slyth, too, was dealt with swiftly by the blades of two Talishars, with the first taking his head almost as simultaneously as the other blade separated his torso, as each Talishar stopped on opposite sides of him.

In passing one to the front of him, the other standing at his rear, he fell where he stood. While the slaughter raged on Soya, the Sanulite king, quickly turned and attempted to escape.

He avoided the blows that surrounded him as his warriors fell all around—most consumed by flames and the others met their end at Talishar hands. He miraculously found a pathway free of flames and any that pursued him.

He took that route as quickly as he could until there was no one around. He then stopped and looked back as the smoke from the fire filled the air. It was that very smoke that had gotten him that far, but all this was no more than an illusion.

All the escape routes were mapped out and closed when he shifted his face back to the direction of his escape. The last thing he saw was the swovel blade of Theor, who was standing there, waiting, ending the life of the Sanulite king.

Meanwhile, amid the slaughter, Kromus, the king of the seven clans, had also somehow remained standing, scorched and battered. He was now standing face-to-face with the boy king he had sought to destroy.

In the midst of the heavy smoke, two silhouettes of two kings stood ready to decide which one would survive. Norval looked at his warriors, commanding them to stand down, while he faced the large gray behemoth.

With a sickle-shaped sword made from stone, Kromus took his battle stance with the same arrogant smile he had on when he had ridden into battle as Norval stood before him, expressionless, before slowly taking his stance.

Kromus's smile turned into laughter, then he said defiantly, "Boy! My army may have fallen this day, but by my hand, you shall follow the fallen. You are indeed your father's son, but you are only half the scum he was. Since I was denied his head because of an untimely fate, I shall have yours before the breath leaves my body."

Norval looked into Kromus's eyes before taking a crouched stance. Drawing back to the side with his leg extended and the other leg slightly bent, he held a perfect form and balance. His eyes never leaving his opponent, Norval held his swovel slightly behind him while extending his foreblade in front, as if preparing to dance. As Kromus began to move forward, Norval, too, began to go into motion, crossing his steps as he began to circle the gray semigiant very carefully. As he circled, he spun his swovel with one hand, as if it was a baton, before grasping it and taking hold with two.

He twirled it twice as fast as before, taking it over his head and then around his body as it spun almost effortlessly. Kromus took pause as he stood with a look of befuddlement, for the swovel was known to be a bulky and awkward weapon, but the Talishars were the masters of it. It was as if it was a part of them, one with them. But the Kraggan king held his form, and with his stone sword in front of him, he attempted to keep up with Norval's movements. Like a dancer, Norval moved with balance and grace. His movements seemed to almost hypnotize the Kraggan king while he moved within striking distance.

As Norval slowly moved closer, he was now within Kromus's reach. The Kraggan then lunged forward to deliver his blow, but Norval spun his body around 360 degrees, using his momentum to counter Kromus's attack.

As the Talishar's blade of the swovel and the metal-laced stone sword of the Kraggans met, the sound of the collision replicated that of a lightning strike, as sparks from metal and stone flashed, along with the thunderous sound of an oncoming storm. Each of the two kings made an equal attempt to end this as the Talishar soldiers looked on by their king's command.

Back and forth, they dealt their blows with neither gaining the advantage. But with each attempt, the blows of each came closer to finding their mark. The Kraggan king was also highly skilled as he attacked with extreme ferocity. No quarter was asked or was one given. This duel was driven by pure hatred and rage. There could be but one outcome, which was death.

But as the battle raged, the agility of the young Talishar king began to become prevalent as his blows began to graze the armor of Kromus, knocking away chips at a time, causing Kromus to move backward. With each blow, the Kraggan king felt its impact as he grunted, displaying obvious pain with every blow that grazed his armor. Norval's speed and agility had begun to take form as the advantage began to move to the young king's favor.

Norval had begun to chip away at Kromus's defense with the blade of the Talishar proving to be much superior to that of the Kraggan's stone-chipped blades. They were stronger and far more durable.

With one massive collision, the two blades met with such force that the Kraggan king's sword shattered into rubble, leaving only splintered metal veins that had once held it all together. As it exploded, the sound echoed across the valley.

It had been compromised by the accumulation of blows that were delivered in this contest. But there was still enough to kill if Kromus could get close enough to find his target. With two hands holding his broken sword, Kromus swung with all his might.

Norval then slipped under him, leaving the Kraggan finding nothing but air. Norval countered him as he used the spear end of the swovel atop the spinning ax blades while he spun his body around to the left, burying the blade deep into the center of Kromus's chest, finding his heart.

Bringing him to his knees, leaving him gasping for air, Kromus dropped his sword. Then without hesitation, Norval withdrew his blade from his chest and then spun around, slicing the throat of Kromus with the second of his spinning blades, causing him to choke in his own blood.

Finally delivering the coup de grâce, he spun once again, this time to his right, dealing the final blow by burying his ax deep into the center of Kromus's skull while still spinning, splitting it in two, like a melon, with Kromus's blood splattering like a shower back on Norval, who was unfazed as he watched Kromus fall facedown to the ground in a pool of blood.

Norval stood over him, staring down at his corpse. Through the entire contest, he was unscathed and unmarked. As he watched Kromus take his last breath, he then draped his swovel across his back. Then silently, he surveyed the battlefield of what had been a slaughter of two armies—the annihilation of the armies of the Kraggans and the Sanulites. Kromus lay dead at Norval's feet with his enforcer, Brotos, lying in the midst of the fallen, with both armies spread across the Mautaur Valley, forming a blanket of death and rivers of blood. No one survived, with only a sparse collection of Talishar warriors sprinkled among the dead.

Emerging through the smoke and flames that were rising from the burning trenches surrounding them, Theor rapidly approached with nearly a dozen warriors riding close behind him until he was finally face-to-face with Norval. Theor acknowledged his king and then looked at his feet, seeing Kromus's body lying face down in blood. Then he said to him, "It is done, my lord. Their armies are no more. The Sanulite king, Soya, has met the same fate as that of the Kraggan king that is lying before you. He, too, had met his fate at the end of my swovel, with his head separated from his body."

The few that managed to escape the gauntlet of both swords and swovels met their end beyond the valley enroute to their home, only to find the Talishar forces there hidden among the trees and bushes to greet them before sending them to join their comrades in what would be their final destination—death.

Norval then said, "There is but one more task that must be completed, then it will be finished."

Instantly Theor knew what must be done, as he saw the hidden pain that was evident in his king's eyes. But it was a command that would not waver. Norval then said to him, being true to his word, "Gather the army. We must march again and finish what they have started. First, we march to the wasteland then the Northern Mountains and finish this forever."

Theor then said to the king, "Would it not be better to split the army while you return home so that you are not exposed to any unnecessary risk?

Norval looked at him with a half smile on his face before returning to a more somber expression and saying, "This decision I have made carries an enormous amount of weight, a burden that I must carry on my shoulders, along with my men who must carry out my command. It is not for me to peddle off this responsibility to someone else, for I must learn and feel the full weight of my decision as king that I may know the true meaning of that responsibility."

CHAPTER 11

The Final Solution

AFTER GATHERING HIS army together, Norval set his eyes on the Sanulite Kingdom of Mordune.

This task would not be quite that simple. They would have to follow a specific path to reach the Sanulite realm. There were places within this barren realm that even the Sanulites feared to tread.

There were creatures unseen that dwelled beneath the sand, like those beneath the ocean surf, which were deadly and attacked without warning. As the Talishar reached the edge of the desert, Norval held them at its edges and addressed his army, "Beyond these edges where land and sand meet, remember the dangers beyond what our eyes can see. Stay along the structures of solid sand. To venture were the sand is loose and fine will bring us unwelcome guests.

"Follow behind me on the path in which I set. In twos, we must travel and remain silent, for we cannot win a battle against an enemy that is unseen. We must not bring attention to ourselves to that which lurks under the sands."

Norval turned as he exchanged eye contact with Theor, each acknowledging the danger they were to face without speaking a single word. What was it that brought such reverence from such a mighty people?

The answer was one none were willing to ask. Silently, each of the Talishar peeled off into a straight line, one behind the other in pairs, as they entered the desert until they formed a line that reached more than a mile. After hours, they saw what they had come for.

Silently they encircled the city. It was without a real force to protect it, and without warning, Norval ordered his warriors to attack in which the slaughter began. The Talishar rained down on what remained of the Sanulite shifters.

With no army left to defend them, only those who were either too young or too old to fight were left to protect what was left of the Sanulites, who proved to be no more than a minor disturbance. They were the only barrier between the full might of the Talishar army and that of oblivion.

With little or no resistance, the city of Mordune was laid to waste. Under the blistering heat, nothing was left alive. True to his word, every female, every child, and everything that crawled or moved was put to the blade and swovel, slain where they stood, whether in their dwellings or in the street.

They hunted down those who fled into the sand and killed them all, crumbling all structures that remained standing, turning the Sanulites' greatest city into ruins. They thoroughly searched everywhere until Norval was satisfied there were no survivors.

Like a ghost, they entered the land of dunes. And like a ghost, they left in the same manner in which they came. Then it was time that they turned their attention to the north and to what remained of the Kraggan clans.

After the massacre of the Sanulites, Norval, true to his word, led his army back to the Kraggan lair high up into the northern highlands with great vengeance. Finally, his goal of lasting peace was in his reach with one last task to complete it. Entering the mountains without any show of mercy, he and his army destroyed everything that dwelled there. They searched every crack and crevasse, killing everything that breathed life until none born of Kraggan seed remained alive.

Nothing but shattered bodies of a once formidable race were left in their wake. Like the Sanulites, both their females and their young were beheaded and scorched by fire. Not even the hands of the Talishar king were free from the blood of his enemies.

Norval led in the destruction of the clans with unrivaled relentlessness and efficiency until he was satisfied that all his enemies were completely destroyed. Though the acts were cruel and calculated, in his eyes, they were necessary. He was doing what he had to for the future survival of the existence of the Talishar people.

The campaign had taken months. Finally, they returned home. As the great Talishar army came into view in the distance from high up on the fortress wall, the trumpets began to sound as everyone in the city hurried to greet them.

All were in celebration throughout the kingdom. Their army and their king had retuned victorious. Entering the gate, the streets were aligned with thousands of cheering people,

all sounding a salute to their king, along with his army, as they began shouting, "Norval! Norval! Norval!" Theor then stepped from the ranks, having fought by the side of his king and his father, and said boldly, "There has been no greater king before him. He is King Norval! King Norval the Great!"

The crowd then erupted exuberantly, following his words as they began to shout the same, "Norval the Great! Norval the Great! Norval the Great! Thousands chanted his name over and over again with swords and swovels raised high in the air.

Norval, along with those who were greeted by his side, had not the words to express the honor he felt. But the king had one thing on his mind that he had not expressed—that of his wife, Pricillica, and that of his child she was bearing.

He looked up as he arrived at the gates of the palace. There he saw his wife holding his child. During the months he was away on his campaign, she had given birth, only weeks before his arrival.

He dismounted his steed and rushed up the palace stairs to greet her. Once he entered the chamber, he slowed and then carefully approached her. His delight could not be measured as he gently placed his hand on the child's head with pride and then leaned over and kissed his wife. She then handed the child to him as he gently grasped him with that of a father's pride.

He then said, "I wasn't even here to name my son." He then looked at her and asked, "In my absence, what name did you give him?"

Pricillica looked into her husband's eyes and said while they exchanged stares of love and smiles, "Our child is nameless. He awaits the arrival of his father to give that honor."

Norval then looked back at his son and said, "Cyris, his name shall be Cyris after the rising sun, the symbol of hope." He then extended his arm that was not holding his child to his wife as he affectionately held both his wife and child.

In the days ahead, the celebration of a new king would be greater than any time before. For not only did they have a new king but also an heir who would one day follow his rule.

After the great campaigns and the destruction of their greatest threat, peace ruled throughout the kingdom and the lands surrounding them. No longer on alert from constant threats, over time the kingdom began to relax the security of their borders while maintaining that constant edge that made them great, and the great Talishar Empire flourished.

CHAPTER 12

Obizar's Trek into the Land of Holes

THIRTY YEARS LATER, unknown to the Talishar king, Norval, and his people, it had been nearly a year that had passed since Troguare scouts had quietly entered their lands without their knowledge. They roamed throughout their lands, gathering as much knowledge of their culture, their strengths, and their weaknesses, along with their way of life, before returning to their overlord after a long desolate journey, giving their report of all that they had seen to their king.

For months, Obizar and his enormous army were spread out across the vast ocean of endless sand under the blistering rays and drooling heat of the twin suns that hovered up above. Everything was as it was described—its stinging sandstorms that relentlessly battered them, along with its torturous heat with temperatures reaching above 120 degrees—but they were prepared to deal with these obstacles as the wizard king pressed his army relentlessly.

But despite their preparation, all this combined took its toll, weeding out the weakest of an army of powerful, hardened warriors, leaving many of them littering the sand with their enormous bodies. Not willing to risk losing any more of his army, Obizar commanded his army to stop. Looking up to the sky, Obizar closed his eyes and then began chanting words of an unknown language. With it, the sky began to darken to nearly the pitch of night, as lightning danced across the sky. With it, the heavens opened up and the rain began to fall, like a flowing river, in a place that had not seen water in more than a thousand years, replenishing the strength and the hope of a fleeting army.

It could not have come at a better time. With many already lost, others who were soon to follow found relief as the harsh conditions of the place was ready to claim even more of them. As the rains fell, pools of water formed all around. Many submerged themselves, cooling their overheated bodies while drinking their fill, both giants and their beasts. But Obizar stood there among them, both anxious and impatient, while he waited for his army to regroup and replenish themselves.

With anxiety pressing on him, Obizar no longer was able to bear the wait. He mounted his liborox while he found the highest point on the sandy terrain where he was visible to all. He then began to speak, raising his voice so that it rivaled the very thunder that brought the rains. He shouted, "It is time! Gather yourselves. We have stalled long enough. Let us begin our march once more, for our destiny awaits us beyond the horizon."

With Abithar and his scouts leading the way, they did not stray from their previous path. But those who had gone before them revealed a different and an unfortunate fate. Both travelers and beasts who lost their way left hard reminders of the reality of this unforgiving desert. With their bones as markers, they served as both a reminder and a warning of the harsh reality of this unforgiving land as they lay bleached under the fury of the two suns.

After hundreds of miles, they finally reached the ruins of what was once the great city of Mordune, which had been vacant for quite some time. Knowing that once they reached this point, Abithar reminded his king that their journey across the desert would soon be at its end. Looking back at his master, he said, "My lord, we are nearing the end of our journey. We are no more than a day's journey before reaching the lands in which we seek. You shall not have to wait much longer." Obizar looked at him without an exchange of words and nodded to acknowledge him but remained silent and focused.

They passed the lifeless city and the evidence of the dead scattered about, fossilized by the desert heat, depicting the unfortunate events that had once taken place. Obizar, having no interest in either the cause or the results of their demise, barely took notice. It was only the living that fueled his interest and the kingdoms that lay beyond these unforgiving lands. It was that in which he could build an empire on.

Finally, they had reached the limits of the fallen city and beyond. After a few hours, they came to the place his scouts deemed as the Land of Holes. Once they arrived, many were amazed by the abundance of craters that littered these lands, resembling cottage cheese. It was laden with hundreds of holes in the ground, filled with sand, as they marched through it.

Many of these Troguares marveled at the formation of stone curved like claws. Even they were impressed by these formations. But Obizar showed no interest as he simply moved on, barely taking notice. Unlike their scouts that preceded them, the Troguare army showed no concern toward these strange lands as the whole army, like their master, remained focused on what they had come so far to accomplish. As they moved through this strange land, a few of the liboroxes' behavior became erratic.

One had begun to snarl while swaying its head from side to side and then raising its snout in the air, as if it was detecting a scent. Then in an instant, it broke into a gallop, moving in the opposite direction from where the others were traveling. Despite his efforts, his rider was unable to gain control of him.

Known for being unpredictable without reason, it simply took off from a gallop into a full stride. In the midst of this chaos, it rammed into another beast, causing it to lose balance and driving it onto one of the large sand craters.

With its rider pulling on its harness, trying desperately to gain control, it was to no avail as both it and its rider began to sink quickly, like they had fallen in a pool of water instead.

Its rider called out in desperation, "Rope! Throw me a rope!" Nearby one of his comrades hurled a heavy rope toward him. Desperately he reached over but barely grabbed it. He was nearly out of time before others rushed to his aid. But his beast was not so fortunate.

All its struggling efforts was useless. Already submerged, it had drowned in the fine-grained sand. As others pulled, all was certain he would be rescued, but something seemed to be pulling him under. The harder they tugged, despite their great strength, it was like something was pulling him back under.

In the midst of the confusion, no one saw the strange thin objects protruding up from the sand. But slowly it disappeared without much notice, and so did the mighty Troguare they were trying to aid until, like his liborox, he, too, found his home in the graveyard of sand.

Without further delay or thought, they moved on. As quickly as the ordeal came about, so did their thoughts of losing their comrade fade from their memory. Rambling forward with every step they took, the ground shook beneath their feet.

The sheer weight of their armor and the girth of these warriors rumbled along like thunder. With the sound of armor rattling about, they were unable to hear the faint sounds of sand shifting to even notice. But their liboroxes were on edge and uneasy. Something had unsettled them. They snarled and roared with the bellow of an ox mixed between, a sound they only made when coupled with fear.

It was a sound that was rarely heard from these fearsome beasts. They had sensed something, and not even their riders could calm them. Obizar sensed a presence that they were not alone and that they were being stalked, not by anything above ground on top of the desert floor, but below.

He raised his hand high above for all to see, halting his army. Obizar knew there was something around them, something close, but not even he knew what it was. With his sight into the future blurred, unable to look into the unknown to forewarn his army—a gift taken from him long ago—he was unable to see beyond his natural sight, not even the use of sorcery could aid him. With his army waiting in tow, he commanded them to slowly begin their advance.

The deeper they moved into this strange land among hundreds of these sand craters, the sand within them rippled like waves on a river as the Troguare army weaved around them in a steady direction.

Looking around, they saw nothing, only vapors created by the heat as it rose up from the ground, distorting their view of their surroundings, causing their sight to waver while seeing images around them that did not really exist. Suddenly, one of them cried out, followed by the roar of one of the beasts that was typical when they were in pain.

As he cried out, he shouted with a heavy, gravelly voice, saying, "I've been struck by something! I feel like I'm burning inside!" Then all went silent. Something had grabbed hold of him, pulling him under the sand. Even though their numbers were in the thousands, they were widely spread apart. The close proximity of the sand craters that varied in sizes and shape posed a danger to each of them. The sand was so loose and soft that it prevented them from traveling together in hordes.

The sand within these craters was soft and loose and extremely fine. A stone thrown in them sank beyond sight in moments, and even among the thousands of warriors, no one saw anything. Everything happened so swiftly. No one saw what had taken him, as his liborox dropped to the ground where it fell dead where it stood. It only had a small wound on its belly, one that was minor for a beast that, like many, had seen worse in battle or in conflict with one another.

But there was something different about this wound. A thick yellowish fluid oozed from it. But what was it? What could have caused or have done this? It snatched a fully armored Troguare soldier while killing his beast so quickly, all the while remaining unnoticed even while being surrounded by an entire army on alert, watchful of their surroundings, before dragging him under the sand without anyone seeing or getting a clear look at what had happened.

Those who were closest to where it all took place stood confused and confounded. But as they stood there, before their eyes, a large dark creature rose out from one of the craters as it burst from under the sand in a blur and grabbed hold of the dead liborox, pulling it under and into the hole, as if it was a cub, before any could react to challenge it. Moments later, it happened again as another cried out in agony before going silent, disappearing into yet another of these large sand craters.

It was all happening so quickly. Even with their weapons drawn, they were unable to prevent or aid their fellow comrades. There was simply no time to react. One after another, they cried out, followed by the roar and bellow of yet another of their powerful beasts, then there was silence.

It was beginning to happen all around them. One by one, these massive warriors were being killed and dragged down from where they stood into these craters all around them. In the blink of an eye, they were being pulled under and devoured. It was the Troguares that were now under siege and nearly helpless to prevent it.

But it didn't come from an advancing army but from something unseen and immensely powerful. Obizar reached around and grabbed hold of the battle ax he kept draped across his back, removing it as he dismounted his liborox.

Dropping to one knee, Obizar first placed his ax to the ground in front of him, then he placed two fingers on his temple while he placed the other hand to the ground before closing his eyes, as if in meditation. Then he stood up after grabbing his ax, rearing it back. He began directing his head while having his eyes closed, as if he was gauging where to direct a blow. While those closest to where he was standing watched the movements of their king, no one dared to break his concentration to ask what he was attempting to do.

Suddenly he released his weapon, hurling it with all his might in the direction of the closest crater where nothing was in view. As it spun through the air, a large black creature rose its body high above the sand, a creature that was called a cennidon. This subterranean predator was both blind and ravenous.

They had two large antennae, were striped with yellow markings, were equipped with a set of giant bone-crushing mandibles and rows of razor-sharp teeth designed to strip flesh from bones, and displayed crab-like claws on each section of their legs.

With an impeccable accuracy, the ax found its mark in what could be perceived as the center of what appeared to be its forehead, just above its mandibles and between where its eyes should be if it had any, killing it instantly as it sank deep inside the creature's head. Its lifeless body then slowly sank back into its lair. Obizar, not yet satisfied, repeated his actions, kneeling to the ground, closing his eyes while once again placing his hand to the ground.

"I feel them moving beneath us," he said with his weighty voice, "tunnels that link each of these craters together. Over there." He pointed not more than fifty feet away from him. He then commanded twenty of his bowmen that were standing just a few paces from him, "Direct your aim toward the crater's edge that is closest to where we stand." It was about twenty feet away from where he was kneeling. Still having his hand to the ground, he said, "On my command, release your arrows."

All remained silent while the intensity escalated; no one made a sound. With only the sound of the wind interrupting the silence while blowing specks of sand violently against them pugnaciously, the hair streaming from beneath their helmets blew violently into the wind.

Breaking the silence, Obizar opened his eyes and shouted, "Now!" His bowmen released twenty spear-sized arrows into the air, taking flight toward an unseen target. In that instance, once again another cennidon raised its body out of the sand, only to find itself riddled with these massive arrows. And like its predecessor, it, too, met its end but at the hands of the Troguare bowmen.

Still wary, many throughout the Troguare ranks were still unsure. They stood ready while they looked around for signs of movement from within the craters that surrounded them. They stood quietly. The entire army was still on edge, but they were ready. After a short wait, it was time to move as Obizar climbed onto his liborox to move on.

Not more than fifty feet in front of Obizar, bursting from beneath sandy ground, one rose about forty feet into the air. Larger than the two they had just killed, the creature rose out onto the surface with a battery of clawed legs, facing the mighty wizard, Obizar. But he simply smiled, while his soldiers began to surround the beast, drawing their weapons to put an end to this ordeal.

Obizar shouted, "Lower your weapons. This prize belongs to me." With his weapon of choice, he drew his mal-lace from his hip and expanded it to its full range. Its spikes were freshly polished, allowing deep penetration with little effort. With a smile still fixed on his face, even though he had the power to summon demons, he chose to forgo this talent.

Though the most powerful wizard on the planet, he was equally skilled as a warrior. Choosing to put aside sorcery, this was a rare opportunity to take on such a formidable challenge that would push his abilities to its limits—a challenge he would relish. Obizar admired these subterranean beasts, and the one he now faced was much larger than the others.

This one, unlike the others, had fully exposed itself. It was at least sixty feet in length as it stood their perfectly still, with only its antennae moving independently and randomly, as if it was determining its next victim. It was the roars and bellows of the liboroxes that seemed to confuse it. There were so many to choose from and so much to eat. The war beasts snarled, baring their teeth and claws with their horns pointing downward, ready to charge.

Slowly it began to move forward, then it raised a third of its body twenty feet off the ground, exposing its full arsenal of deadly weaponry. Its exoskeleton was a dense leathery texture, much thicker than the others. Standing there for all to see, it revealed what made it truly deadly—two giant spear-like spikes protruding from its rear with thick yellowish poison oozing from them. Seeing this, it was clear why death was so quick. Moving from side to side, it dropped back to the ground. And with a burst of speed faster than any had anticipated, it charged into the ranks of at least a dozen warriors who were too slow to react in time.

As it charged, it turned its rear slightly in an angle exposing its poison-laden spikes as it ripped through nearly a dozen soldiers before turning its attention on Obizar himself. As it turned, eight Troguares and three of the liboroxes fell dead where they were standing while another was being crushed within its viselike mandibles. Not even these powerful warriors were a match for this creature. It had chosen its victims carefully, and now it was the Troguare king it had set its sights on.

Obizar moved away from his war beast, giving it the command to move away, as he had his mal-lace in hand. He stood ready for one of its bursts when it attacked. Charging at full speed, Obizar stepped aside from its charge, avoiding both snapping mandibles and its two poisonous barbs.

Obizar was far more agile than he appeared as he avoided a second charge, outmaneuvering the huge creature once again. But on the third attempt, Obizar grabbed hold of his mal-lace, smashing downwardly on the head of the cennidon while avoiding its snapping jaws, stunning the beast. But in one fluent motion, he spun his body to avoid yet another attack while the momentum of the creature caused it to pass by him.

In one motion, he drew his sword from his hip, slicing off the poisonous spikes that protruded from its tail, eliminating the possibility of becoming impaled by the creature and, therefore, crippling the great beast. Though wounded, it was still far from helpless as it rose once again in the air, exposing its pincer, attempting to move in for the kill.

With the Troguare king now standing within striking distance, it lunged forward, attempting to grab hold. But once again, it was much too slow, as it grabbed nothing. This time, Obizar avoided its attempt and once again sidestepped it and leaped on its back, unleashing the power of his blow to the back of its head until the creature fell motionless from the repetitive pounding as Obizar opened a large hole in the creatures head. Then Obizar took his sword and beheaded it.

It was not known to Obizar how many of these creatures dwelled in the tunnels. He did not give an account or a reason to anyone for his next set of actions, for they were kept to himself. But it was time that they moved on.

Already claiming his prize for his victory, he closed his eyes, raising both arms to the air, and chanted words of the dark magic he commanded. It commanded silence among his ranks as he caused all the creatures that dwelled below to rise up from the sand.

Nearly fifty cennidons were erected, like living pillars, motionless. They almost seemed frozen in place while dark black clouds began to roll in from every direction as they rapidly approached their location, with lightning flashing above.

Obizar stood with his arms raised and his eyes closed, with the rumbling clouds above as they flashed lightning, accompanied with ground-shaking thunder. All stood there in awe of what they were witnessing, but no one was certain what would happen next. Only Obizar knew.

Once all the creatures were aboveground and exposed partially, lifting themselves out of the sand, Obizar opened his eyes and quickly lowered his arms, releasing bolts of lightning from the sky as it became a light show, striking each of the cennidons and causing them to explode on contact as parts of the beasts splattered everywhere, raining down on his army.

Seeing the results of his acts, he was now satisfied with the results as the stench of the burned flesh of these creatures was nearly suffocating. He, therefore, turned once again and was about to give the command to press forward when he noticed movement in the beheaded corpses of the cennidons he had just killed.

Looking at one of the giants, he said, "Take your sword, and cut open the belly of this beast so that we can discover why that creature that is already dead still moves as if there were other occupants."

As his master commanded, one of the soldiers proceeded to follow Obizar's command as he walked over and rammed his sword in the creature's belly, opening it up and releasing a smell so foul even the Troguares had to turn away. They were no strangers themselves of being foul-smelling creatures.

In the belly were dozens of young. The cennidon was ready to give birth. Seeing the fierceness and how deadly these subterranean creatures were firsthand, Obizar looked at his commander and ordered them to be caged and to be taken with them as part of his menagerie.

They were to be bred for future sport. After that, Rolo humbly approached the wizard king and said, "We are close, just beyond the horizon. No more than a few hours' ride, we shall reach the lands the Talishar. It will be another kingdom that you shall claim as yours, my lord." Hearing those words, Obizar smiled. And without further delay, Obizar pressed forward, eager to meet what he had believed would be his destiny.

CHAPTER 13

A Sea of Armor—an Enemy at the Gates

UNDER THE BLISTERING heat of the dual suns above and at the edge of the sands, a lone vanguard sat upon his ramsteed on top of a hill, overlooking the vast open space. There he sat quietly and aloft. All was silent around him.

Until rumblings in the distance could be heard, as if a storm was approaching. With the sound of thunder, the very ground began to shake, yet not a single cloud could be seen. So he focused on the distant horizon, and there he noticed the sparkling of light.

It was that of the stars reflecting off the ocean at night. As their approach became closer and louder, he could see that it wasn't thunder but distant figures intertwined with dust and that of armor reflecting off the double suns, a number that rivaled the stars in the heavens.

Immediately, his steed reared up. And he, like a bird in the wind, turned and pressed forward to give a report and a warning to the king about what he had seen of the coming advance of this large army. The walls of the city were a little more than a three-day ride with haste, but he would make it in two.

Back in Tajheire, it was a great day of festival in honor of the prince. It was tradition among the Talishar that when the prince became of age, or what was known the season of manhood, it was time to pick a bride from among the lovely maidens from the esteemed families throughout the kingdom.

But the young prince, Cyris, had his sights on a common girl he had known from his youth, a beautiful young woman named Leela. They had fallen in love from the time of their youth. In their secret place behind the vine garden, they would meet, embracing each other and greeting each other passionately.

On this day, it was an early sunrise. The young prince had arrived in the garden, but to his surprise, he already found her waiting. It was an honor that was normally his, but this particular morning, she was the first.

Dressed in a pink-and-white woven gown, her beauty radiated around her. The young prince stood and gazed at her, captivated by her beauty, before moving closer to her, with his eyes never leaving her. As he drew near, so did she. Before, they had embraced each other, as they had since their youth. But now it was different. They were now adults, doing the things that adults could now do.

He grabbed her by the waist and pulled her to him. Then she wrapped her arms around his neck as they drew closer together, kissing each other while passionately embracing. He then pulled back slightly as he looked into her eyes and said, "I love you with my very essence and will not love another."

Leela looked back into his eyes and then replied, "I love you even more, my prince. No other shall possess my heart as long as I live."

Cyris then said, "It's settled. I will go to my father and tell him I'm going to break with tradition and marry the woman who has captured and tamed my heart."

Leela looked with a glow and a smile as she felt a joy she had never felt before, then she replied, "I love you more than life itself, but your father would never accept this. It is against our tradition. And that, my love, has never happened."

He then said to her, "Do you not love me?"

Leela replied, "How many times must I answer that question? You know I do."

Cyris then replied, "Then you have to trust me, and you will be my bride." Silence then seized the moment before passion took over, and once again both became lost in a kiss.

Meanwhile, within the palace walls, in the chamber of king, Norval stood solitary on the balcony, overlooking the city streets, focused and troubled as though he was carrying an untold burden that was difficult to bear.

The queen slowly walked up behind him, placed her arms around his waist, and kissed him on his cheek. "My king, you haven't slept well the past three nights. The ramblings in your sleep, the words I'm unable to understand, your restlessness during your slumber. What troubles you?"

"Dreams, nightmares, shadows of dark figures that stand before me in hordes, the sounds of agony, hellish dreams with me being helpless and powerless to stop them. Night after night, the same questions without answers, and all but real, unlike any I've ever had before. I see nothing but destruction, and I feel fear."

The queen then said to him, "You are the bravest man I have ever known. All who has raised arms against you have learned to fear your swovel. The mighty Kraggans from the caves of the Northern Mountains, you wiped from existence, along with Sanulites who shared their fate.

"Together they believed themselves to be invincible, but you returned them both to dust. All that had ever stood against you have fallen. Now peace circumferences the lands, and a calm has been felt throughout the land for more than thirty years. Now you are a just and humble king and warrior loved among us all."

The king looked at her and smiled. "You have always known the proper words to calm my spirit. You are my queen, my wife, and I'll love you forever." Then he leaned forward and kissed her.

At that moment, Cyris, the prince, entered their chamber. "Mother, Father, greetings," he said upon entering the room.

"Welcome, my son," the queen replied.

"What a great day! My son has become a man this day," the king replied. "Do you have your sights on your lovely wife to be? Which of the Elites have the good fortune to marry the prince?"

"None of the mentioned. I'm in love with Leela, a common girl. I've been in love with her since the days of our youth together."

The king then said with a most troublesome expression, "The tradition of our people dictates that the prince of the Talishar shall take up with that of an Elite bloodline."

"No, Father," the prince replied. "I don't want anyone else. You have taught me to follow my heart in all things and to be true to myself, and in this I am being true."

The queen then walked over to her son and gently embraced him, then she reached up, placing both hands on the side of his face, and leaned his head forward where she laid a gentle kiss on the top of his forehead. Then she asked, "Son, you have never mentioned her to us before in this way. Do you truly love this woman in your heart?"

"Yes, Mother," the prince replied. "I feel her warmth inside my heart, and as long as I live, I shall have no other love."

"Cyris," the king spoke, calling out his name, "we have traditions and laws set in place and rules that govern order throughout the kingdom. One day you shall be king, and how can you rule if you cannot follow the very rules and laws you set forth to govern others?"

"But, Father, this is not law. This is tradition. It is not the same," replied the prince. "This is the private matters of the heart and a tradition that needs to be broken." For a moment, silence filled the chamber as tensions between father and son began to settle.

"Cyris, you are my son and heir to the throne. It isn't lightly that I bare these words into your ears, but perhaps time is needed by us both to settle our thoughts on this matter."

The queen then said, "Go and prepare to celebrate this day. For the day is very young, and your father and I have much to discuss."

"Very well, Father, Mother," Cyris said, turning in haste as he left the chamber.

"My husband, maybe it is time that we change our thoughts and begin a new tradition. After all, the world is forever changing. Why not?" Pricillica spoke as she smiled at her husband. The king looked at his wife as a calm came over his face, but yet another word was not spoken on this matter as silence prevailed. Cyris went back to Leela and told her all that had been discussed. Though the conversation was disturbing to the young prince, they found comfort in each other's arms.

All the while, the festivities were reaching their peak as people from all parts of the kingdom began to fill the streets. The Elites and their families began to take their place among the people. Musicians were performing while the children were playing all around with their families present. Some being mischievous, as children often do, but joy and laughter undoubtedly filled the air.

This was a time of peace and plenty that prevailed throughout the land. As the trumpets sounded, the king and the queen appeared, with the prince returning to take his place beside his parents as they sat up on their balcony, overlooking the streets below. The king arose, looking down at his people that had gathered to be in their presence, and then began speaking, "People of Talishar, it has been my honor to serve as your king and leader of the mightiest warriors and people in all the land, that of the Great Talishar Empire. And it is also my honor to have Prince Cyris as my son. A father could have no greater prize, one who loves his people as he loves his mother and father. And on this day, we honor him as he steps into manhood."

The crowd immediately erupted after hearing those words with cheers and chants, as they cried out, "Long live Prince Cyris, and long live King Norval the Great!"

Cyris turned to his father, who stood alongside him, then said, "It has been my honor to be your son and for you to be my king." Once again the crowd cheered. The prince looked down into the crowd where Leela was standing and smiled down at her as she smiled back, forming her words in silence, "I love you." Even those words in silence filled the air, like a trumpet sounding, in the mind of the prince.

At that instance, the warning trumpet sounded. In the distance, a lone warrior was in full gallop while waving his warning banner. As he approached the gate, he gave the guards the signal to sound the horns of war, which was of a different decree than that of the warning trumpet.

Silence then overcame the crowd as the warrior road through the gates into the city's street toward the palace where the royal family and that of the Elites were sitting. The king rose to his feet as the rider came closer before dismounting his steed and bowing to one knee. The king then gave the command to rise. "What is your report and the degree in which the war horn was signaled to blow?"

The soldier then said, "My lord, a large army approaches from the great desert. Numbers I have never seen before, countless numbers, my lord, countless."

"Do you have more?"

"Yes," replied the soldier. "As they came into view, they appeared to be giants of steel and armor riding even larger horned beasts with deafening roars. They are but three days' ride from here. I pressed it in two."

"Sound the alarm for the armies to assemble," commanded the king. "Relay word to all the four corners of the kingdom that once again, we face the threat of war." Then he turned to one of his guards and said, "Send scouts to where they have been seen. Cover all possible routes regardless of how obscure they may seem. There will be no surprises from our foe on our soil."

D. R. SIMPSON

At that moment, Norval and his wife then retreated into their quarters. As the crowds dispersed to make themselves ready, Cyris went to Leela and held her tight, then he said to her, "There can be no better day than today to welcome manhood. It appears that our time of peace is fleeting, and once you embrace it, it slips through your grasp.

"With the defeat of the people of the sands and those of stones before I was born, I grew up believing the last threat to our people fell with them. I was barely born during that struggle, but memory serves me well when my father placed me upon his knee and told me the tales thereof. But now my time is at hand to be a participant, and all that I have learned shall be put to the test. I shall return to you a complete man and a tested soldier."

"No matter your state of being, I'll love you with all my heart," Leela replied as she stepped toward him and kissed him.

Standing there as they looked into each other's eyes, Cyris then said to her, "Go back to the safety of your home. I shall return, but I now must go and join the men as we prepare ourselves for the possibility of war." With one last embrace, she watched her prince walk away before turning to her home.

Back in the palace chambers, the king spoke to his wife, "Seems that my dreams may be more than such. The reality of it is now prevalent. Once again we must gird ourselves for yet another invader. But who are they? As they are described, they are like no other people we faced or have known. An army of giants upon our gates, but these are not the enemies of my dreams. There is a much-darker force that drives my thoughts, one I have not the answer to nor are they the ones that drive my fear."

The queen replied, "My lord, they are nothing but dreams, just another foe to fall before you."

"When will this madness end?" replied Norval. "Another army raises arms against us, and another follows and fall."

At that moment, Prince Cyris walked into their chambers, along with two of his top commanders and advisers. "The word to assemble has been set forth, Father. We are ready to lay strategy and await orders."

The king called council with all his commanders and laid out his plan. Then afterward, he stood before all. All the commanders stood in front of him with his son, Prince Cyris, at his side. After all were assembled, he spoke to them, "The time is now at hand, and once again an unknown force stands at our gates. There hasn't been much time to plan a calculated strategy, only what we are naturally accustomed to—the raw savagery of our ancestors before that had never failed them, the instincts that makes us who we are—for those instincts have never failed us in the past nor will they now.

"We will take our standard formation. It has been told to me that we face far greater numbers than ever before, along with an opponent nearly twice our size in stature. Whether it be giants, men, or manlike beasts, it shall not matter, for we shall prevail against all. Though our kingdom and our lands are now threatened, we are Talishar, and all who have dared to raise arms against us have fallen by the wayside. And these shall fare no better.

"There is no army that can defeat us in this world, and a lesson shall be taught when they face our might, when they stand before us, for we are Talishar. Let our cry be heard through the ages. We are an unbeatable foe!"

After the king spoke, everyone chanted, "Norval! Norval! Norval! Hail the great king!" Then the chants erupted into cheers. Afterward, the king ordered his army to assemble as they awaited his forces from other parts of the kingdom to arrive.

While the Talishar was in preparation, Obizar was unaware that his presence was known as he steadily pressed what was a three-day march into four to the fortress city of Tajheire in the hope that he would catch them by surprise. Moving slowly reduced the thunderous effect of his heavily armed giants and, therefore, the chance of giving warning of their approach. Unlike in the past, he decided to forgo the summoning of the dreaded smoked warriors, being that they took a significant drain of his powers.

In front of him, his commander and scout, Abithar was still leading the way. Obizar then called out to him, ordering him to slow down beside him. Then he said to him, "We have come across nothing resembling a civilization, only forest trees, tall grasses, and thickets. Beyond that of the menial life forms we have encountered, I see nothing to rule. "Where are these great cities and dwellings and all the people you spoke to me about?"

Looking over at Obizar, Abithar could see in his eyes that he was not pleased. This brought fear to his heart because he knew if the right words were not spoken, it would be his last. Abithar then replied, "We surveyed these lands, and I have chosen the path of least resistance, one devoid of civilization, a route through their vast and most isolated wilderness. They will not know we are coming."

Obizar looked at him with a piercing stare and said, "How do you know we have not already been scouted?"

Abithar replied, "Because the nature of these people would have been to greet us long before now, my lord." Obizar reluctantly accepted Abithar's answer and then ordered him to proceed on his path.

Outside the gates of Tajheire, Norval had assembled his army. Forces from around the kingdom quickly began to arrive. This was a warrior-based race, and everyone remained prepared and on constant alert, regardless of their demeanor. It took all but a day for the word to spread. Vast numbers of his forces began to arrive from the outer kingdom, with more forthcoming—from the north, the south, and the east. It would be at least another day before the Troguares arrived. But Norval was not going to wait and face them at their home. He ordered his army to begin their march, with thousands of his warriors ready to face the Troguare threat. No one but the first rider that gave warning had ever seen one, much less an entire army of giants.

These beastmen came from far-off, unknown lands beyond the unyielding desert, but none of this mattered. They feared nothing, though not an army had slain many giant beasts single-handedly that would dwarf their foe. But they kept moving forward in the direction of the southwest.

Norval had been given word of their approach by those he had sent out earlier that they were advancing. Finally, they reached the place that had formed the highest ground. There Norval ordered his army into position where they waited. Beside him was his son, Cyris. After the death of his most trusted adviser and loyal friend, he stood alone. He left that position vacant until now when his son had come of age on this day.

Like his father before him, Norval carefully trained him of the ways and the skills to be a great warrior, along with the humbleness it took to sit on the throne. The time had come sooner than expected that all that he had taught young Cyris would be tested by an unknown foe.

Norval looked at his son and asked, "Do you stand ready to defend the ways of the Talishar?"

Cyris then replied, "From my youth, you have prepared me for life. That, too, will cover in the event of facing death. For only under the fire can your metal be tested, words you had taught me that had never left my thoughts. And yes, I am prepared to do everything that is asked of me. To give it my all, including my life, if necessary, to protect my king and my people."

Norval looked proudly at his son, placing his hand onto his shoulder, then he said, "You shall do well, my son."

Cyris replied, "I shall never disappoint you, Father."

Norval replied, "That, my son, I have no doubts." His father looked at him and smiled as both continued their preparation.

As Obizar and his army advanced, they saw in the distance an army already waiting. Surprised that he was already known and forthcoming, he became angered. He then looked at Abithar in silence, then he said, "You told me no one knew that we were coming, that their nature would have brought them to us long ago. What more of your words can I trust?"

Abithar then replied, "My lord, I have. We were careful in our steps and followed your words as commanded, my lord. All that I have seen of them would have dictated that they would have faced us long before now. But even so, the route that I had chosen should have given us the advantage of surprise."

Flanked by another of his scouts, one who went by the name Rahlu spoke out, saying, "Master, the fault is not ours. In these vast lands, eyes could be everywhere."

Obizar then chuckled and said, "An error any could have made." He then looked over to one of his guards that was directly behind Rahlu and nodded. Immediately, the guard drew his axe and, without warning, swung it with all his might as Rahlu's head separated from his body while his body fell from the back of his liborox onto the ground.

Then Obizar said, "Errors are made, but those that fail me will not live to make another." Obizar then looked at Abithar and said, "You owe him gratitude, for he suffered the fate that was set aside for you. The question was yours, but he chose to answer, and his answer was not satisfying to me."

Looking on silently, Abithar nodded to his king and then replied, "You have my gratitude, my lord, for sparing me." Obizar simply grunted before turning his attention on the task at hand, halting his army, ordering them to take position. It was now a standoff, as the two great armies that were assembled there faced each other.

CHAPTER 14

The Undefeated

KING NORVAL SAT atop of his steed in front of his army. Across from him, the king of the giants took the mantle in front of him as he sat upon his liborox and smiled. The two kings faced each other from a distance, both glaring across the field at each other. Both waiting as if it was a chess game. Both believing their armies to be invincible.

But on this day, one would learn who had made the error in judgment. The Troguares had the advantage of numbers, more than three to one, which boosted the confidence of the Troguare king. But the Talishar were legendary, and the truth would soon come to light as both armies formed to prepare for their attack.

Obizar was sure his forces were superior, giving the order to form their usual tactic—lining their liborox shoulder to shoulder and horn to horn as they awaited Obizar's command. Obizar then called one of his warriors and said to him, "I will show mercy this one occasion. I sense no fear in the air. An army that valiantly awaits its destruction should be given a chance to surrender. We will be in much need of strong servants and slaves. Why waste them on the battlefield? There they serve no purpose lying dead."

The soldier then acknowledged his master and rode off at full speed as he and his beast rode off to deliver his king's message. As the giant approached, all saw him in plain view. Massive and robust, he was an intimidating sight to most. Many armies that faced them trembled in fear at the sight of such an army, but the one the Troguares faced had no such fear. Neither were they fazed. They just stood ready, awaiting their king's commands.

As he became closer, Norval rode up from among the ranks and said, "Come no farther." Behind Norval, his bowmen stood ready with their arrows already drawn and aimed. The Troguare then halted his advance, as he began pacing his beast from side to side.

In the distance, Obizar and his forces looked on quietly and curiously. Then the Talishar king said to him, "I am King Norval of the Talishar. Speak, giant, or your time on this world will be over before another breath is taken." The Troguare smirked with arrogance that was spread across his face for all to see, then he said, "My master, Obizar, ruler of the mightiest army on this world, requires your surrender. He wishes to spare your lives to become willing servants to the Troguare Kingdom."

Those words brought laughter that broke out among all the ranks of the Talishar, so much so it could be heard across the field from a distance that all appeared as minute shadows to the ears of the Troguare army. It was something Obizar did not find to be amusing but wasn't surprising or unexpected, coming from the army that stood before him.

Along with his army, Norval also found the messenger's words just as amusing. Looking back and all around at his forces, he adjusted himself on his saddle atop of his steed. Then he turned toward the giant and looked into his eyes and said, "I see that your king likes to amuse us with ridiculous words. Therefore, I have words for him that he may not find as amusing. Turn yourself around and return to your king. Tell him to turn his army around and return to the pits in which you came. And if he chooses not to, we will fertilize the ground with your bodies and water the dirt with your blood. And this I shall promise, if my words are not heeded, every one of you I shall destroy, laying waste to your entire army.

"Tell him that word for word, for we are Talishar." Norval spoke in bold words, then said, "God is the only one to whom we shall bow, and your king is by no means a god. For no man, no matter how great his illusion in his mind may be, he is not anyone's god. And we shall never bow to the likes of him or anyone else as long as breath remains within us. Now go tell him this. Let us see if he finds my words amusing."

The giant then said, "I shall tell my master, and you and the rest of your dogs shall drown in the river of your own blood."

He then turned to deliver the message. Norval then sharply turned to his warriors and said, "Prepare to meet their attack. Unleash all your fury onto this enemy. Let them know the error in their judgment when they chose to invade our lands."

He then turned back, looking into the direction of the massive army of giants sitting there before his army as they anticipated the Troguares' next move.

Returning with the message, the warrior stood face-to-face with his master, Obizar, and repeated what Norval had said word for word. Obizar became so angry he growled like a rabid beast, then he took his mal-lace and split the skull of his messenger.

Angrily he turned to his army and roared. He then gave the command, saying, "Ready yourselves to attack. We will teach these defiant vermin the cost of disobeying my offer and not willfully accepting their inevitable fate. Gather in formation!" Immediately, the Troguare lines began to form with their great beasts locking their horns together as they formed row after row of seemingly endless horns, claws, and teeth.

As they formed, Obizar gave the order to advance, in which they began slowly before picking up the pace. The massive beasts then began to gallop across the battlefield. Their numbers were hard to fathom while deathly roars from both giants and beasts, along with their mass, shook the ground as they were now in full gallop as they began to cross the battlefield. This was a tactic that normally broke the ranks of their adversaries.

But the Talishar were different; they knew no fear. And as the enemy approached, Norval the Great, as he was affectionately called, raised both sword and swovel and ordered a slow advance, a tactic that was unusual on the field of battle. Norval then looked at his commander Sabore and said, "Their numbers are far greater than ours, so we will conserve our energy. On this day, these fields will heap mountains of dead giants and their beasts."

Furiously the Troguares approached, and when they got within the distance of a spear throw, the Talishar pressed forward at full speed until they clashed into battle. Roars of the beasts rang out as the Talishar began to mow down their forces, moving in harmony with their blades, swovels, and long spears. First, they disabled their liborox with agility and speed as they amputated the limbs of the beasts while avoiding lowered horns and slashing claws. Though many of the Talishar steeds were unable to avoid their deadly claws, many being disemboweled, the Talishar warriors were agile enough to avoid their blows.

With unrivalled reflexes and strength, they were more than an equal to their giant opponents. The Talishar had a method they used when fighting their larger adversaries—a tactic they learned in past wars. Experienced in fighting both man and beast-like creatures, they had long since learned to outmaneuver and exploit the weaknesses of their much-larger opponents, posing little obstacle. They easily outclassed the Troguare forces. Their strength and agility surprised the Troguares. Never before had they faced such an opponent. Decades of arrogance and overconfidence had blinded their judgment, causing them not to recognize the need to fall back and regroup.

Obizar also saw this as he began to fade back from the battle lines. Not far from his father's side, the young prince, Cyris, displayed all the skills his father had taught him, downing his opponents one by one, sometimes in twos, with little effort. Swift and agile, he pressed forward alongside his fellow warriors into the fray, drawn into battle as a bee is drawn to honey. It was not long before Obizar had engaged into battle himself.

As the Talishar brought the battle to him, he proved that he was a formidable warrior himself. Obizar demonstrated skills that were superior to any that were in his army. He held his adversaries at bay as he wielded his mal-lace, defeating every Talishar warrior that he faced, proving his skills were superior to those he faced.

Outwardly delighted, Obizar was thrilled to engage an enemy in open battle. The fire that was within him had not yet extinguished as he pressed forward, wielding his mighty mal-lace, mowing down his opponents as if they were weeds. His physical stature was misleading. Despite his size and bulk, he, too, was agile, much more than those of his kind. It would take more than an ordinary fighter of the Talishar ranks, even those who were of a superior class of fighters.

Wielding his mal-lace and swirling it around with both hands, when Obizar struck an opponent, death was swift. All around, there were cries of agony and the roars of beasts and of the battle as the ground turned red with blood, caused by the savagery released on this day. But it was the blood of Troguares that was the most dominant.

With the sound of bones breaking and the splitting of skulls, Obizar battered his opponents senseless, with some nearly ripped in half by the powerful blows released from the giant king. Pressing forward once again, he now stood face-to-face with the Talishar king, Norval. Obizar shouted out to him, saying, "Today I shall have your skull as my most prized necklace, a trophy I will indeed cherish forever!" Laughter followed his words.

King Norval replied, "Let us see, for words will not win this contest. The test of skills is what will prevail."

Without a further exchange of words, the two kings clashed in battle—mal-lace to swovel, foreblade to ax—each glancing the other's blows. Neither was able to gain the advantage until Norval found his mark, slicing off part of Obizar's ear. This infuriated the giant king as his aggression rose and became more intense, launching blows with more intensity and fury.

Norval evaded the blows of the wizard, and with each miss, he countered his moves with those of his own, finding his target. With glancing blows off his armored plates and finding flesh, Obizar began to slow and became more vulnerable. This game of chess between the two monarchs went on until Norval found the opening he was waiting for. Poised for the kill, he quickly moved in until something distracted him before he could deliver the fatal blow. From his peripheral view, he caught a glimpse of a liborox running free of its rider, charging straight at him.

Norval quickly avoided its attack as it lowered its head with its horns aimed directly at him. Norval quickly avoided both its horns and its slashing claws before he sidestepped the ten-foot beast, then he leaped onto its back as it passed in a single bound while avoiding the kicks of its hind legs and deadly hooves. Rearing his arm back with his foreblade in position, he sank it into the beast's thick skull and horn casing, penetrating it with enough force to instantly kill the beast.

By this time, Obizar had regrouped and was being pressed by other Talishar fighters on the attack, diverting his attention to those now facing him. Never before had he faced an army such as this. No longer holding back, the wizard warrior began to revert to the use of sorcery.

He now began to use it to repel his attackers. Obizar extended his hand with his palms open wide. He halted the Talishar's advances using an unseen force, then he closed his hand as to make a fist, crushing them as if they were crushed metal, discarding them as if they were waste, and killing them where they stood.

But he only used his power sparingly as if saving it for a greater purpose. Even his army was puzzled with his reluctance to use it, but he had never revealed that. Despite his army being repelled and driven back, Obizar had begun limiting his use of magic mainly on himself, healing his own wounds and repelling those who were in front of him. But he had a hidden purpose.

CHAPTER 15

A Bitter Taste

HIS NEAR DEFEAT and possible death at the hands of the Talishar had Obizar, for the first time, cast doubt upon his own forces. Seeing this, he turned to his trumpeter and roared at him, "Blow the horn to retreat. We must regroup!" He stood there as he watched his forces begin to withdraw.

Seeing this, Norval contemplated on continuing his attack. But he decided to hold his line as he had driven his opponent miles behind the point of battle and well into the forest. Cyris came to his father as Norval sat atop his ramsteed on the front line at the edge of the open plain leading into the woodlands. There he watched the retreat of the enemy forces crashing through trees and bushes, leaving an open trail to follow if they so desired and leaving their dead spread across the battlefield.

Sitting on top of his ramstead beside his father, Cyris asked, "Why do we not pursue?"

Norval turned to his son and said, "Their numbers are much greater than ours, but their army is wounded. They have come to realize that a grave mistake was made when they underestimated us." Looking directly at his son, he said, "I will save our strength rather than waste it in one ongoing battle against such numbers. The giant king made a grave error in judgment."

"What is that, Father?" Cyris asked once again.

"He didn't commit all of them, holding a great many in reserve. He was testing our fortitude, but I think he learned a lesson he did not expect—a lesson taught with Troguare blood. I have known those such as these. He will return but, this time, with his greater force. And we will slowly cut them down, like the weeds in the field. We will reduce their numbers with each passing attack until their numbers are nearly equal to our own. It is then we will pursue and destroy them all."

Back in the Troguare camp, Obizar and his forces were still digesting an unexpected defeat. Speaking with his generals, an enraged Obizar looked at all his commanders and said, "How could this be? Of all the armies we have laid to waste, how could this one whose numbers are less than any we have faced be allowed to humiliate us, driving us back as if we were nothing?"

Obizar, frustrated and flustered, paced back and forth, looking at each of his generals that were lined in attention in front of him, addressing them all as he walked down the line. They all stood silently and were in fear of their master, not knowing if a life was about to be taken from among them. With the displeasure dripping from his voice, he said, "I shall not succumb to such defiance."

Without a pause to think or gather his thoughts into words, he continued, saying, "It is my destiny to be ruler of this world and all that lives in it. Though they have driven us back this day, I shall not be stopped. I shall have them before this struggle has ended. They will bow before me, as did all those before them. And I shall have their king's head as a trinket attached to my necklace of skulls. At dawn's first light, I shall release our entire force, unlike our first encounter. And if they do not fall on the next wave, I shall do it again and again until they are no more."

True to his word, on the dawning of the first light, Obizar released his forces, sending them in waves. But this time, the wizard king held to the rear of his forces to better assess the events taking place on the battlefield. Finding the highest point in which to survey the field, there he waited as his army attacked. The ground shook from the weighted mass of the Troguare charge. Norval and his warriors stood ready to greet them. Looking back at his army, Norval gave the command to hold. When they were but a few meters away, he then let them greet their guests once again, welcoming them fully with Talishar blades.

With a ferocity the Troguares had never seen by any that had faced them, the battle was even more brutal than before. This time, Norval and his son were fighting side by side in another bloody affair. With each pass, the Talishar proved why they were the ones that should truly be feared. Not only did they defeat the Troguares with relative ease, they also slaughtered their mighty war beasts without even the powerful liborox, without any distinction between the two.

Obizar asked himself, *How could this be?* For a second time, his forces were driven backward despite alternating them in waves, as he watched them give up more and more ground. Everything was going as Norval had plan as the bodies of Troguares began to mount. But on the contrary, this was not as Obizar had foreseen or had planned. The thought of using his sorcery to a much-greater extent had begun to filter through his mind, but his reluctance to use it continued to prevail.

The struggle went on for weeks till the Troguare army began to break ranks and fall into a full retreat. Large numbers of Obizar's soldiers had fallen, while there were only small Talishar losses in comparison.

The superiority of the Talishar forces was now clear in all comparisons. Though the Troguare numbers were far greater, it wasn't a factor when facing the catlike warriors. It was now evident that one Talishar warrior was equal to any two Troguares and their beasts. They were slow and predictable, a brutal lesson that was taught to them from the start. None of the Troguares could foresee these events unfolding, not even the great Obizar himself. Regardless of the reason, these events served to do no more than to increase the wizard's anger and determination. Obizar could never digest the thought of defeat. Therefore, he could never stop as long as he remained alive.

The Troguares were now in full retreat. It was the first time that they learned the true meaning of fear. King Norval stood his ground, covered with the blood of all he slew, for he wielded his metal as fluently as a bird flying with a breeze, killing giant after giant. After one fell in death, another quickly followed its path. He was the greatest of all the Talishar. He looked at his commanders and said, "Prepare yourselves, for this is just the beginning. Great are their numbers, and they have many more to follow their fallen comrades until they leave our lands or join the dead with their last."

Meanwhile, the giant king, angered by his soldiers breaking ranks, ordered three of his commanders before him. Using sorcery, he summoned a shadowy aberration of flame and smoke and consumed them where they stood in front for all to see as an example of the price of failure.

Then he replaced them with the next in command and then spoke out, "Failure brings death, either on the field of battle or before me." Seeing this, all were even more afraid of their king and were ready to leave everything on the field of battle than to return and face a horrible end before all.

At early light, once again with the twin suns at their back and determined to defeat their enemy, they charged forward, fueled by fear and blind fury. But this time, a different tactic was awaiting them. They were showered by arrows—a tactic rarely used by the Talishar armies. Unlike other armies, the Talishar people had far superior strength, hurling a barrage of arrows as they filled the sky. Because of that great strength, they could kill from much-greater distances long before reaching the battle lines.

Wave after wave, the giants fell, until finally, their numbers began to dwindle. But they were so driven by fear and the price of failure they continued at full charge. When the arrows ran out, the Talishar cavalry mounted upon their gnores, which were lean, shaggy four-eyed beasts with ram-like horns set on the bridge of their elongated snouts. Also known as ramsteeds, they were known to be very agile and swift.

Quickly they closed their distance until they reached the hard-charging Troguares, avoiding the slashing claws and stabbing horns of the liborox that would surely have killed them. Swiftly, the fighters were able to move in and out between the Troguare ranks, inflicting deadly wounds as a result of it.

Though the giants fought fiercely, it was to no avail. The Talishar king and his forces were far too skilled, while the roars of the beasts and the grunts of giants could be heard for miles as they lay dying on the field of battle, being after being sliced apart.

After weeks of slaughter by Norval and his army, Obizar and the Troguare army now stood at the edge of the sea of sandy desert from whence they had crossed. Driven back on the verge of defeat at the hands of the Talishar, this was a feat no other army had ever accomplished under Obizar's reign. Neither could they have imagined that it would be possible.

Seeing that his forces were now cut in half, this enraged Obizar. He realized that he was facing a foe whose skills were far superior and could not be overcome or defeated by strength of might or numbers. Despite this, Obizar once again ordered his forces to attack. With a sense of desperation, the Troguares fought with an unrivalled intensity even greater than before, unleashing the fury of giants onto their foes. Driven by arrogance and rage and accompanied by their fear of the mighty sorcerer that commanded them, they engaged the Talishars. The battle was brutal, even more than before. As the battlefield began to fill, it was littered with the bodies of both Troguare and Talishar alike.

Even though Talishar's fallen were greater than all the previous battles, it was to no avail. The giants were once again overmatched and defeated as they fought in retreat.

Obizar, realizing the futility of his attacks, was no longer willing to risk sacrificing his entire army at the hands of King Norval and his army. All but defeated and once again driven back into the desert, distant memories of a place he had never been to began to surface within Obizar's mind—a distant past that served as a mystery even to his own people.

Though his heart was as dark as a lightless pit, deep within was the light that gave him his immortality and enhanced his strength—a secret known only to him, which he had shared with no one before or since.

It was a knowledge of an earlier time, one that brought with it a dark secret that once shook the foundations of the world a thousand years before his birth, but none of this was known to anyone.

CHAPTER 16

A Dream of Darkness—
Enter the Demon Kreel

E VERYTHING REMAINED A blur in his mind, except one thing. It was the evil he now had at his disposal, one that was far greater than anything he had ever conjured before. It was something that would take great power to control, but he was willing to take the risk.

For Obizar, defeat was no option, and that which he now decided to call would tip the balance forever in his favor. With that knowledge, the Troguare king stood in front of his army and said to them, "Withdraw back within this barren land beyond the dunes of loosened sand. Do not let your feet touch solid ground, and remain silent. Or you, too, shall become consumed by that which I am about to unleash onto the flesh of the living."

As commanded, they did so. With a wave of his hand, a fire sparked from nowhere as it burned on a fuelless ground. Many whispers of astonishment and awe at the power that he wielded could be heard throughout the Troguare ranks.

Standing before the flames, Obizar turned and commanded his forces with authority, shouting, "Silence, you fools! Lest you all will die!" He then closed his eyes while raising both hands in the air with his palms up. Then pausing before uttering words in a tongue unknown, he began to speak in words all could understand.

Across mountains of bodies and blood that seemed to take up every inch of ground, the Talishar forces stood ready, waiting for Norval's command. While they waited, Cyris looked at his father, who, like himself, was splattered with blood that had dried from their prolonged encounters, and said, "We have driven them back beyond the sand.

Shall we not pursue them and finish it or wait until they regroup once again?"

Norval sat silently with his eyes never leaving the direction of his enemies, then he replied, "No, we will wait. I am certain the answer that we seek will soon be upon us."

Cyris then said, "This may be an attempt to lure us into some type of trap. Why else would they stop and wait after being defeated at every turn?" Norval had a troubled look on his face. Something had vexed him deeply in a time that victory was nearing its conclusion in his favor. His son noticed the expression on his father's face and then asked, "What is it, Father? Why is it that you appear to be perplexed and hesitant? We can finish this now. Why do we wait?"

Norval then looked at his son in silence, which served as his only response. While the Talishar looked on, awaiting their king's orders, Obizar continued to speak the words. Suddenly, the ground began to tremble. With the depth of his voice, even the Talishar could hear him from where they stood, as his voice echoed about over great distances.

While Obizar spoke, everyone heard the giant's voice as clearly as if he was face-to-face with them. The sky started to darken, while the ground began to shake. Forcefully Obizar began to chant, "I call upon the darkness from the pitch of night. I summon Kreel to awaken, along with his legion of demons, the masters of flight, from their prison of stone from which they are held in slumber to come forth. By the power of the light that is within me, I release you from your bonds to do my will. Come forth unto me. That I command!" At that moment, countless unknown eyes came open, as all the Troguares stood by and waited.

The sky began to get darker and darker. Dark clouds began to bellow in from the east, like a storm. They were a gray so dark they appeared black, rolling like a thundering ball as lightning flashed within it and all around it. It was a display of light as it danced across the darkened skies. It was a light show of yellows and whites flashed as day became night. The clouds had smothered the rays from both suns, making everything feel so very strange.

This was unlike any storm any had ever seen, for there were no winds blowing to propel the clouds. Armies on both sides took notice, reaching both far and near that of the field of battle. Throughout the countryside, all that were awake looked up to the skies. Many were amazed and confused.

Obizar stood on top of a dune with the slightest smile as one of his generals approached him with his head bowed, saying, "Master, what is happening? What has been brought upon us?" Obizar looked at him and smiled, then he said, "In moments, your question will be answered."

Across the field, Cyris asked his father, "What is happening?" Norval just stood quietly. Then Cyris's expression on his face suddenly changed, then he asked, "Father, do you hear something?"

Norval paused and looked around and then back to his son and said, "It's the sound of wings. This is the vision that I saw in my dreams."

As the clouds rapidly approached, propelled by a windless sky, a force of supernatural origin no one could answer but the wizard that commanded the Troguare army, Obizar himself, appeared.

Back at the city of Tajheire, the queen and one of her maidens stood atop the palace walls, looking across the blackened horizon in the direction that the war was being fought while the clouds moved above their heads. One of her maidens then asked Pricillica, "What is happening here?"

The queen replied, "I do not know." As they looked up, they saw shadowy images that they could not make out as they swiftly passed overhead. Not only did the queen notice the unexplained sights but people spread across the kingdom also saw something that no one could explain.

Unknown to King Norval and his army, death was on the horizon, and a foe not of this world approached. The maiden then said to the queen, "I think it would be wise if you take shelter in case rain may follow."

The queen looked at her and smiled, then she said, "That would be wise for the both of us." Her maiden smiled back, then both took shelter inside, away from the view.

Meanwhile, back at the edge of the desert, Norval and his army stood ready as they looked across the plain that separated the two armies, believing that this conflict was nearing its end. The king sat there as if lost in his thoughts. Cyris then said, "I ask again, Father, what troubles you? For I am your son, and I know my father quite intimately. You cannot hide the fact that something beyond our enemy is troubling you."

Unable to hold his silence any longer, Norval looked in the eyes of his son and said, "This is the moment I fear the most."

Then Cyris replied, "Father, why?"

The king then responded, "This is the moment that reflects my nightmares. It is not the enemy I can see before me but the darkness that follows and fuels my fears."

In that moment, the heaviest clouds were now upon them. Everyone paused as all came clear into view. Cyris looked, now wearing a face to match that of his father's expression, and asked, "What manner of evil is this?"

The king then cried out, "Prepare yourselves, for we face a new foe!" All were astonished at what was approaching. They all drew their weapons as the sky seemed to fall upon them.

Kreel and his horde of demons were unleashed upon them as they seemed to fall from out of the sky, like rain from out of the cover of the darkest clouds. Obizar stood back in delight as he commanded a new army—the demon horde.

He cried out, saying, "Destroy them all! It is your time to feed. Now have your fill. Feast on all you can while they are all before you." Like a plague across the land, not only did they fall upon the battlefield but they also fell on the lands far beyond its boundaries of wherever the darkness cast the shadow of night. The demons were free to roam.

Obizar then looked at his army and said, "They will cleanse the land of its vermin occupants, and after they have their fill, we shall lay claim to it all." Throughout the land, no one was spared—not humanoids nor beasts, not even the smallest that crawled. These demons of darkness had a ravenous appetite to appease, and they were relentless in their pursuit. There would be no mercy or anyone or anything to be spared in their attempt to devour it all. Only the place where the Troguares stood held refuge, protected by the power of their overlord, and Obizar found delight in it all.

While Kreel's legion placed havoc across the land, Norval and his army fought this evil with everything they had. Though they fought with all the skills they had acquired since the time of their youth, for the first time, they now faced a truly unbeatable foe.

Prince Cyris stood before a demon with teeth and claws. He fought valiantly, but it was for naught. He moved quickly as he avoided strikes, placing his swovel in places that would kill any living foe as did all who fought beside him, along with the king. But the natural was no match for the supernatural.

Until finally, he, too, was struck with a blow that sent him to the ground. But before he could be dealt the final blow, two of his comrades came to his aid. "Stay back, demon! You shall not have him," cried out one of the warriors as he confronted the creature with all his fury. The other comrade looked at Cyris and asked, "How do you fare, my prince?"

Grimacing in pain, he replied, "As soon as I gain my breath, I shall help you return these monsters to their rightful place." Struggling to regain his feet, he could see his father engaged in battle nearby. But he turned, hearing the scream of one of his defenders, just as the beast sank his claws into the chest of one of his warriors, ripping out his heart and tearing through his armor as if it was paper.

Cyris watched him fall as the other kept pressing his attack just before he was swept up into the air by another of the creatures and was torn apart by two others that wished to join in on the meal. Though they fought gallantly and fiercely, it was to no avail, for not the foreblade, sword, arrow, or the mighty swovel could harm them.

They tore through flesh and armor as though they were nothing, with Talishars being feasted upon while they fell. For the first time, the mighty Talishars were helpless in their stand. Cries of agony filled the air all around as these great warriors, with all their abilities, were rendered helpless. Obizar and his army watched the massacre, filling them with delight as many cheered on, knowing the inevitable end was soon forthcoming. And that time was finally upon them.

Descending down from the sky, the four-winged lord of the demons hovered just above the fields of the fallen. Standing amid the mound of bodies, King Norval now stood before the creature of the darkness, awaiting its next move. Floating on the wind, the dark-gray demon hovered in front of Norval, displaying all his glory.

With a voice that echoed to the very depths of one's soul, it was the ancient evil and the ruler of the flesh-starved legion of winged demons. Its name was Kreel, having a head with three faces. To the right was the face of a female. Another to the left was that of a male while the face in the center had the features of both, each sharing an eye, four eyes in

D. R. SIMPSON

all that they interchanged with one another when they began to speak. All had separate minds, and when they spoke, it was in turn. But they had a voice that echoed as if three were speaking in tandem.

The king looked into their eyes, which were cold and glassy and silver in color. It was reflective, as if one were gazing into a mirror. A reflection was cast of his own death while facing the fear that reached deep within the soul. Kreel stared at the Talishar king and began to smile with each of its faces, displaying its daggerlike teeth that were spread unevenly across its faces.

With every exhalation, the air around the creature had the smell of brimstone mingled with that of rotten flesh as it reeked from its pores and its breath. His breath was so hot it singed the hairs of Norval. Its flesh was as if it was woven atop its torso, like braided hair. Its skin was riddled with oozing sores and clusters of bumps atop its flesh.

While they stood there facing each other, screams and cries of extreme suffering were heard all around them as the mightiest warriors ever known were being ripped apart and eaten while blood was still being pumped through their veins. But the old titan was not fazed, looking into the eyes of the demon. Norval saw no such reflection, for there was no fear in him. The only thing he saw was the cold glassy eyes of a monster. As the creature moved closer, Norval lifted his foreblade behind him with his left arm and his swovel in front of him in his right, taking his stance in preparation for a battle, while he awaited the demon's next move.

Kreel came forward and began to speak, with each of its faces speaking in turn. With a sense of eternal delight, the flames arising from its pupils began to intensify, which was followed by a deathly laugh. The face of the female first began to speak, saying, "Ahhh! We savor the taste of living flesh—the very essence of life—oh-so-sweet!" Followed by that which resembled the man, it began to speak its own mind, saying, "To be consumed by us, everything that makes you who you are and what you are brings nourishment to our infernal soul."

Before the third could speak, two winged demons swooped down from above out of the darkness to share in what would be a feast, but they suddenly broke off the attack as their master glared at them as if to dare them to interrupt that which the demon lord had chosen for himself. They went their way to seek out other prey.

Kreel quickly turned his attention back on the Talishar king. And with the center face, it smiled once again, speaking in the voice of both male and female, saying, "And we shall find our greatest pleasure dining on the flesh and soul of a king deemed so mighty." Slowly the king climbed on the body of a dead liborox to gain a vantage point, not once taking his eyes of the creature before him. With mounds of bodies of fallen giants and their beasts lying all around, most of the Talishar army now joined them and mingled among them—not by the swords of giants that they slew but by the hordes of demons summoned by the wizard king, Obizar.

Now in position, Norval stood in his stance, holding a swovel before him in one hand and his foreblade behind him in the other. Standing bold and fearless, Norval did not flinch. Norval then cried out defiantly to Kreel as he lashed out, saying, "There is no fear in me, demon! With my last breath, I will fight a thousand such as you." The king then shouted out once again to the evil one, saying, "Come to me, you unholy abomination! I pray God guides my hand and strikes the blow that shall return you from whence you came."

Kreel replied with laughter as it spoke. As they fused together as one, saying, "God will not help you this day, old king. I shall have my special treat—your flesh seasoned with blood. I shall savor its sweet flavor and pick my teeth with your bones."

"You shall try, demon!" shouted Norval. "Come forth! Let us embrace that you may taste the blades of my swovel—the only flavor that you may savor." Swirling his swovels back and forth and around his torso, his movements were so fast one could barely keep his motions in clear view. The king then let out a roar and launched his attack, striking the demon over and over, raking across its scale-covered hide.

But this was to no avail as the demon barely flinched. With claws thrashing through the air and with its stabbing tail, for a time, it was unable to find its target. The king moved with fluency and a wave of grace, striking the demon with every pass, causing him to become more agitated. But despite the king's great strength, it was useless against a creature of this sort. Dancing between the fallen, trying to avoid what certainly would be death if struck, Norval began to tire.

The demon's claws became closer with every pass till finally finding its mark and tearing into the flesh of the king with his powerful claws, Norval fell to his knees before keeling over on his side. At that moment, a voice cried out, "Father, no!" Not far from his side, his son saw him fall but was unable to come to his aid, for he, too, was facing death as his time was rapidly running out.

With life slowly leaving Norval's body, the eyes of the greatest of all the Talishar warriors began to go dim. While the demons were ravaging the countryside under the veil of darkness provided by the wizard king, the drain on him was severe. The longer Kreel was loose, the greater the drain on Obizar's power, and he knew he wouldn't be able to contain it if it remained free much longer.

Believing that the Talishar were all annihilated, Obizar knew what he had to do. The demon, Kreel, had done what the evil wizard had needed for it to do. Now it was up to his army of giants to do the rest. The time had now come to return Kreel while it was still within his power to do so. Controlling Kreel was a great drain on him. The longer it was free to walk among them, the more it would be impossible to control. He knew that if Kreel was free to walk around Tyrus, all would be a part of the feast, including the master that had set it free.

Standing over the fallen king, Kreel, with a deathly smile and pointed teeth spread across its faces, said to the dying king, "I shall have great delight feasting upon your heart." Before the flesh of the king could be consumed, Obizar recalled Kreel, the demon. Kreel then let out a deathly roar. It angered it that it could not eat of its fallen prey, for it had only the power to obey the command of its master. Kreel and its army screamed out as they returned to their place and, with it, the curse that imprisoned them until the time it could be called upon once more.

CHAPTER 17

Talishar No More

P RINCE CYRIS, BLOODIED and wounded, lay there with a winged demon standing over him, who had just finished eating the heart of one of his men. It looked down at him, ready to finish him as it prepared to strike the deadly blow. It, too, shouted out a bone-chilling scream before flying off to join its master.

Gathering his strength, Cyris went over to where his father lay. He kneeled over his father's body with a silent stare and a burdened heart. Mortally wounded, Norval looked into his son's eyes and said, "My son, this day you are now king. We cannot survive attacks against such creatures. Leave me here with my fallen comrades and save your mother and what's left of our people. Lead them far away from these lands to the Shadowed Forest where they can never be found. One day our people shall rise again and our glory shall shine once more. It is your light that will now lead them. Everything I have taught you shall now be within you to guide them.

"I have taught you all that I could. It is now up to you to complete their journey—a task I know you are more than capable of. My love, my hopes, and my dreams now rest on your shoulders, my son. Now go."

With those words, the light in his eyes went out as his breath left him. Burdened with sorrow, Cyris leaned over and kissed his father above his brow before honoring his father's request. Looking at the few that survived the onslaught, Cyris said, "I will honor my father's wishes and leave him with our fallen."

Standing close to Cyris, one of his warriors said to him, "My prince, there isn't time, for it is fleeting. Those that remain of our people, we must lead to safety or perish, for there isn't enough of us left to protect them. The giant must have summoned them then called them to return to their place, believing all of us to be dead. Why else would they leave?"

Cyris stood silently, contemplating the words of his warrior, then said, "There is truth in your words. Though my pain and grief are beyond measure, as well as those that remain at our side, we must move quickly before the giants discover that we have survived." Cyris looked around at the few that remained standing and said, "Gather yourselves. We must act quickly and return to our home and gather what is left of our people and leave this place."

Now king and remembering the words of his father, Cyris led what was left of his people as quickly as he could. Back to Tajheire, he returned with what was left of his army. It wasn't until he returned to the city and the surrounding countryside that he saw the full scale of what had happened. His people were also ravaged by the demon invasion, and only a few were spared.

Returning home in haste with only a remnant of what was a mighty army, they gathered all that they could carry, along with the survivors. Cyris knew that they would no longer be able to defend themselves beyond the destruction of their race from any Troguare attack that was sure to come. Cyris went to his mother, Pricillica. As he rode into the courtyard, he found her already there, waiting. As she watched her son approach, nothing had to be said. She had already known as he walked up to her, pulling her close. Holding her tight as she wept on his shoulder, he told her that the king was dead. He then said, "No man or giant took his life but that of the unholy summoned by some dark force."

His mother looked at him and said, "This I know. Your father shared with me his dream before the evil came. I tried to comfort him, but it remained firmly in his mind." Looking her son in his eyes, she continued, "We watched the evil shadows as it passed overhead hidden amid the clouds, but we were not clear of what it was that we had seen or for whence it came. We heard the distant screams of terror as they became louder as it rapidly approached all around. But as quickly as it all began, it had also ended. Just as abruptly before, all became silent."

Responding to the queen, Cyris said, "The Troguare king was also a sorcerer. It was he that brought the demons down upon us. We could hear his words from a distance as he called upon the darkness. He has a power we could not fight nor defeat. But we have wounded his mind, that of which believing that his army was invincible. And with that veil lifted, he will not rest until we no longer exist. We must leave this place without a trace that any of us have survived. We shall take nothing beyond what we can carry."

One of his warriors that stood closest to him asked, "Shall we set everything aflame?"

Cyris looked at him and said, "No, leave everything as it is. If we set fires, they will know that there are survivors. That would incite an endless search for our whereabouts, and I shall not have my people forever pursued. There's not enough for us who remain to give the slightest resistance, let alone defeat his army. It won't be long before they come searching for survivors, and we shall give them nothing to find." Cyris turned his attention to that which now burdened his heart—to find his one love, Leela. And he would not have to search far. He heard her gentle voice in the distance, calling out his name, "Cyris!" And his heart was relieved.

He looked as she approached him, running as quickly as she could. It was a sense of relief filling the air around him, a moment of joy as he ran over to meet her. She threw herself into his arms, shedding tears of both joy, sorrow, and that of relief wrapped all into one. She then said to him, "My lord! I didn't know if I would ever hold you again. I prayed to God that he returned you to me. Life without you would be unbearable to even think of."

Cyris smiled and then replied, "Nothing in this world or even beyond this could prevent me from returning to you, my love. But now we must go and save our people. Most of our people have died at the hands of the evil that has fallen upon us. We must now leave this place, our homes, the lives we have lived, and begin anew far from here, never to return. One day we will rise again and avenge all that has been lost, but today death has cast its shadow upon us. For our survival, we must either leave or stay and fight to the last, upholding our freedom, for we shall never fall to slavery by the likes of giants or any other."

With those words, Cyris turned to his people and led away what was left of them, telling them what had to be done now. Taking what they could carry, they left their homes and their lands, as well as their memories, and ventured into the unknown, never to look back.

He was to lead them far from there to the place that he had journeyed with his father when he was a lad, to a wilderness that was so vast it could swallow an army without a flicker. It was a place known of shadows called the Shadowed Forest, one so thick that light barely reached its surface. So began their journey, a small remnant of survivors of a once great and mighty people known as the Talishar, leaving both their name and their lands behind to what they hoped would be their new home. Without a trace, they vanished, leaving the Troguare to search in vain.

After returning Kreel and his legions back to their place, Obizar had become weak. The power to summon and control a demon such as Kreel dwarfed that of any he had summoned before. Though still possessing great power, Obizar became more and more fearful of depleting the power that still remained within him.

He was so driven in his lust for power that before he faced defeat, he was willing to sacrifice everything. To once again call upon the great evil, which was Kreel, he knew he would no longer be able to control it or its army. With that knowledge, he knew that everything alive, including himself, would be consumed by the irrepressible hunger for flesh by the demon and its hordes.

Though drained of a great portion of his power, he was still more powerful than any sorcerer alive, but he was in need of rest. He ordered his army to make camp, being too exhausted to move on. As he lay in his tent, Rolo entered. Once in Obizar's presence, he bowed, clutching his chest. He then said, "We have begun our search for any survivors. So far, we have found nothing but half-eaten and tattered bodies."

Obizar then replied, "Continue searching. I want not one of the Talishar dogs to remain alive. Find and bring me the head of the fallen Talishar king."

Rolo then replied, "Place them with the rest of the skulls of kings that dared to defy you."

Obizar then said, "No, this one I shall mount upon my necklace of skulls to be remembered as one of my greatest triumphs. If there are any survivors, kill them, but I trust that the demons did what they were summoned to do. If any exists, I shall seek them out and destroy everyone of them—may it be male, female, or child. I shall kill the memory that was once Talishar, for no one will ever know the history that had befallen between us."

But there was a truth hidden in Obizar's mind—the fear that his army was not invincible and that those of Talishar descent must never be allowed to exist so that they could never rise and seek revenge upon him.

This was the truth that would drive him for as long as life remained. Before the Troguares broke camp, Rolo returned to Obizar with the head of the fallen king. Filled with delight, the Troguare king laughed and said, "I shall sleep well tonight knowing that they are no more."

Obizar then rose to his feet and said, "It is time we begin." Obizar and his army pressed forward as he moved across a sea of bodies, stopping only to allow their liborox to gorge themselves on the dead till their bellies became too bloated to walk. The stench of the fallen was so great it filled the air for miles. For the scavengers, this was a time of plenty. Obizar scoured all the lands of the fallen Talishar and found not a trace.

After a long and tireless journey, the last of the Talishar had finally reached their destination—the Shadowed Forest. No longer would they be a people of the plains as they now withdrew into the cover of the forest.

Making a vow to his people, the new king, Cyris, spoke to them and said, "I am now your king. The name Talishar died on the field of battle with my father and our beloved brethren. He shall be known as the last of the great Talishar kings, for we are now a people of the forest, and so shall our new heritage begin."

With that, he swore an oath to his people and said, "Never again will I allow our people to be subjected to such evil where there is no hope in defeating them. Until so, guided by the light, we shall retreat to the shadows of the forest forever."

And so was the fate of the once-mighty Talishar as they faded from memory, and the name Talishar faded along with them. Over time, they became a tale of myths, a people of legends known as the Shadowed Warriors.

CHAPTER 18

A New Order—Troguaria, a Rising Empire

THE TROGUARES NOW laid claim to Talishar lands. With them, they brought a multitude of human slaves from the conquered lands beyond the wastelands. During the tumultuous journey, with their livestock nearly depleted, they turned to the multitude of human slaves to supplement their diet to survive the journey.

Pleasing to the taste, harvest camps were formed of humans and humanoid species as a supplement food supply, along with their livestock. Wherever there was a Troguare settlement, there was a harvest camp.

Regardless of how great the supply of livestock there was, Troguares preferred the taste of human flesh above all else. Those who were spared from the butcher's blade were used as servants and slaves under conditions that were too unbearable to imagine.

Children were seen as pets and playthings. When broken by the Troguare young, they were discarded, as one would do with an unwanted toy. Those who lived to be adolescents found no relief and were now subjected to the hardships of being a slave to brutal and unyielding masters. The life of women were short and agonizing, becoming pleasure items subjected to the brutality of unimaginable acts.

Many of their slaves died during the long trek across the wastelands, and the Troguares sought to restock their supply through the conquest of new lands. The thought of defeat, or how close that had come to fruition at the hands of the Talishar, never left Obizar's mind.

The possibility that there might be any survivors would haunt him through the ages, and in his mind, his search would never end. When Obizar arrived within the city walls, he marveled at its design. It was here he decided that the nomadic ways of his people would end but not within these walls.

He looked around and said, "We shall settle in these lands, but I shall have a city of my own. Put to the torch everything they have built—every structure, every shrine. We shall replace all that was once theirs into the images of our own. It is here that a new city in my name shall be built, and I shall call it Ozaria."

As commanded, the Troguare set aflame anything that would burn. Those things that could not be burned, he commanded them to be destroyed. And all markings were removed, erasing whatever history remained of a people that he wished to forget, until not a trace could be found so that future generations would have no knowledge that they had ever existed.

The life of the nomadic conquerors had now come to an end. The Troguares had now found a home, and it was here that the birth of the Troguare Empire was spawned. And it was here in these newly acquired lands that the reign of Obizar would truly begin.

With the blood, sweat, and lives of human slaves, the great city was built. In the center of the city, he had them erect a giant statue of himself. It was a giant fortress that was magnificently built. One could not help but be in awe at the sight of it, and as he had commanded, he named it Ozaria.

It had a chamber especially built to his specifications. In it, he kept his most prized possessions. He so named it the Hall of Skulls. There he had hundreds of skulls of kings from the kingdoms he had conquered, with space to include many more.

Most of the kings, their kingdoms, and their names had been lost and forgotten over time. Those he remembered and were his most prized, he had their crowns mounted on their skulls. They were worn around his neck, serving as his crown.

From here, he would control all the lands, as far as the mind could stretch, without mercy, centralizing his rule of terror. The Troguare Empire slowly began to spread, like the lands they had conquered before. The Troguare king broke the spirits of all he had conquered; no one was spared.

From man to the humanlike races, they were either killed, enslaved, or made sport. Everyone suffered the same fate, while those who dared to resist Obizar's rule were wiped from the face of Tyrus forever. As Obizar's merciless hand tightened, an entire world wept as hope evaporated as quickly as a shallow pool under the scorching heat of the suns.

It had been nearly a thousand years after the defeat and the fall of the Talishar Empire, and Obizar and his empire had slowly spread across the vastness of seemingly endless frontiers. With no kingdom powerful enough to challenge him, he refrained from his use of dark magic that constantly drained him.

The summoning of the demon Kreel took a heavy toll on his powers, which had weakened him. He now relied solely on the might of the most powerful army known in existence.

Kingdom after kingdom, both mighty and weak, tumbled as the Troguares moved along like dominoes, crushing everything in his path. With nothing but time at his disposal, Obizar expanded his empire. With a grip like a vise, it could not be broken. Man once again had begun to lose his identity, along with his freedom.

Generations upon generations of both giants and men had lived and died. Their names had faded through time, but there was one constant that remained—the name of Obizar, the immortal giant, the only name any could remember or had ever known. Many believed it was magic that one would live so long.

It was a question no one could answer and a mystery that was unsolved. The only one who knew this secret was Obizar himself, and the answer he never shared. Under his reign, there was only misery and despair, and none could ever forget his name.

The empire had finally reached the steps of the great Center Mountains. With their approach, thousands attempted to flee the Troguare onslaught. Most were hunted down and captured and enslaved. Some fled into the wilds to an uncertain fate. The creatures that stalked them were even more deadly.

There were a few who knew of a passageway leading through the great mountains called the Three-Valley Pass. It was a maze that led to three valleys but only one that led to the other side. Many had been lost, never to be seen again. Without the knowledge of its paths, only a few merchants and travelers had ever known the way.

Beyond its ranges, it had been rumored that there were three great kingdoms that remained outside Troguare rule. Obizar had learned this from a slave he had tortured, who told of stories by merchants who had journeyed there from beyond the other side.

Seeking answers once again, he stood before the flames. Using his powers, he opened a portal into the darkness, seeking answers from his masters from the dark realm. As before, these shadowy figures appeared to him, emerging from out of the shadows. They appeared one after the other according to the position of their power.

Where there were once four, three had now appeared before him. The one whose eyes burned of yellow flames was not present. The wizard did not ask but kept his focus on those who were before him. Coming forth was the one whose eyes burned brightest, the most powerful of the Dark Ones.

With flaming white eyes and in a low whispering voice, it asked, "Why have you summoned us? What answers do you seek? Have you found a way to bridge the barrier that keeps us from entering into the light?"

The mighty Obizar bowed and said, "No, master, I have not. But I am seeking the answers. My vision remains clouded. I only see the shadows of three kingdoms. Beyond that, I see nothing."

The passage that was called the Three-Valley Pass was also revealed to him from those he had tortured in this region. It was a single corridor that led into three narrow canyon valleys that merged back into one. It was large enough to allow an army to pass through. He learned it was the only passage and gateway to the other side for the impenetrable mountains stretched for thousands of mile in either direction.

It had been used by merchants and travelers for generations. To confirm his sight, he brought before him nine of his best scouts and warriors and commanded them to split up in groups of threes, each taking a separate course to the three kingdoms.

He instructed them to remain unseen, finding the kingdoms' weaknesses and their strengths, and to kill anyone that could witness to their presence. They rode out as they were commanded through the great mountain passage until reaching the other side.

There they split into three groups—one to the north into what was the Kingdom of the Norstar, one to the south to the fertile valleys and the magnificent Kingdom of the Niejar, and the other far to the east until reaching the land of the Lakes deep within the forest—each doing as they were commanded to do, out of sight and mostly under the cover of night.

For several months, they remained within the Norstar, and they learned they were hardy and brash people, direct in their approach and their fighting styles. They observed that many of its people would train at early dawn and well into the afternoon suns in the open fields daily. They also observed that they were excellent stonemasons, building many fortified positions throughout their lands, which were kept heavily guarded and always ready to defend. But they also learned that their weakness was, they were spread thin and were vulnerable if under mass attack by great numbers.

To the south, it was learned that the Niejar had a more relaxed stance. It was a great trading empire, and people roamed more freely. Its armies were highly mobile, excellent with the bow, and fearless. But they were vulnerable to surprise attacks under the perfect condition, mainly at night.

The Kingdom of the Lakes, which was hidden deep within the forest, revealed no real obstacles other than the forest and the distance it would take to reach its castle walls, which was its only strength. They reached it without any difficulty. Its only real strength was that it provided many places to hide under its thick foliage.

But what they were unaware of was that they were also being watched—everywhere, every step. Finally seeing all they had to see, the scouts began their journey back to the land of giants, as did their companions that traveled to the Norstar and the Niejar. After nearly a year, Obizar's envoys returned to him with their awaited report.

Standing before their king, they told him everything they had seen and learned, confirming that his visions were true. After sending them away, Obizar stood there, pleased with all he had heard. With a smile on his face, he called to his guards and told them to summon all his generals and commanders to meet with him within his war chamber.

As he sat there, waiting for them, he thought to himself that the whole world would finally be under his boots. As they arrived, the room was finally filled with his commanders and generals.

Rising to his feet, he called three of his top and most trusted generals before him. General Koshier was his top general and most trusted and was his second-in-command. Ruthless and brilliant, he was the greatest of his strategists and his most trusted. General Zhorr was patient and cunning but excessively brutal and efficient. Then there was General Troxus, who was volatile and reckless, evoking fear everywhere he treaded and was totally unpredictable.

As they approached him, they stopped, clenched their fists to their chests, bowed their heads, and dropped to one knee. Obizar, standing before them, told them to rise. As they stood motionless, Obizar began to speak, saying, "Beyond the mountains lies a new frontier, three kingdoms, with the belief that they are safe and free, that there is nothing to fear. But fear will soon be a reality, and freedom will be but a dream. Everything that they ever knew will soon come to an end, for the shadow of the Troguare Empire is now upon them. And when they awaken, they will find they will already be under our boots, like the insects they are. Koshier!"

"Yes, my lord," he responded.

"You shall take one hundred thousand warriors and riders to the south and conquer the kingdom of the Niejar!"

Koshier, looking at his master, replied, "It shall be done."

He then called General Zhorr.

"Yes, my lord," General Zhorr responded.

"You shall take another hundred thousand warriors to the north to the Kingdom of the Norstar and rain our might upon them." Bowing to Obizar, he, too, replied before stepping back to his place. Looking at General Troxus, Obizar said, "You shall have one hundred and fifty thousand at your disposal to take with you to the Kingdom of the Lakes. The additional fifty thousand soldiers are to prevent escape within this forest realm."

"Yes, my lord," General Troxus replied, as he bowed before him.

After giving his orders, he released his commanders to gather their armies and leave as quickly as possible.

CHAPTER 19

A Titan's Love

OBIZAR STOOD ATOP the fortress walls. He had long since put his armor to rest. He was adorned in a quilted gold robe with crested shoulders that curved upward. With the skulls of kings around his neck, he was now wearing a wardrobe that was fitting for a king, even one that was as massive and brutal as he. He watched his generals lead their armies to the lands he had called the new frontier. His mood was one of exuberance. Looking at his guard, he said, "I shall have pleasure tonight. Bring me a human female."

The guard looked at him and said, "Yes, my lord. Do you have a preference?"

Obizar paused in thought for a moment, then he replied, "Tonight I am in the mood for one of the darker sort. Bathe and perfume her, then bring her to my chambers."

"Yes, my lord," the guard replied, walking off to find his master what he had requested.

As commanded, the guard brought to him exactly what he had asked for—a slave woman from a faraway land of people whose identity had long since vanished and been forgotten. Obizar looked into her light-gray eyes and was fascinated by her smooth copper-toned skin as she stood before him.

With the stare of a wild animal, it seemed to sear straight through her. She was different than any of the women he had before. Unlike the rest, she stood proud with her head up as she looked the giant in his eyes, an act punishable by death. But she showed no sign of fear.

Taller and sturdier than any woman ever presented before him, he slowly walked around, inspecting her, reaching out as he twisted her long black locks at the end of his fingertips, drawing them close to his nostrils as he sniffed the ends of them. Boldly she stood firm, following his every movement until he walked behind her. She turned her head and stared straight ahead until he came around to the other side of her.

Obizar was intrigued by her boldness. He leaned forward until he was face-to-face with her with a snarl that would send chills down one's spine, but the woman did not flinch. He sensed no fear within her nor did he see it in her eyes. Obizar then said to her, "Woman, what is your name?"

She hesitated for the briefest of moments, then she replied, "Azola."

Obizar then repeated her name back to her, saying, "Azola." Then he made a gesture before responding back to her with a remark, saying, "Hmmmm, interesting." Looking her in the eyes, he said, "Humans bow before me. Never do they look into my eyes, but yet you do. A crime punishable by death, and you do so defiantly. Do you not fear me, woman?"

She responded, "Why should I? My fate is the same whether I do or do not, master." Unlike those before her, he found her to be most interesting. He saw a strength in her that excited him. Not even before his time as an immortal being was gentleness found in him, but yet there was something about her that stirred emotions that he had never known to exist within him.

Gently he reached down and grabbed her by her hand, leading her into his sleeping chambers, and said, "Come." Never once taking his eyes off her, he slowly closed the drapes behind them, giving the command to his guards that he was not to be disturbed before sunrise.

Night after night, she was summoned to his chambers. Unlike most human women, she survived the experience. Never once was she harshly treated. As weeks turned into months, she had become his most precious possession, pleasing him at every turn.

The Troguare king had begun to fall in love with his beauteous prize, sharing with her his deepest thoughts as she escorted him wherever he went. For months, she toured the lands with her master, reminding her of the plight of her people. With a heavy heart, she whispered in his ear, hoping to relieve their burdens.

For a moment in time, the heart of Obizar softened, and it was noticed throughout the kingdom. Even his own people witnessed the change. It was an act that was indeed most dangerous in a culture built on fear and cruelty. The heavy hand that all had experienced under Troguare rule had taken a pause.

These acts would have been deemed a sign of weakness, one that would have prompted any rivals to take advantage and seize the opportunity to rise up. But Obizar wasn't one of ordinary lineage. He was the most powerful sorcerer known, and despite his actions, that alone prompted fear that was beyond comprehension.

With that knowledge, no one among them would dare even the slightest to challenge his might, for failure in an attempt would surely end in a most horrible death. It was during this time that even Azola, whose hate had once stirred within her for the Troguares and their king, had mellowed.

Azola found herself falling in love with the same monster responsible for centuries of atrocities against her people and the rest of the known world. No longer kept in a cage, she lay by the giant's side every night.

It was early morning. She rose with heavy thoughts as she stood by the window to watch the dual suns rise. Noticing that his bed was empty, Obizar rose up and walked to her and stood by her side, towering over her as if she was a small child, then he asked, "What troubles you?"

Azola looked up to the giant's eyes and simply asked the question, "Why?"

Obizar looked at her, puzzled by the question, and said, "What is the question that you ask, woman?"

She then replied with a tremble in her voice, holding back her tears, saying, "Us. We are two different creatures. You are the master of this world, and I am but a slave. You show no mercy to anyone save me. What is it about me that I am deemed so special?"

Obizar stood silent. Not even he was sure of the answer, so he pondered it for a moment and said, "Woman, walk with me." As the two left the king's chambers, they walked down the long corridor of the palace.

Ceilings reaching twenty feet were adorned with an array of designs and odd shapes. As they walked, he said to her, "From my youth, I knew I was destined to rule. I come from a place as harsh as the most desolate place on this world and a people that mirror that fact. When I was young, my father was killed in a futile war of clans. My mother had died the previous year.

"I was left to roam, beg, and scrap for food to survive on my own. I even killed to do so. One day I slipped into the sorcerer's tent when he was absent to find whatever I could steal. Others were afraid of him and his power, everyone except me. He caught me as I was leaving out of his dwelling and beat me to nearly an inch of my life. Bloody and battered, I showed no fear, even attempted to fight back rather than to flee. This had impressed him, so he said to me, 'Boy, who cares for you so that I may take my wrath out on them instead of an insignificant child?'

"I replied, 'No one, for I care for myself and need no one to look after me.' The wizard looked at me with a puzzled look on his face and said, 'Boy, I should kill you where you stand, but you have courage beyond any youth of your age that has ever been in my presence.' He then asked when had I last eaten. When I told him I could not remember, he told me to stay. And from that moment, I was taken in by the sorcerer of my kind. Later I asked why he took me in. He replied that I was bolder than the others of my youth and that he saw something in me.

"Day in and day out, I stayed under his watchful eyes as he began to teach me the darkest secrets of the arts, but we are of a harsh and brutal people. With a heavy hand, any and all discipline that was administered to me was relentless. He was amazed at how quickly I learned and how well I took punishments for anything he deemed insubordinate. It was through him I learned to master the dark arts."

Azola then asked, "What happened to him?"

Obizar smiled and replied, "I killed him, but that is a story for another time. The power that now and, to some extent, that resonates within me brought me to the realization that any and all things are beneath me and my race. We lack the warmth in our hearts to know anything else but war or conquest, which makes us stronger than anyone else, a trait my kind is born with." For a moment, he became silent and then looked down at Azola and said, "There is something in you that sparked something different within me. Something I had never known or felt before. Something that gives my life added meaning. Something I care not to relinquish for as long as you are by my side.

"Troguare woman also lack warmth or love nor are they desirable to live with. It is only duty that we mate to continue our species. Love is not in them or a part of our people. You, Azola, bring with you everything that I want but the one thing I truly desire the most from you."

Azola looked at Obizar and asked, "What is that, my lord?"

Obizar replied, "A child."

Azola then replied, "Master, since my youth, I have despised my Troguare masters. You, above all. The loathing I had for you and your kind was beyond measure. By your cruel hands, I have witnessed the deaths of many I have loved through the years. Over time, I had grown accustomed to this harsh and bitter life, so much so that I had begun to grown numb to it all until all fear had left. I realized that one day I would experience the same fate. When I first stood in your presence, it did not matter to me what was to become of me.

"The thought of death meant freedom from my bonds, and in my heart, I would have welcomed it. But there was something deep inside you that I saw, buried beneath that blackened heart, something that needed to come out that was beyond your cruel and merciless demeanor."

Obizar stood quietly to listen. For a moment, not even he was sure how he would respond, but he stood patiently while he contemplated what would be his next words as he waited for the conclusion of her thoughts.

"My lord," she continued, "you were the first male of any kind I had ever been with, and I truly believed you were going to be the last. I have known only a few women that have survived a night with a giant. Tales of horror and brutality filled my ears. Therefore, I had no reason to believe that my fate would be any different. After all, I was to be with the king himself. That night you showed me what I believed would be impossible."

Azola paused, staring Obizar in his eyes, then continued, "A gentle hand that was opposite of anything that I had ever heard. To my surprise, I found pleasure in every moment. I felt protected by your strength, and with that, I became most infatuated by it. Over these many months, I have grown to love and desire you. To bear your child is something I thought would sicken me, but now I wish it could be true. But what you desire is truly impossible."

Obizar replied, "Yes, that is true of our two species, but I am not like the others of my kind." He then became silent, looking down into the windows of her light-gray eyes as he gently placed his massive palm on the back of her head.

Azola then replied, "What do you mean, my lord?"

Obizar simply smiled. Then he said, "I have chosen you above all others to be by my side. My affection for you is great, and if I am to be presented with a child, it is you that I have chosen to be its mother." Upon finishing his words, Obizar's smile turned into focus as he looked her in her eyes and said, "My powers go far beyond nature. What is impossible for all others is but a simple gesture by me. Stand silent, for I shall turn what is impossible into a reality."

As commanded, Azola spoke not another word. She simply stood in silence as she watched her lover begin to speak. Standing before her, he began to chant a language unknown to her.

She watched with amazement as Obizar's hands began to give off a bright-red glow before placing both of his giant hands on her stomach. Instantly she fell into a trance, which lasted but a few moments before she came out of it.

Feeling dizzy, she grabbed her head as he reached out and drew her close to his massive body. Wrapping his arms around her, he held her close to his chest as if she was but a doll. Soon afterward, he took her into his until she had conceived, bringing life into her womb. Only time would tell, for the future would be uncertain.

Nine months had passed since Azola had been by Obizar's side. A slave queen bearing the king's child, she was viewed with loathing, but no one dared to utter a word of defiance. A lowly human was having the heir of the most powerful ruler that had ever ruled the likes of the Troguare.

Any other who had attempted such a thing would have long since been challenged or murdered in their sleep. For a king who could summon demons with merely a thought, no one dared to challenge his will.

Over the time that Azola had traveled with the Troguare king throughout the kingdom, it reminded her of the horrors she had faced growing up since she was a child. It was a mystery to all how she could have fallen in love with such a monster. Even she inside was lost for words.

Traveling from village to village, she witnessed the endless horrors of her people. Children, like birds, were kept in domed cages, many broken and hurt by the rough hands of the Troguare youth.

Some survived only to grow into a life of slavery, and some with a fate that was even worse, ended up on the menu of some masters that preferred their taste over the beasts that were raised for that purpose. Those who did not end up on the menu were discarded, only to serve as appetizers to many of the feral beasts.

As the life inside her continued to grow, all that Azola had witnessed served only to sadden her, knowing her words would carry her voice only but so far. Looking into a mirror, she was reminded of who and what she was. It was the love for a monster that had imprisoned her, keeping her clinging to an uncertain future.

D. R. SIMPSON

CHAPTER 20

The Wanderling

FOR SEVERAL MONTHS, a large caravan was returning from lands far away beyond the Center Mountains. Stretching for thousands of miles in both directions, its ranges climbed straight up vertically, making them nearly impossible to climb.

Having steep jagged walls with ridges and cliffs more than a thousand feet straight up, there was only one direct passage leading through to the other side. Many had become lost, attempting to find their way. Many perished in the attempt. But there were a few who had the knowledge, who could find their way, mostly merchants and traders with knowledge that had been passed down to them for hundreds of years.

It was a maze of corridors leading to a single passage called the Three-Valley Pass. Stories of an advancing army beyond the lands they had left behind followed these merchants by those fleeing the enemy's advance.

They headed north to the city of Hiendore, the capital of the Norstar Kingdom, from which they came. They brought back with them treasures of unmeasurable worth. With them, there were also tales of the Troguare army led by their wizard king, Obizar—the immortal able to summon creatures of darkness, consuming anything that dared to defy him. No one was safe; they enslaved everyone unfortunate enough to have crossed their path.

Just before the setting of the second sun, Ashma, the leader of the caravan, and all its merchants were worn out from their long journey as they pressed on with great fervor, putting as much distance between themselves and the lands they had left behind them until they couldn't press on any farther.

Exhausted along with the others, Ashma decided to stop and make camp at the forest's edge. Once settled, he summoned Orthimar, the leader of a group of mercenaries hired to guard the caravan and its bounty.

The gruff middle-aged warrior, with long straight hair sprinkled with gray, was as tough as the terrain of the rugged mountains they had just passed through. With a scar across the right side of his face, he was accustomed to the dangers of his trade. With forty or so men like himself, they were well suited for the task they were hired for. Ashma came up to him and said, "We shall camp here for the night. You are as familiar with these lands as I and the dangers as well as the risks."

Orthimar looked at him and smiled, then he said, "There hasn't been an incident in decades."

Ashma replied, "That may be, but I expect you to do what you were hired to do."

Orthimar looked back at him with a smirk on his face and said, "You have no worries. There are none any better than us. I shall take added precautions if it will put your fears to rest." He bowed his head, making a waving gesture, with his eyes fixed on the head merchant.

"Let us pray that you do." Ashma briefly looked back at Orthimar before he turned and walked away, leaving the old mercenary with a smile of sarcasm spread across his face. The evening soon gave way to the darkness as the last glimpses of sunlight faded over the horizon.

Fires throughout the camp now ruled the night, providing the only flicker of light as storm clouds rolled in from the west, causing an unusually dark and starless night. While his men were preparing themselves for their duties, Orthimar stood among them while they stood quietly, awaiting their orders.

Looking at each, he said, "These are lands in which the Triclore roam, three-eyed brutes who will attack—" Abruptly interrupting Orthimar's words before he could finish his thought, someone among them shouted out in jest, drawing laughter among each of the men, "Sounds like that Omerion woman I was with on our last adventure together."

Orthimar looked at him and said, "It is pleasing that you are in such a light mood." Walking over to him without a smile, all became silent, along with the one who made the jest. Now face-to-face, Orthimar looked him in his eyes and said, "Have you ever encountered a Triclore?" The warrior looked at him and shook his head, not sure of what actions the old mercenary would take.

Orthimar then said, "If you did, there would be no jest in you." Slowly pointing to the scar on the right side of his face, he said, "This is the mark of a grazing blow of a bone-end spike of a Triclore's club. Before I sank my blade into its chest, it merely slowed the beast. It was the arrows of my comrade that found its mark deep within its third eye that sat atop its forehead that brought it down. An inch closer, I would not be here telling the story."

Looking at Orthimar not only commanded the man's attention but also all those who stood around listening. Looking around, the old warrior shouted, "Be alert! Though they may seem to be mindless brutes, they are deadly. Attacks are swift and without warning. A single blow can detach your head from your body. They move silently in the darkness despite their bulk, and you will be dead before you can even make a sound."

Looking around at each of his men, Orthimar said, "Some of you claim to know no fear. But once you encounter one, you shall know the meaning of it." Of all his men, he was the only one that had ever engaged a Triclore.

Though his men were battle-hardened and resonated little fear, this was something that they were not accustomed to. After his speech, he then focused on the task at hand, giving the order to his men, saying, "We shall post forty feet apart, each in view of the next man until we circumference the camp. There shall be three shifts through the night. I suggest that the rest of you get rest, for this may be a long night. If any are caught asleep, the punishment will be severe."

As the evening wore on, everyone throughout the camp remained uneasy. Though this was a common trade route, none had dared to stop to make camp in these lands after nightfall.

Everyone knew that to stop here was of great risk, even Orthimar himself, though he attempted to conceal it from Ashma. A few hours had now passed, restlessness gave way to weariness, and all eyes were heavy.

The long journey began to take its toll on all of them. With all the sights and ramblings of their travels, they had pressed on harder than they had ever done before. Even the most hardened of these guards felt the burden.

Exhausted, they fought the temptation of sleep. But they managed to remain awake until the eyes of one of the guards posted on the fringes of the camp fell shut. It was only for the briefest of moments, only to open to what would be the very last image within his mind, which was a large gray figure, before everything went black.

Like the sound of an ax striking a tree, the echo of the strike filled the air all around before his body fell to the ground, followed by heavy grunts from manlike beasts.

The caravan's biggest fears were now realized. Standing nearly seven feet tall, the Triclore were large and gray, having skin textured like leather. These three-eyed beasts, with three ridges along the top of their sloping forehead, were the raiders of the night that everyone had learned to fear.

They came out of nowhere, but yet they were everywhere. Moving through the caravan and wagons, their number was about twenty in all. Armed with wooden clubs and with bone spikes protruding from them, they also had daggers that were made of bone.

Smashing everything in their path, they were driven by their attraction to gold, silver, and precious stones. They took anything that gleamed or shined, but for reasons that were never known.

No one knew from whence they came or exactly where they went, only that their tracks always led somewhere within the thick forest—a place all declined to follow.

The attack was swift and savage. They were all over the camp before a warning could be sounded. Only the cries of men echoed through the night, revealing their true brutality.

All efforts to stall the attacks failed, with sounds of clubs crashing through shields and swords. All attempts by the guards to stop them proved futile. Orthimar fought bravely and valiantly in the defense of the camp, causing injury to several, but was killed by an unseen blow.

From the rear, he was impaled by one of the Triclores before being thrown several feet out of the way, like a used rag, by the brutish beast. Unlike before, he wasn't as fortunate.

A few feet away, concealed by the darkness and unknown to all, a separate set of eyes watched silently. Patiently they waited while the sounds of death spread across the caravan like a ripple in water.

Many fled the assault, while the broken and maimed bodies of men who weren't so fortunate lay dead or dying, scattered about everywhere. Many of the survivors fled into the woods and the fields, staying hidden and petrified, trying to avoid the Triclores' assault.

As quickly as it all began, it also ended. The Triclores then pillaged through the broken wagons and bodies that were lying all around. They took with them as much of the gold, silver, and precious stones they could carry, leaving only a few glistening stones of the once hefty caravan scattered about.

Among the chaos, out of the shadows emerged a stout muscular figure. Seeing that all was now clear, he moved silently through the rubble. There was still treasure that was overlooked, and he could've taken all he could carry.

There was no one to guard the bounty who could've stopped him, only that of the dead scattered about. He was tempted to take what was left. After all, that was why he was following the merchants.

Unexpectedly, the Triclores had beat him to the prize. His name was Cyrikhan. The Wanderling was from a people known to be opportunists and assassins, having a knack for acquiring information for such things.

He had been following the caravan for days. There was one stone in their possession that held his interest in particular. It was called an orophyx. Rare and extremely valuable, it would demand a king's fortune, and he knew it was headed to the palace.

This was the reason he was there, but he had not the time, believing a much-greater bounty laid in the possession of the Triclore lair. In his mind, he could return later to claim the stone. Keeping at a steady pace, he didn't miss a stride, having other intentions and following a trail only a fool would consider.

Stealth and cunning were the traits of his people. They were born with superior senses greater than that of most humans, having three scent flaps along the bridge of their noses. Wanderlings were a tribe of people having no alliance or allegiance with any kingdoms.

Moving to and fro whenever, wherever they willed. They were both fearless and feared, taught from youth to be most efficient with the sword. Cyrikhan not only mastered one, he was also twice as deadly, being the greatest of his people using double swords. Having shoulder armor, a battle ax on his back, and a hatchet on his side, along with two daggers wherever he could readily reach them, the oval-eyed warrior was equipped to handle any situation that might arise in his line of work in which he excelled.

He had a bald head, a painted tattoo over his left eye, which was a symbol of his status as a warrior, and a yellowish skin. He also had a ponytail curled into a bun. Known by his people as the Killer of Titans, both great and small had died by his hand.

He roamed places not even his people would go. He had been stalking the caravan for days. Learning word that they would come, he patiently waited along the trail until they arrived. Along with the rest, he, too, was unaware that the caravan would come under assault by a different sort of bandit.

This proved to be as an unexpected opportunity he hadn't counted on or one he could pass on. Going to the lair of the Triclores was a thought of a fool. But for him, it was an opportunity.

For generations, these three-eyed creatures had raided caravans filled with precious stones and metals. No one ever knew from whence they came or went. He figured wherever they took the treasures, it would be enough wealth to build one's own kingdom, and he was willing to risk it all to find out.

Keeping a distance from them, he stalked them for hours until he found himself deeper and deeper and within the boundaries of these heavily forested and uncharted lands. He had faced Triclores before and prevailed.

Traveling through these lands, he was one of the few that had survived the experience, barely escaping with his own life. Triclores had keen hearing and smell. Despite having three eyes, their eyesight was poor.

Remaining downwind and silent, he used his own senses and tracking abilities, allowing him to keep a fair distance without losing them, stalking them as if they were his prey. Traveling in a single file, Triclores remained quiet and on a steady pace, neither straying nor wandering from their designed route.

They showed respect for these lands. Though large and powerful and aided by numbers, there were creatures here that they paled in comparison to—giant creatures. Some were mythical in nature. Despite this, even they were vulnerable to an attack from creatures that were just as mighty.

For hours, he followed them with ghastly sounds echoing all around as the cycle of life and death was being carried out all around them. With all the distractions, they remained steady in their movements— both Cyrikhan and the unsuspecting Triclore brutes.

They moved quietly through the underbrush and tall grasses, careful not to lose their scent in the air. Never once did the Triclores take a moment to stop. They defecated while they shuffled along, leaving trails of dung as they went.

Cyrikhan knew that once they reached their lair, he would no longer have the ability to get close enough to remain undetected. Scooping a handful of the foul substance, he smeared it all over himself, his weapons, and all he had with him to mask his own scent.

Finally, they reached their destination—the Triclores' lair. Cyrikhan remained hidden in the shrubbery but found himself surrounded by dozens of them. They were all around him. Lying perfectly still and silent, not moving a muscle, he waited until the opportunity presented itself. Even with the activity, his eyes remained fixed on his target.

Torches were lit sparingly throughout the entrances of their dwellings. Between the shadows of the flickering lights produced by their flames, the Wanderling watched through the tall grasses as the Triclores, with the treasure, entered the cave.

Cyrikhan lay and waited motionless for hours until they began to tire and fall asleep. It was then he made his move, moving stealthily around slumbering bodies and piles of dung until he reached the cave entrance.

Under a lit torch at the entrance of the cave, one of the gray beasts had sprawled out and fell asleep at the entrance. Smeared with Triclore dung, he silently moved past the resting behemoth, knowing his scent would be concealed by the stench as he followed the path deep within the cave.

With a superior sense of smell, Cyrikhan's scent flaps on the lower bridge of his nose allowed him to focus on whichever scent trail he so chose to follow. Moving along the narrow passageway down the tunnel, Triclore dung littered the ground along with puddles of urine.

While the cave reeked of the foulness thereof, the Wanderling was still able to follow the trail of those who brought the treasures with them. Finally, he found the chamber where they kept their prize.

Those who brought it there themselves were scattered about the cave, lost in heavy slumber with snoring that was so loud one could hardly hear their own thoughts. Cyrikhan had seen and been to places a lot worse and was not fazed by any of it.

Finally, he entered the chamber that was full of gold, silver, precious stones, and jewels of all types. The chamber stretched as far as he could see. It had also been lit throughout by torches.

They had been collecting treasures for generations, all lying dormant with an unknown purpose. Cyrikhan pulled from his belt a folded sack where he loaded up as much as he could carry. When he was done, he quietly made his way over and around the slumbering oafs.

After a while, the smell nearly became so unbearable he could barely think. Eventually, even he found difficulty keeping his breath as he passed the last of the slumbering creatures sprawled at the cave's entrance. In his bag was a small tear, an opening barely noticeable until a tiny gem, the size of a small pebble, slipped through the opening, falling onto the ground.

To the Triclores, it was like an alarm had sounded. They arose quickly as they began their pursuit of the Wanderling. Though they weren't fast, Cyrikhan himself was weighted down by the bag of treasures he was carrying.

Steadily gaining on him with their clubs in hand, Cyrikhan was forced to drop the sack, but he had no intention of leaving his bounty. The thief had now become the assassin and drew both of his swords.

Knowing he couldn't make a stand against an entire clan of these beasts, he dealt with the ones that were the closest at hand. The first to arrive swung with such force that when he missed, it turned him completely around, finding one of Cyrikhan's sword buried into its mouth and out the back of its head.

Quickly removing the first sword, Cyrikhan spun around using his other sword, beheading the second brute. Quickly he snatched the bag filled with his bounty before the bodies of both creatures could hit the ground while trying to make his escape.

Moving swiftly, trying to buy himself a few precious moments, he found three more Triclores that were now blocking his path. Somehow maneuvering himself between two of them, one of the club-wielding beasts aimed for his head as it attempted to deliver its blow.

Bellowing under, it flailed over Cyrikhan's head, smashing the head of the other Triclore and killing him. In one motion, the Wanderling thrust his sword through the throat of the other beast before he could recover to make a second attempt, leaving him lifeless before he also fell to the ground, motionless.

With his path now clear, he sheathed one of his swords and took hold of his sack with his free hand. For a moment, Cyrikhan had put some distance between himself and that of his pursuers until he ran directly into what felt like a stone wall.

Falling to the ground awkwardly, he lost grasp of his sword, along with that sack of jewels. Standing over him with club in his hand, an even larger Triclore, larger than all the others, just stood over him and watched.

Cyrikhan looked up at it, poised, anticipating its blow, knowing he wouldn't be able to draw his second sword in time. The two locked eyes on each other for a brief moment. To Cyrikhan's surprise, it stepped aside, allowing Cyrikhan to regain his swords and bag before passing by the Triclore to make his escape, all the while being puzzled as to why.

Making his way back through the forest, he was still being pursued by the enraged clan. Cyrikhan proved too elusive, evading their efforts to track him as he escaped. With his path now clear, Cyrikhan finally made it back to his steed at the edge of the thorn forest. Now safe, he rode off with his bounty, along with yet another adventure under his belt.

Back at the Triclore lair, the returning Triclores directed their anger toward the one that allowed the human to pass by him. The leader of the clan looked at the one and pointed his club at him as he let out a series of grunts, directing the others in their way to attack him.

With a size advantage, along with being more powerful than the others, the first of the brutish beast that attacked him was killed with a single blow. With so much power, its blood spattered over fifty feet from where it was struck.

Not deterred, another rushed in as it shared the same fate as its predecessor, then another followed, and then another, with little effort. With three of them lying dead in front of them, fear finally came over the rest of his would-be attackers.

The clan leader stood there but did not attack. Instead he allowed the large Triclore to leave. None of the brutish beasts wanted to share the fate of the ones that had challenged him. Now forced to leave the clan, he roamed alone without a place with his kind or that of man. He now wandered the lands as an outcast, with no place he could call home.

The next morning after the rise of the first sun, the merchants went back to the caravan to gather what was left. With most of their bounty lost, along with those hired to protect them, they buried their dead and gathered what remained of value.

Ashma stood silently over Orthimar, remembering the last words that had been spoken between them as he looked around at those who were not fortunate enough to escape or survive the Triclores' attack. With many lost, he commanded those who remained to burn the bodies and move from this place as quickly as possible, in case the beasts decided to return.

After a month's journey, Ashma and what remained of the caravan were still recovering from their misfortunes from the Triclore attack. They arrived back at the Norstar city of Hiendore with a minimal bounty of treasured goods and other items of value.

Though their loses were great, there was still a profit to be made among the merchants who had survived the ordeal. They also brought with them tales of terror from the far-off lands they left behind them— that of conquering giants and a powerful sorcerer, along with other nightmarish events that filled the ears of the many that would listen. The news spread rapidly throughout the entire kingdom and beyond, even reaching the ears of the king himself.

CHAPTER 21

Clash of Titans

ARRIVING ABOUT THE same time, a more inconspicuous traveler quietly entered the city, also having shared knowledge of the events surrounding the caravan's encounter. Cyrikhan had already hidden the prizes he had stolen from the Triclore caves, but he had yet one more treasure that he wished to claim—the orophyx.

It was a prize fit for a king, and by now, he figured it was already in the king's possession. There were more stones of great value that made it back to be sold, but it was that one he desired the most.

For weeks, Cyrikhan watched, finding those who had purchased the merchandise from those merchants who had returned to sell their goods. He found out exactly where those of wealth were residing and were they stored there possessions.

Not known for conservatism, greed was a prominent trait of the Wanderling people. He wished to steal it all and turn a profit elsewhere. His plan was to slowly rob these aristocrats of their gold and jewelry a little at a time without them noticing.

Anything large would bring unwanted attention by those enforcing the law. While he drained the wealthy of their gold and precious stones, he was planning his biggest challenge—retrieving the orophyx from the security of the palace vault before moving on.

It had been a while since he had operated within these walls. Everything changes as time moves on. No matter if guarded or not, no one ever knew he was there.

He was no ordinary thief but one exceptionally skilled at his craft. Unknown to him, everything did not go unnoticed. There were eyes that remained on constant alert. His name was Honduro. He was both captain and champion of the guards, the most trusted of all who were charged in the protection of the king and the city.

Undefeated in the tournament that took place every year that determined the one who was deserving of that title among them, Honduro was the finest warrior and fighter of the Norstar people. He was the master of the broadsword, and he wielded it with perfection.

Reports had been brought to his attention of valuables that had been missing while they were positively secured. There were no signs of entry or evidence of any break-ins, simply mysterious disappearances that had left their owners puzzled.

No one seemed to have had an answer. To Honduro, this had a very familiar flavor to it. He recognized the craftiness of the work. After seeing such things years back, he exercised patience as he waited.

He believed it would be only a matter of time before the source of these mysteries would eventually reveal itself. A few more weeks had passed since the last reported incident when a silent figure moved like a ghost in the night through the streets and alleyways.

He passed by open windows with the sounds of nightly pleasure being heard, interrupting the night as he passed by. Cyrikhan was once again on the prowl. He had chosen this night to claim his greatest prize.

He knew the palace from a few years past, on a prior visit. Nothing of value was beyond the grasp of a Wanderling. Their skills were far above all others of this trade.

He had once entered the palace late one evening and had taken a jewel-laden necklace off the necks of several sleeping guests of royalty, with guards being present outside of their sleeping quarters. No other people alive possessed such skills, and nothing was going to deter him from his goal or stop him from reaching his destination.

Now he was at the base of the grand walls of the palace. They were heavily guarded by elite palace guards alert to any movement, no matter how slight. They were skilled at what they did, but this would indeed be a challenge for them.

They were dealing with a master that specialized in the art of stealth. Cyrikhan had chosen this night to demonstrate his mastery, robbing the palace of its most prized jewel. He used the tools of his trade, attaching himself against the forty-foot walls, scaling them with little effort, as if he was an insect.

Without making a sound, he slipped past the guards, concealing himself within the shadows cast by the dimly lit torches spaced along the lavishly designed architecture and arched hallways.

Not taking a conventional route, he used specially designed tools made for this purpose, skills taught to him from youth by his father, which were the ways of a Wanderling.

Slowly moving along with great care, displaying exceptional strength, he wedged and braced himself along the corners where the walls and ceilings met, like a spider remaining out of view.

He passed over the top of the guards in which none of them thought to look up. Fortunately, his visit wasn't one with a darker intent, an assassination, or anything of that sort. His was one of a more profitable purpose, one in which he was highly skilled to perform.

Finally, he reached his point of interest. Sliding down the cornered wall, he slipped behind one of the large planted vases used to decorate the hallways. Unlocking the latch to the door, which was only a few steps from where the sentry was standing, he entered the chamber.

There, well hidden, was a vault that had been built there without without the knowledge of any but a chosen few. After breaching the doors of the vault, he removed the quilted sack he had draped across his back and grabbed the glimmering orophyx before preparing to make a silent but hasty exit.

To his surprise, his escape route was interrupted. Blocking his path was the silhouette of a most formidable foe, like a statue with a short winglike helmet. It was the captain of the guards, Honduro.

He was adorned in silver armor that was so highly polished it glistened even under the sparsely lit corridor of flickering candles, almost appearing godlike. With his broadsword in one hand and a silver-spiked shield in the other, Honduro looked at Cyrikhan with a stare as cold as a frozen lake that pierced through him without expression.

The two simply stood, silently facing each other. Cyrikhan was free of the restraints of a bulky armor. He had only a shoulder guard on his left arm to protect him. With Honduro blocking his path, he thought to himself, How could anyone have known of his presence? This was the first time he had been in this position or was discovered.

He showed little concern despite the gravity of the situation he was now facing and despite being discovered. He was fearless and unfazed by it all. After hearing the reports and studying the patterns of these acts of theft for weeks, Honduro had noticed the pattern of thievery soon after the return of the caravan and the dispersion of their goods by the merchants to those wealthy enough to afford to purchase them.

The finest stones and that of gold and silver, which held the greatest value, would disappear without a trace despite being secured and guarded. This was a task too great for an ordinary thief.

With the purchases made by the royal family, Honduro knew it was just a matter of time before an attempt on the palace would be made. Only that of a fool would dare such an act, unless one possessed the skills of a Wanderling. It was their pattern, and it was known throughout the land that only they possessed such skills. So he set a trap for a most cunning thief, using himself and his sword.

Even though these thieves were exceptional in what they do, they were also excellent fighters, and the one that stood before him was the greatest of his people to ever wield a sword. He was well-known, the one they called the Killer of Titans. To the eyes of the champion of the guards, he was no more than a common thief.

"Surrender your swords, thief, as well as that which you unlawfully possess—the king's treasure."

A half smile slowly crept across Cyrikhan's face. Quickly he secured the crystal around his waist. He had no intention of releasing his prize.

"Stand down and place the jewel and your swords at your feet or feel the taste of cold steel upon your flesh."

Armed with double swords with a razor edge that was light and polished, Cyrikhan slowly drew one then the other and then replied, "Even statues fall, you overbloated bag of wind. I do feel merciful this day. If you wish to see morning, it's best you pretend I did not exist and step aside."

"Don't allow two swords to give you false hopes, believing that you have the advantage. One blade is more than enough for me to extinguish your hope," Honduro replied.

Before another word was spoken, Honduro drew his sword and with it first blood as the blade kissed the Wanderling across his face. A slight turn prevented grave injury. In retaliation, Cyrikhan countered, raking his blade across Honduro's shoulder while the second sailed over his head as he ducked beneath it.

Honduro then rolled back into his stance as the two exchanged blows with deadly intent, unable to find their mark, displaying equal skill. As the scrimmage went on, it gained in intensity until the arrival of more palace guards.

Now knowing the skills of his opponent, along with arrival of added swords, it would tip the balance in this contest and place Cyrikhan at a disadvantage. Therefore, Cyrikhan sought an exit, seeing there was a window a few feet away. In the midst of battle, the Wanderling flipped over a flaming lantern hanging in the hallway onto the path of Honduro and the remaining guards.

With their path now hindered by the flames, with haste Cyrikhan hooked the windowsill with his scaling rope from his pouch, pausing as he looked at Honduro. "We will meet once more," he said before rapidly sliding down the forty-foot wall into the courtyard below and then disappearing into the shadows as the warning trump sounded.

Finally reaching the window, Honduro leaned out, looking at the courtyard below, fueled with anger. But silence was upon his lips.

"My lord," one of the guards spoke, "we shall find him. He can't get far."

Honduro replied, "You won't find him."

"My lord!" the guard replied, "He's a Wanderling. Only a moment is needed for him to vanish without a trace. How can we not identify him with the mark on his face from your sword and the patch tattooed around his eye?"

Honduro responded without an exchange of eye contact, simply repeating his words. "It doesn't matter. He's a Wanderling. You won't find him." Infuriated, Honduro simply walked off, not uttering another word, knowing that not only did Cyrikhan get away but he also got away with the jewel.

Within himself, Honduro's pride and ego was tainted. Another of the guards of high rank approached and gave his report of the inventory and to what he knew that was taken, then the guard said, "I will go and give report to the king."

Honduro replied, "No! I'll go." Then he turned and walked away without uttering another word. He was now fueled with hatred for the man that had now humiliated him.

At the rise of the first sun, the king awakened to begin his early morning exercise, with the queen still asleep peaceably within their chambers. Still practicing his form, he was an older king up in his years, no longer strong enough to lead his army into battle. He was once a mighty warrior in the days long since passed.

Honduro, his trusted champion and the captain of the guards, always remained close, for he was loyal and valiant. Without hesitation, he was willing to give his life in defense of the king and his family, along with the kingdom of the Norstar itself.

More than capable to lead their army, the king instead chose him to guard the family of the king. Everyone in the kingdom knew that there was none of higher importance but the king himself.

Entering into the garden, standing before the king, Honduro bowed as he approached. The king then told him to rise as his captain stood before him, standing firm and straight.

His eyes were straightforward and without expression. The king looked at him and smiled, then placed his hand on his shoulder, and asked, "Why such a stern face on such a beautiful morning? Relax such a pruned face."

Honduro responded, "There have been acts of thievery within the city walls of items of great value. It had been brought to my attention, and I have been pursuing all courses within my power to resolve them."

The king then said, "Thieves will always be present as long as people exist. That is an act no one can fully end."

Honduro then replied, "That is true, but these are the actions of one of great skills. I recognized the patterns and had set a trap. He breached the city walls, climbing forty feet into the palace despite added security. In the shadows beyond the notice of our own guards, it was only by knowing the ways of a Wanderling through previous encounters was I able to recognize his pattern and set a trap of my own before confronting the thief as he attempted to make his exit.

"It was a Wanderling having great skills with a sword, and this one wielded two of them. I placed my mark upon his face with my sword, adding to the tattoo he wore over his left eye, yet he still escaped."

The king smiled, looked at him, and said, "His skills are obvious, I see. He also left his mark on my greatest fighter." He then took his hand off his shoulder and walked a few steps away to gather his thoughts.

The king then let out a sigh before he began to speak, "There are events unfolding beyond these walls that outweigh the motives of a thief or any such acts. Word has reached my ears, as well as many throughout the kingdom, of an upcoming threat."

CHAPTER 22

Rumblings in the Wind—Deadly Deals to Be Made

"RUMORS OF AN army of giants and other things not yet mentioned. Is it true?"

"That I cannot truly answer, but a good king must always consider the threat, for the well-being of the people must always be weighed. And rumors must be considered if they are of this magnitude.

"War has not been at our doorsteps for many decades, but I will prepare to make cautious moves. I have begun to ready the army and prepare the people in the event that such an act becomes prevalent. I have set up watch throughout the kingdom along our outer borders that we may have early warning in such an event."

Honduro then replied, "The rumors have also passed through my ears. And as always, I am prepared to defend you, my king, your family, and the kingdom, together with all the guards who have sworn to protect you. I shall go and prepare for the unknown that when the time comes, and I pray that it never shall. But we will stand ready until the end of days." Honduro bowed and walked away while the king watched and thought to himself, *I hoped he was right and that day never comes again.*

After having the palace robbed of one of its most prized treasures, soldiers had been searching the city and the surrounding lands for the thief and the stone he had confiscated from their possession. Every part of the city had been searched, but they found nothing.

Even with a bounty on his head, Cyrikhan's talent allowed him to evade detection and avoid capture as he moved about among them. He knew the value of the stone he had in his possession. Despite the risk of being caught with it, he knew there were those within the city that would be willing to take that risk and take it off his hands, one in particular with whom he had past dealings with.

Disguised as a simple traveler, he moved about, carefully surveying his surroundings. Covering his head was a red-hooded cloak. Cyrikhan carefully covered his face, hiding both the scar given to him by Honduro during their encounter and the patch tattooed around his left eye, though an ointment was used to help blend the mark.

The soldiers and guards had been searching for him for weeks. With a bounty on his head, anyone that got the chance would turn him in. Carefully moving through the city streets, concealing his weapons and quilted sack beneath the bulky cloak he was wearing, he had a clear direction in mind and a clear idea of who he was looking for.

Two of the city guards were walking casually in his direction. Heavily engaged in conversation, they took little notice of him just a few steps away. One paused a moment as they were talking, looking in his direction. Slowly Cyrikhan placed his hand near a dagger he had covered on his side.

He turned his face slightly away, further covering the mark on his face. Though he used the ointment to cover it, it wasn't completely foolproof. He soon realized the soldier had only paused to gather his thoughts as they passed each other. Cyrikhan couldn't help but think that his presence was in danger of being discovered.

Soon his travels removed him from the main strip of buyers and sellers toward a less frequently visited area of the city surrounded by weather-worn buildings in desperate need of repair and half-paved streets of worn out brick but mostly dirt.

It was a place where society had blinked and had deemed an area of low morals—a place he was well suited for. Those of noble and of reputable character were careful to avoid these streets.

Many of the less fortunate roamed these streets, living a hard life away from the comforts of mainstay society. Filled with muggers and thieves, even those who would not hesitate to kill made these streets their home.

Now square in the heart of them, Cyrikhan, with his hood drawn over his head and his eyes looking downward, remained cautious and careful not to exchange eye contact to avoid being identified. Above him, women stood on their balconies with curtains drawn, shouting down at him and other men as they searched for potential customers, trying to sell themselves for profit.

Both men and women, old and young, all around him were begging for handouts. An older woman with tattered garments and worn-out shoes, whose hair was streaked with gray, tugged on his garments as he passed by her.

She asked for a handout or anything that he could spare, but he simply glanced back at her and kept in a steady direction along the narrow corridor of the back streets. His presence did not go unnoticed among the small crowds of people tarrying about all around.

A group of eyes that were not of any authority remained fixed on him, following his every movement. But he was also aware of their presence and knew that he was being watched. He was aware of everything around him.

He passed a group of men that were standing just beyond clear view. Silhouetted, figures mostly watched him as he passed by. Not once did Cyrikhan turn to look, giving away his awareness, hearing three sets of footsteps that were distinct from all those who were walking around him.

Soon the crowds around him began to thin, and he decided to walk down another corridor, except this one had a dead-end away from view. He then turned around, finding himself facing three men with swords drawn.

The one standing in the center was of slender build, tall, and lanky, with a couple of his teeth missing in the front. The other to his left was bald, with a belly slightly hanging over his belt. The one flanked on the right was a little of both. All were bearded and unshaven, and their stench preceded them all.

With his head still lowered toward the ground, Cyrikhan showed no emotion nor did he sprout out a single word. Arrogant and brash, the one standing in the middle asked jestingly, "What's in the bag, my friend?" Cyrikhan remained silent, with his face remaining downward. The man to the right looked over at his two companions and said, "Maybe he's deaf."

The third man on the far left replied, "Or dumb." All joined in on the laughter. Then the one in the middle stopped laughing and asked, "What? Are you without a tongue, or is it you simply do not wish to share?"

With those words, the men slowly began moving forward. Slowly looking up, Cyrikhan reveal his face as he also dropped his cloak, revealing his muscular frame and his two swords harnessed across his back. Shocked and torn between fear and stupidity, they chose to come together in force.

Cyrikhan drew both blades, twirling them both as he moved forward. As his first attacker attempted to strike, he deflected his blow with his first sword as he stepped to the side, killing him in one motion with his second sword.

Angered that their companion had fallen by Cyrikhan's sword, the others continued with their clumsy assault. Fighting the remaining two with one hand, Cyrikhan drew them closer, then using his speed, he took both of his swords, thrusting them simultaneously through the chests of the remaining two.

The attack lasted for less time than it took one to stretch after a good sleep. He left them to lie dead in a puddle of blood. Showing no concern, he sheathed his swords and continued on with what he had to do without wasting a single thought.

He could hear a scream in the distance from the point in which he left. The bodies had been discovered, but that was no longer his concern. Finally, he found the place he was looking for and did what he had gone there to do.

He met with an interested buyer, one who he had had prior dealings with years ago and one who was willing to strike a bargain that he believed he could not pass on. His name was Barsol, and he has a reputation of dubious dealings with those of the lower end of society—thieves and robbers desperate to relinquish their goods for whatever they could get. Without proof that could link him with the item, Barsol would then resell them to those who lost them at a higher price with a few alterations, an act reputable merchants would not partake in.

Entering the merchant's tent, he was greeted by two burly men. Both had evidence of hard living displayed in their faces. They reached out an extended hand, halting Cyrikhan's advance. Not saying a word, Cyrikhan looked down at their hands and then at their faces. He gave them an unsettling stare.

Barsol immediately recognized who he was. His disguise couldn't fully conceal the tattoo on the left side of his face. This was his most prized customer looking at the two men. He then looked at Cyrikhan and said, "Don't mind them. It's tough around here. Everyone needs a little protection."

Cyrikhan remained quiet, looking at each of the two that confronted him as if he was trying to determine whether or not to take their lives. But he decided on doing business. The two had a history of doing business with each other years ago. Looking Cyrikhan in the eyes, Barsol said, "Wanderling." Before Cyrikhan could reply, Barsol continued, "Meet me in the rear, my friend. Did anyone see you come in?"

Cyrikhan responded, "If they did, no one recognized me."

"That is good, my friend. Dealing with a Wanderling, especially one with a bounty on his head, will bring the king's guards down on me," Barsol responded. "That would be very bad for business."

Suspiciously, Cyrikhan looked at him and his two companions. Trust was never an option in his line of work. Responding with a nod and without an exchange of words, he just simply complied.

Now secluded and out of view and free of surprises, Cyrikhan flashed his merchandise, astounding his potential buyer by the worth of what he had presented to him as he opened the bag he was carrying. Barsol leaned and reached into the bag, pulling out the orophyx, and saying, "Ahhh! This is what has drawn the king's interest. Its value is such it would demand a king's ransom. It would have to be sold away from the kingdom to perhaps another, like, say, the Niejar. But that's hundreds of miles away."

Thinking Cyrikhan would be anxious to remove it from his possession, he said, "I will give you thirty jenarols for it." It was a price that carried a very low value. Jenarols was a common currency among traders and of the Norstar Kingdom, having moderate value. And what was offered was barely enough to feed a man for two days.

Cyrikhan looked at him and said, "Which one of us is truly a pirate?" He took the jewel from Barsol's hand and immediately placed it back into the bag, then he turned to walk away.

Barsol then shouted, "Forty jenarols!" He continued to walk away from him. "Fifty jenarols!" Barsol shouted. "That's my final offer."

Cyrikhan turned and said, "Three hundred jenarols."

Barsol then looked at his two men and then at Cyrikhan and said, "You won't find anyone else that would even risk taking that off your hands. For that price, it's too high. It's too difficult to find buyers for a prize belonging to the king."

Cyrikhan replied, "Do not attempt to play me for a fool." Looking Barsol directly in the eyes, he said, "That in which you have offered me . . ." Cyrikhan snickered as he spoke, "Your head has greater value than the price you have offered, and I deem that to be worthless."

Barsol then replied, "Those are stolen treasures from the king's vault. You won't find another buyer that will take them. I am the best at my craft." Hearing the frustration in his voice, he continued, "Not even I can alter suspicion of its origin. Anyone caught in possession of it could lose their head. Surely, you do not wish the king to somehow get word of such a thing in the possession of a Wanderling." Barsol, with a smirk on his face, stood, flanked by his two enforcers.

Cyrikhan walked slowly toward Barsol, then he took a step backward as Barsol's two men stepped toward him while drawing their weapons. One with a sword and the other a dagger, both lunged forward toward Cyrikhan and attacked simultaneously.

Before either could strike a blow, Cyrikhan had drawn his dagger faster than either could react. The first one received an upward thrust of Cyrikhan's dagger through his throat until it pierced the back of his skull.

Before he could hit the ground, the second assailant had the very same knife with the blood of the first still dripping off it. Cyrikhan had buried it deep into the chest of the other, piercing his heart, dropping both nearly at the same time.

In a blink of an eye, they were both dead. The balding merchant continued to back up until he found himself pressed up against one of the tent's support poles. Cyrikhan leaned forward, with the dagger still dripping with blood firmly pressed against Barsol's throat.

He then whispered into Barsol's ear, "If any should happen to receive word that I was here, you will join your friends. Thank the god that you worship that I may yet have need of you in the future. Despite your treachery, I will allow you to live for that single purpose. Attempt such a thing again, I shall separate your head from your body before it ever knew it was missing."

Barsol stood petrified and shaken, his urine streaming down his legs. Cyrikhan backed away, looking down at his trousers and the pool of piss mixing with the blood of the two men that were lying at Barsol's feet.

Barsol was certain that he would be next and couldn't contain himself. Cyrikhan then said, "I've been in the presence of the foulest creatures you could imagine, but they pale in comparison to the stench that surrounds you. You best clean yourself. Who would do business with one bathing in his own piss and garbage lying around?" Cyrikhan then turned and left the tent. Letting out a sigh of relief, Barsol was sure his time had ended. Looking down at the bodies of the two men, he knew that he was fortunate that he had not joined them.

Putting the encounter behind him, Cyrikhan knew it was time to leave the city and seek his reward for his efforts elsewhere. There was no profit to be gained here, along with the risk being too high.

Back in the courtyard of the palace, disturbed and frustrated, Honduro paced along its pathways. His failure to capture the Wanderling plagued his thoughts relentlessly. Even with a trap well planned and thought out, Cyrikhan had still managed to escape. To add to the insult, the Wanderling had left a scar raked across his shoulder as an embedded reminder.

A proud and honorable warrior and protector, this was now personal. Honduro had never failed in his duties until now, despite the king's understanding and forgiveness. The fact that he did fail burned inside him like a torch that could not be extinguished, and he vowed to himself that he would not rest until the Wanderling was in chains or worse.

Walking along the bricked pathway, Honduro was still wrestling with his thoughts, playing out the encounter in his mind again and again and again. He could find no solace in his mind.

Approaching him, one of his lieutenants had just left the streets of the city to report to him what they had found, along with other news that may have had some interest.

After his approach and salute, he said, "Captain, we have searched every corner of the city and found no sign of the Wanderling. He must be far from here by now. Also there were three men that were found dead in a back-alley pathway in the east section of the city."

Taking interest in this report, Honduro asked how they had died. The guard responded, "All three lay dead with their swords drawn lying beside them. From the look of their wounds, they were killed by a sword. It appears that they had fought a single combatant. The ground around them shows that there was only one other set of footprints other than those of the three, a different type of print that left only a slight indenture in the dirt. "Whoever killed them possessed superior skills. We went door to door, but no one had seen or heard anything. The woman who discovered them could tell us little else."

Honduro then said, "That is your clue."

The lieutenant then blurted out, "The Wanderling!"

Honduro then replied, "Time is of the essence. We must act quickly before he can escape the area as he had done before. Send a squad of your best men to that section. I shall send word to the king of the purpose of my actions. I will join you in the search. There is a score that must be settled between us." In haste, both men hurried to carry out the command.

After securing the perimeters of Hiendore, they found nothing. They searched everywhere, every home, and every business from the more elite sections to the lowest corners of the city. All attempts had turned up empty.

On the opposite end of the city, a young lad working in the city's garbage pits saw an arm partially buried among the rubble. After digging up the body, they found that it was two bodies buried there.

It was the two companions of Barsol. Reporting what they had found, Honduro arrived to look at the two bodies. He knew them both. They were two low-life thugs and criminals, and he knew who they had worked for.

Immediately he mounted his ramsteeds, along with two of his men, and arrived at the merchant's business. Entering the tent and looking around, he noticed traces of blood on the floor.

Sitting at a small round table, Barsol was writing on his ledger as if unconcerned. He then looked up and said, "My lord, Honduro, what brings you here to my place of business? Perhaps you would like to purchase a lovely stone for one that you may have close to your heart or maybe some sweet essence of flavor?"

"Dispense with the pleasantries. I am not here to purchase perfumes or jewels. You know why I am here. We found two of your rats buried among the filth of the garbage pits, a most fitting place for scums such as them, along with yourself. And I do not believe they just happened to appear there without help or your knowledge."

Barsol looked Honduro in the eyes with an expression of puzzlement on his face, an illusion he was well practiced at, but it was as transparent to Honduro as a clear mountain stream.

Barsol then asked, "Who may that be, my dear captain?" Honduro then spoke their names. Barsol then replied, "When did this happen? I've been here in my place of business for weeks. The streets are not safe to be aimlessly wandering about."

Honduro replied, "There is blood on your floor. Would you care to tell me about it?"

"I fell and injured myself, and I must've missed a spot," Barsol replied.

"That's quite a bit of blood. Where is the injury?" Honduro responded.

"It was internal. I spat it up."

"Liar!" Honduro replied. He then began to give the detail of his thoughts. "A short time ago, the palace was robbed of its most precious jewel by that of a Wanderling. He would have a need to make a profit from it. To find a buyer would not be an easy task among the honest merchants of this city, unless he was able to find the right low-life scum willing to take that risk." Honduro paused, staring down at Barsol as the man looked back at him.

"My dear captain," Barsol replied, "you cannot possibly be referring to me. I'm an honest businessman. Conduct a search. You will find I am innocent of knowledge of both the accusations you referenced toward my knowledge."

"Enough of the lies!" Honduro shouted. He drew his sword as he reached down and grabbed Barsol by his throat, lifting him off the ground with one hand, leaving Barsol's feet to dangle in the air above the ground, with his sword pressing against his throat.

The witty tongue of Barsol had ceased and was overtaken by the fear of once again not knowing if these would be his last breaths.

"Where is the Wanderling? I know he was here. He left his mark on your two friends. There is only one place he could go to have a chance to rid himself of the king's jewels, so I ask one last time or tomorrow will not be a possibility." Honduro pressed his sword firmly against Barsol's throat, drawing blood.

"I do not know. I swear it. The Wanderling said he would kill me if I revealed to anyone that he was here."

"You shall die right now if you don't. Your choice," replied Honduro.

"Okay, okay, my lord. It is true he came to me, but a deal was not struck. He became angered and slew my men. The last thing I remembered was that he said he was leaving for other lands to find his fortune."

Looking glaringly into Barsol's eyes, Honduro knew he was telling the truth. He released Barsol as he stepped back, and Barsol then fell to the floor. As Honduro walked to exit the tent, he paused and then turned and looked back at Barsol, who was sitting on the floor with his eyes on the ground, and said, "Thank the Lord that I haven't the time to dole-out the justice that you deserve. If I ever have to return, you shall spend the rest of your days in the dungeon." Honduro, along with his men, then left from Barsol's presence.

After mounting their steeds, one of the guards then asked, "Shall we continue to scour the city and the countryside for him?"

Honduro just sat there, looking off to the distance and gathering his thoughts, and then said, "I fear that the Wanderling has eluded us once more." They then rode off.

Barsol lifted himself off the floor, giving a sigh of relief, then he began gathering himself. Once again he believed his life would be over, but once again he had eluded that fate. Turning to gather his things, it had been a difficult time for the low-character merchant. He was then startled by a figure that lay partially hidden as it slowly emerged from the shadows.

It was Cyrikhan. Before Barsol could utter a word, Cyrikhan removed a dagger from his belt, then he thrust it into Barsol's chest, looking him in the eyes as the old merchant fell to his knees both in shock and in pain.

Cyrikhan then said, "I told you if you told anyone that you had seen me what your fate would be." Barsol fell over to the floor in that instant. He drew his last breath, his eyes wide-open but without life as he lay dead.

Cyrikhan looked down at the body, making sure his task was complete, then he stepped over the body while he looked outside, making sure his escape path was clear before slipping away. Once again Cyrikhan had eluded Honduro and his guards.

CHAPTER 23

The Fall of the Norstar

LOOMING BEYOND THE horizon were matters much greater than that of a wandering thief. There were rumors of an impending threat from lands that were yet far away from those few who had escaped the onslaught and who knew their way through the impenetrable mountain barrier. It was only a rumor. Most believed it to be an unlikely threat, let alone one orchestrated by that of a giant people who were unknown to them.

King Orchard was both wise and brave, but he was also cautious. Rather than being caught unprepared, he decided to prepare his kingdom in the event that this threat would all come to pass. Putting Cyrikhan behind him, Honduro turned his attention from catching a thief to the defense of Hiendore as he began preparing the guards.

Unknown to them, the rumors reaching them were true as the large Troguare force was rapidly approaching. They had just completed their journey beyond the great mountains through the Three-Valley Pass, guided by one of their captive slaves having intimate knowledge of the valley passage.

Once they had reached the other side, the huge force split into three separate armies of near-equal numbers, each heading in three different directions. General Zhorr, along with one hundred thousand warriors and war beasts, headed north to the kingdom of the Norstar.

To the south, Koshier, with an equal force of warriors, marched toward the kingdom of Niejar. General Troxus headed east with the greatest force of one hundred and fifty thousand warriors and beasts to conquer the kingdom of the Lakes. All had a single goal: to conquer all three kingdoms at once and bring their king the prize he so deeply desired—the complete conquest of the known world.

As the Troguares advanced toward the Norstar lands, Honduro, along with the rest of the palace guards, had intensely trained to prepare for the event of an invasion. Driven with a purpose, they were now prepared, as was the rest of the Norstar forces.

The king called on his army to prepare in the event of war, led by a burly and powerful general named Rexthor. He had led the Norstar army to many of its greatest victories.

With the many warrior clans that had once terrorized these lands, he had either destroyed them or driven them back into the wilderness, never to be seen again.

Lightly manned outposts were set up along the outer fringes of the kingdom in the event of war, but no one truly believed it would happen. Weeks had passed, and everyone kept a watchful eye. But all remained relaxed throughout the kingdom.

In the city, Honduro had found his moments to ease his mind. He had his eyes on a lovely maiden named Celene, a woman of the highest order within the kingdom whose position was to escort the queen to all her affairs. She would see to it that those who were subject to her attended to all the queen's needs.

After a day of meditation and mental preparation, Honduro sought the one thing that he could find solace and peace that would sooth his troubled thoughts. In the corridor of the palace, he found what he needed.

Standing there waiting for him to arrive was Celene. Greeting each other with a display of passion, they embraced each other, showing a deep affection toward each other.

After a few moments, they began walking hand in hand, sharing their thoughts and the inner feelings that they had for each other. Honduro said to her, "You are beholding to my eyes, a beautiful flower blooming into its full glory. I find it hard to look away from you or for my heart to ignore the feeling that has grown inside me for your affection."

Her cheeks became as red as a blossoming cherry flower while her smile spread across her face as if it began to bloom. Looking up at him, she became mesmerized.

As his golden hair draped over his shoulders, she looked him up and down without flinching a muscle. To her, he was like a statue made of bronze. Silently she stepped even closer to him, looking up intensely into his blue eyes. She then said to him, "What else do you see that you find desirable?"

Honduro responded, "All that I am beholding in front of me. And what I see, I desire in its fullness. We haven't spoken many words in the passing weeks with the constant preparation for an uncertain threat that may not even exist." Honduro paused for an instant, then he continued. "Our preparations have been put to task, and yet I still feel troubled."

She then replied, "My thoughts haven't left you since I first saw you. We are apart, but yet you are always with me."

"I am frightened at the thought of never seeing you again. It is the thought that you will not return that only causes my thoughts to be unbearable."

"We have drawn closer with each day that passed. Finally, I have my golden warrior possessing my heart."

"Do not fear, my lady. I shall return to you, and nothing will keep you out of my arms." Then he reached down and gently lifted her chin while he bent over and gently pressed his lips against hers as they drew closer and tighter toward each other until they were entangled in a full embrace.

With her quarters nearby, he bent down and lifted her, cradling her in his arms as if she was a child. He carried her into her place, a cloak of privacy they both desired before blowing out the candle as they submerged themselves into the darkness.

As the night set in, Cyrikhan decided that the time had come to leave these walls. Hidden among the masses for months, he had moved about without effort but found difficulties in selling his prized stone because all were in search of it. Taking heed to the words he had spoken earlier, he decided it was time to go elsewhere to seek its value someplace else.

Concealing the stone, he once again slipped past the guards, something he had grown accustomed to since his battle with Honduro, before vanishing into the night.

Throughout the kingdom, all was quiet. They had prepared themselves for an assault that had not yet come to pass. The guards remained on the alert as their fires were seen throughout the kingdom.

While most slept, others remained restless. Under the cover of night, there were other eyes watching the movements of the Norstar watchmen, slowly moving about in the night, like a stalking lion waiting to ambush its prey.

General Zhorr placed his riders in position to ambush the Norstar patrols closest to his forces, knowing that they would have very little time to react. His foot soldiers maneuvered through the high grasses, passing and crawling as low as possible under the cover of night. And with the element of surprise on their side, the Troguare army awaited Zhorr's command.

Once all were in position, General Zhorr gave the signal to begin their attack. The slaughter began throughout the night around the outer boundaries of the city. Despite the preparations made by the Norstar people, it didn't matter. They were silently and, without warning, under an assault.

The Troguare forces moved rapidly through the darkness, gaining ground before sunrise could reveal their position. Moving toward their position, another stealthy warrior was heading straight toward the Troguare ranks.

As he drew near, he caught their scent in the air as they emerged out into the moonlight. Stopping in his tracks, surprised, for the route of escape was no longer clear.

Now facing him was an army greater than that of which he had left behind. As far as his eyes could see beyond the darkness, their numbers were so great and spread apart there was no way to get around.

His skills were extraordinary, but even they had limits. Left without a choice, he made the decision to return quickly. As fast as his steed could carry him, he raced back to the place that wanted him arrested.

With the giants in pursuit, they knew he would give warning of their approach. Unable to gain distance on him, they began to lose ground. This time, Cyrikhan was not trying to be one of stealth or be unnoticed. He gave warning to all he had passed by.

Quickly forming their lines, the Norstar, like many before them, have never faced an army of this type, size, or might. Alarms rang out as they began to relay throughout the land. The outer forces began to engage the invaders and quickly found out they were greatly outmatched and fell quickly. They were being defeated with little effort.

With size, claws, and teeth on their side, the Troguare army were excessively brutal, with the axes of giants tumbling soldiers as a tiller shreds through their wheat.

Men and their bodies were being hacked apart; body parts were flung everywhere, providing snacks for the scavengers and some of their war beasts. The swords of the giants found their place with men. With all their attempts, no matter how valiant their efforts might be, they were truly helpless.

Only the exceptional fighters fared better, but they, too, eventually succumbed to the giants' might. With trumpets blowing, giving warning, Honduro arose from the quarters of his Celene.

Along with the rest of the palace guards that took their position in defense of the city walls, the old king, Orchard, had once again donned his armor and joined his general at the wall, overlooking the land below.

With the Troguare army rapidly approaching the city walls, the main forces formed both inside and outside the city. They formed barriers capable of halting almost any assault, but they were not prepared this night for the size and stature of what they would face.

This night, their mettle would truly be tested. General Rexthor left the side of his king to join his army outside the gate, leaving Honduro and his guards to protect the king who was at his side.

Once reaching the Norstar's defensive front, the supreme commander of the Norstar armies looked up to the top of the fortress walls to King Orchard, awaiting for the king to give his command with Honduro at his side.

Both of these fierce warriors stood ready to defend both king and kingdom. Already in place, his archers and their manned catapults awaited the order to light the fires as the huge Troguare forces emerged from the cover of the trees and hills into the moonlit fields.

They came in hordes with General Zhorr out in front of them, leading them. With the ground being so unleveled, they were unable to use their standard formation, locking horns and plowing and clawing their foes.

With roars like thunder, many succumbed to their fears and attempted to flee. But it was too late to retreat within the protection of the walls of the city. They were forced to stand firm with all weapons ready to defend the city.

General Rexthor stood firm until the king gave the command once they came within range. Heavily armored and massive in size, the ground shook with every step. The general raised his arm, and the king nodded his head, giving the general the command to rain arrows of fire and showers of stones and spears.

With many finding their target, it still wasn't enough to slow the march of the giant hordes. Giving out the battle cry, the valiant warriors of the Norstar nation pressed forth on their attack to defend that which was theirs.

Their homes, their families, and all that they had ever known were at stake. As the two armies clashed, the once mighty Norstar army found themselves treaded under the giants' feet.

Long swords and their users found themselves equal in their fate, with neither able to withstand the violent attacks of the Troguare beastmen. The roars of the liboroxes mixed with the grunts and cries of men as they fell while claws ripped through their armors as if it were tissue.

Despite this, a few giants met their deaths. But they didn't seem to notice. Thousands of Norstar fighters fell that night as the giants finally reached the walls and as they prepared to lay siege upon the city and to breach the palace walls.

With archers still lining the walls and releasing arrows upon them, the giants and their army released their spear-like arrows that also found their mark with an even more deadly effect.

They began to batter the walls. All attempts to stall their attacks failed. In the midst of his antagonist, Honduro's enemy had now become an ally. Cyrikhan had made it back to safety inside the city walls.

Cyrikhan stood his ground with both swords drawn, ready to face the inevitable once the gates caved in. Just above him atop the city walls was Honduro with his sword drawn. Everyone awaited the final blow that would cause the gates to shatter.

As both warriors stood in wait, Honduro looked down at his defenders below at the same time that Cyrikhan looked up, seeing those atop the walls. Spontaneously, they spotted each other, both having lingering stares and both wanting to battle each other as the hatred they had for each other was greater than the force they were now about to face.

Suddenly, the gates gave way as they were leaped upon by two of the liboroxes. No longer strong enough to withstand the combined weight of the two beasts, the gates collapsed.

Rushing in behind them were the Troguare army, killing everyone in their path. Charging straight at Cyrikhan was a snarling liborox and his rider, with its head bellowing toward him, head down, poised for the kill.

Cyrikhan leaped into the air to meet the huge beast and its rider, thrusting one sword between the eyes of the beast while walking up its muzzle onto the top of its head. Its momentum continued to move, making its Troguare rider vulnerable while the rider was still leaning forward. Cyrikhan drove his second sword through the Troguare rider's eye into his skull, killing both in a couple of movements.

With men dying all around, he believed his time had finally come, but he was determined that he would take as many with him as he could. Meanwhile, up above him, another battle was raging.

After breaching the walls, the giants climbed the stairwell into the palace. The Troguares batted their enemies aside, as if they were gnats, over the outside walls and into the courtyard below inside the walls.

Honduro fought furiously to protect his king who, in turn, was fighting beside him, avoiding the mighty swing of these massive giants. Turning to help assist the king, Rexthor fought his way back within the city walls.

As he looked upward toward King Orchard, the king was struck in the chest by a giant's spear directly through his heart. With sword still in hand, he fell a few steps away from the stairs. Nearby, while engaging his foes, Honduro kept up his movement, evading blow after blow while finding weaknesses in their armor, killing giants almost as easily as he would a man, which was no ordinary feat for a human against such odds.

His battles were taking him farther from the side of King Orchard. Realizing this, he tried to get back to him, but he was too late. The king met his end, and he was helpless to prevent it.

Of all the palace guards, Honduro was the only one that remained standing. Enraged, he fought as fluidly as a poet recites her words. He rolled under passing blows, thrusting his sword into whatever opening the giants presented before him until all went black from a blow to the skull from a liborox's paw.

Witnessing all this while still engaged in conflict himself, Cyrikhan had no intentions of surrender. He was prepared to fight to the last breath until he was netted by giants that came upon him on his blind side.

Death was all around. The Norstar forces were all but defeated. The Troguares moved quickly through the city, setting to fire anything that would burn and raping women they captured. Most died during the brutal affair before being carted off to places unknown, along with the children that they captured.

Unlike many of the other Troguare generals, Zhorr didn't readily kill all that fought against him. He was constantly looking for the strongest and the fiercest of adversaries to capture and take away to the mines.

He also knew they would be best for entertainment if they refused to work or do as they were commanded. The once mighty Norstar was now laid to ruin. Those not strong enough to travel had a preset fate, while others were put in chains. A few hundred miles to the south, another saga was soon about to unfold.

CHAPTER 24

The Kingdom of the Niejar

HIGH UP IN the western highlands of the southernmost part of what was once three sovereign kingdoms left standing was that of the Niejar. Unknown to them there, it was now two.

Twelve of the finest warriors and trackers in the land lay hidden among the thickets. Just beyond them was a small clearing. In the center of it tied to a post was a huge creature called a callet. It was a large cowlike beast used for beef and labor.

It had four antler-like horns and a nasty temper to match. On the ground around it were two huge heavily woven nets covered with leaves and grasses, concealing their presence.

Several feet from the clearing's opening, a huge pit was dug with large wooden stakes pointed upward at the bottom. Among the men was the greatest bowman in all the land—lean, muscular, with short flowing locks, and a dark complexion with a short shadowed beard.

His name was Kalee, son of the great King Abbah. So great were his skills, Prince Kalee had once emptied a pouch of arrows two hundred yards away through a small hole the size of a fingertip without touching its edges once.

His skills with the sword were nearly as impressive and formidable. He was the commander and the leader of the great Niejar army. It was an honor bestowed upon him by his father—not because he was the son of the king, but because his skills as a leader were apparent and unparalleled by any from his days as a young lad.

He commanded the respect of the mightiest of men in the kingdom. He was naturally skilled with the use of all weapons—the sword, the spear, and an assortment of others. But it was with the bow that he had excelled in the most.

It wasn't uncommon for him to mingle among common people, for though he was the son of the king and the heir to the throne, he experienced great comfort with the purity and humility of the lives of the common masses. This allowed him to become one with them in understanding their struggles.

This humbled his spirit, and for that, the people loved him. For several months, a huge unknown creature had roamed these forests and lands, preying on travelers and the unsuspecting that lived there.

Day or night, the attacks occurred. People were living in constant fear. For weeks, the men had followed its tracks until they lost it within the boggy creeks that were common around these lands.

They then went back to the place that it most frequently traveled and where most of the attacks occurred. There they waited to ambush the creature. For hours, they lay motionless and quiet, barely taking breaths.

As time went on, the callet became restless and uneasy, pulling and tugging and letting out a long series of snorts that trumpeted the woodlands. Despite this, the forest remained quiet from all unusual sounds.

Then Kalee thought to himself, *It isn't the beast it wants but that which it had an appetite for.* He then said to his men, "Perhaps it isn't beef it seeks but something more of the two-legged sort."

After sharing his thoughts with the others and with a smile that spread across the prince's face, he then said, "I'll give it what it seeks." Slowly rising to his feet, one of the men reached out and grabbed his arm and then said in a low voice, "My lord, you must not be the one to take the risk in the open and be exposed. I'll go."

"No, I will," Kalee said, grabbing the bow he had crafted, made with a rare weaver oak made of reinforced fibers, giving it unparalleled flexibility. He also designed it with double drawstrings, giving it many times the torque of any bow, allowing it to launch an arrow with enough force to penetrate the thickest and heaviest objects.

Uniquely armed, Kalee wore a long metal arm brace made by the finest craftsman in the kingdom. It was made from a mixture of the strongest metal alloys known, making it nearly indestructible. It was formed to the contour of his left arm from his biceps to his wrist.

Extremely flexible and lightweighted, he could move it without hindrance, as if it was a natural part of him. When using his bow, he was able to lock it into place, giving him stability whenever launching his arrows and being added protection for defense against sword or blade attacks.

Along with it, he also crafted three specially designed arrowheads, each with its on purpose. One was sleek and narrow with two small wings protruding just behind the arrowhead, allowing it to reach distances that were far greater than that of any other arrow.

Another had a spread tip that he made to open upon entry, tearing apart tissues and ripping the insides of whatever it penetrated, causing great internal damage. And finally, there was the one he took great pride in crafting, the one he called the slayer.

It was made with serrated edges and a much-longer head and shaft than the others, but it was far lighter than the rest. It was designed to kill the largest and heaviest creatures, penetrating the toughest hides and even the densest armor.

Not knowing exactly what they were hunting, they only knew that it was large, armored, and equipped with a short powerful spiked tail with rows of large curved teeth and claws to match.

This was from the reports of those who were fortunate enough to escape with their lives, leaving them delirious at best. Kalee silently maneuvered his way between the woven nets, careful not to trigger the traps until he reached the bound beast. He placed his hand on the animal's muzzle, careful not to remove his hand off the animal, calming it as he gently moved along its side, along the neck and shoulder, before carefully mounting the beast.

Once on the callet's back, he slowly reached back, carefully removing one of his arrows and placing it on his bow, ready to strike when the time arrived. Once in position, he yelled out a series of calls in intervals with the hope it would attract the creature.

For about half an hour, he did this until he became weary. He then remained quiet for a time shortly afterward. While all remained silent, he began to think to himself that maybe they should call it a day.

The hours were long, and it had turned up no results. Just as he started to call out to his men, a faint sound could be heard from a distance, which was moving in their direction. With the intensity of the moment building, the sweat began to stream down their faces and across their brows.

With their hands firmly on their weapons, each stood ready as the tension steadily began to mount. Slowly drawing his bow backward, locking his armored arm in place, Kalee waited for that moment that they all had anticipated. With all eyes focused on the prince, each were prepared to give their life if necessary to protect him if the need arrived.

Suddenly, a sleek antlered beast leaped out of the woods through the heavy thickets, miraculously avoiding the traps and not fitting the description of the creature they were hunting. Their traps were set for a much-larger prize. It scampered off across the small clearing, disappearing into a nearby patch of wood just beyond where they all were waiting to ambush.

At that moment, a collective sigh of relief spread out among the hunters, breaking the intensity of the moment. With each of them beginning to relax at that moment, even a few chuckles could be heard in the midst of them.

As the mood had begun to settle down, abruptly the chained beast became erratic, rising up, jumping, and bucking. Attempting to free itself from its bonds, it threw the prince onto the ground in the process and into one of the nets that drew him up into the air where he dangled about helpless and vulnerable.

Quickly, the men began to rise to help him, but it was at that moment that the large creature they had been stalking came crashing through the trees straight at them. It was a creature not of these lands. It was called a wantu and was fully armored from head to tail.

It stood about seven feet tall at its shoulder and about fifteen feet long from nose to tail. At full gallop, it shook the ground as it rambled forward. Claws gripping the ground as it built up speed, it headed straight at Kalee.

Ignoring the callet that was still bound to the post, it appeared to prefer the smaller and less formidable meal that was there for an easy taking. Tangled and trapped, the prince struggled to reach his dagger that was on his hip to cut himself free. Only his men stood between the beast and certain death.

With spears jabbing at its eyes and the more vulnerable spots on its face, they slowly drove it back as it growled and clawed. The men skillfully avoided its attack just enough to cause it to step into a second net.

The mass of this creature was too big and heavy to lift it, rendering the net useless. With its bulk and power, it tore through it as if it was like thread. Growling, snarling, and clawing, it turn its body, swinging its huge spiked tail about like a club.

The men moved in circles, alternating their patterns in and out, keeping it at bay. Though their weapons did little more than to annoy it, they were unable to penetrate its thick armor.

Their only course of action was to move in close enough to drive their spears or swords between its armor plates, but that was easier said than done. For such a large and heavy beast, it was surprisingly agile and quick. As they kept it from focusing on any one person and keeping it off balance, one of the warriors moved in too close, anticipating that the wantu would not see him.

As he approached from the rear, at that moment, the beast turned its head slightly, seeing him before driving its powerful spiked tail into his belly, killing him instantly. Suddenly, it rose up, standing on its hind legs and using its tail as a brace.

Now they were facing the wantu head-on. It raised the tightly formed scales up off its neck, like wind flaps exposing a very small portion of its flesh along the back of its head. Boldly, another of the warriors moved around to its rear. But this time, he leaped onto the creature's back, thrusting his sword between its scales, wounding it before it shook him free.

It threw him a few feet away where he fell into one of the spiked ditches, impaling himself. While the creature's attention was being occupied, engaged in battle with the warriors, the prince was finally able to reach his dagger, freeing himself by cutting through the netting.

Enraged and injured, with rows of razor-sharp teeth on display, the creature pressed his way aggressively, disregarding all the men's attempts to stop it. Until eventually, it struck one of them with its powerful claws, knocking him a few feet backward to the ground before pouncing on him as it began tearing into his flesh and crushing his bones.

While the man screamed out in pain in depths that were hard to describe, filtered with cries for help as he was being shredded, all were fervorous in trying to aid their companion. But all their efforts were for naught.

They paid little attention to the others as they were furiously attempting to aid their companion. By this time, Kalee had gathered his bow, remembering what he perceived to be the vulnerable spot when the creature raised its armor. With every attack, it would immediately raise its flaps behind its head. Choosing a spread-tip arrowhead from his pouch, he then circled around with his bow drawn and ready. When the trackers continued pressing their attack, it once again raised its scales.

Immediately, Kalee took careful aim and then let the arrow fly dead, finding its mark as it went the only place it could. Penetrating deep within its skull, it was designed to open after penetration, dropping the beast immediately.

Leaving a small portion of the tip protruding from its forehead, it lay there, releasing its final breath before the prince jumped on its back, driving his sword between the armored scales on top of its head, finishing it.

Relieved that they had finally killed the beast, all were stricken with grief. Three men lost their lives in the attempt. Kalee stood over the dead beast and looked over at his comrades that had fallen. The pain was clearly obvious to everyone that their deaths had deeply wounded him.

Looking around at those who remained, he said, "It is done but with a great cost of lives. Gather our fallen comrades, and place them on the supply wagon. We shall deliver their bodies to those with families, and those who do not shall have a proper burial. Without the aid of their services, many others may have been lost to the appetite of this beast." As commanded, they gathered the bodies, with all sharing in the grief in losing their companions and friends.

During their return to the city, they came across a group of travelers entering their land. During their encounter, the family told them stories they had heard of an army of giants beyond the great Center Mountain divide.

Rumors had spread throughout the land from the accounts of the great caravan and those who were a part of it that had returned from beyond the other side.

Tales of giants, death, and destruction filled the ears of those who listened and chose to believe. But these stories seemed so far away. Not many had ever ventured to the other side of the great mountain divide.

Many had attempted the journey without guidance or already knew the way without becoming lost through the only passage known as the Three-Valley Pass. With a wrong turn, one could be lost in the maze-like valley, never to be seen again.

These accounts were vague and seemed to be more of a rumor than a fact. Not even those who had returned had actually seen these giants, for they, too, had only heard the stories that had preceded them. After hearing these tales, the prince and his men pressed on, not sure how much of it could truly be digested.

After a few days, they were now in sight of the great city of Umar—the capital of the Niejar Kingdom. As a mecca of trade and culture, people throughout the land and beyond its borders came to trade and enjoy its culture. It was a magnificent and beautiful city.

With walls resembling crystals as they sparkled from the light of the suns, the richest kingdom in all the known lands, this was the place they called home. Once they arrived, as promised, Kalee and his men took the fallen to their homes, as they were greeted by the families of those who had died.

Showing great compassion, the prince did what he could to comfort their grieving families. And for those reasons, the people loved him for it. His strength and compassion for his people and for his kingdom earned him the respect of all—both great and small.

There was no one throughout these lands that would not give their lives for him or follow him if need be. After delivering their fallen comrades to their families and loved ones, each of them went their own way until they were called again in the service of the king.

Before heading to the palace, Kalee had another stop to make. Just beyond the city walls in a small village was a woman who had long since captured the heart of the young lion. Her name was Tylah.

Leaving his steed outside of a small fenced gate, he walked up to a small house adorned with a beautiful garden and fragrant flowers. There he stood in front of the doorway and gently knocked, but there was no reply.

Softly he called out her name several times, "Tylah!" But there was no answer. Disappointed, he turned to leave, but standing there behind him, smiling, was who he had come to see. Her skin was smooth brown and flawless, with long black hair streaming down her back.

To look upon her, one could not resist or refuse anything she asked as she had a smile that could bring an army to its knees. Kalee was mesmerized by her beauty as it was unrelenting by the look on his face reflecting his joy.

As with the love she had for her prince, that also illuminated from her smile. Both shared the same feeling as passion drove these lovers toward each other and into each other's arms.

Kalee reached out, grabbing her by her waist before pulling her close, as they stared into each other's eyes before firmly pressing their lips together. Slowly they exchanged kiss after kiss as they became lost in the passion they had for each other.

Tylah then leaned back, looking Kalee in his eyes, then saying to him, "I am glad you are safe. The weeks you were gone were sleepless ones. My greatest fear is that you might leave and never return to me. I love you so much." She kissed him once more.

Kalee replied, "I shall always love you. I shall always return to you. You are what drives me. You are what makes my life complete."

He then lifted her off her feet before opening the door to her house, then carried her through her doorway and closed it behind them as the sun began to set.

Early the next morning, Kalee arose from her bedside, leaned over, and gave her a gentle kiss on her sleeping lips before she awakened. Staring back into his eyes, she then reached out, grabbing him around his neck as he leaned over to embrace her before having to leave her side.

He then said, "I shall see you soon. It is time that I return to the palace and give my report on the events that took place in the western highlands." He then left, mounted his steed, and headed home to the palace to confer with his father and see his family after he had departed a few weeks.

Once he arrived at the palace, he saw his mother taking an early walk in the midst of the budding flowers decorating the garden, something she often did. Queen Aniyah's beauty had only blossomed with time.

Her wavy white hair was pulled back into a ponytail. Her dress was long and flowing, laced with fine stones as she enjoyed the warmth of the sun as it blessed her face. As Kalee approached his mother, he extended his arms to greet her.

You could see the sparkle in her eyes and the love of a mother as he drew closer. Gently he pulled her into his arms, leaning forward to kiss her cheek, then said, "Greetings, Mother, you are as beautiful as always. There isn't a mother more beautiful in a hundred kingdoms." Kalee spoke with a smile.

She then replied, "You make me blush with such kind words for an old woman." She smiled back in return. She then said, "Welcome home, my son, I prayed to God for your safe return. Your presence was sorely missed by both your father and myself but, most of all, by your sisters. They call your name each morning and are saddened by your absence. I do worry myself when you go off on these excursions with such danger involved."

"Yes, I know, Mother," Kalee replied. "The cries of the people must be heard and accounted for, for they are close to my heart. I am here to serve them. They do honor me and our family."

The queen then replied with a smile, "That is why you are so loved. You are blessed with such a beautiful heart."

He then said, "I must go. I have many things to discuss with Father."

She replied, "He's in the council chamber, discussing the needs of the kingdom and that of the people."

Kissing his mother on her cheek, he turned and entered the palace where he was affectingly greeted by his twin sisters, Enieya and Olieria. They were nine years old, both holding the woven dolls their big brother had made for them.

Both were beside themselves with joy at the sight of their brother walking toward them. The prince had the dolls made on their sixth birthday. To them, Kalee was their hero.

He was adorned in a long-hooded cloak, a silver breastplate, and a silver metal armguard that glistened in the sun. Tall, lean, and muscular, he was a giant in the eyes of his sisters. Everywhere he went in the palace, they would follow him. Running up to them, he greeted each with a hug and a kiss, lifting each off the ground and dividing his time between the two of them.

On this day, his mind was far from home, and he was compelled to speak with his father. While in the council chamber, the king was conducting his duties, addressing the various issues brought to his attention by the representatives of the people.

The chamber was nearly full as the king was in the process of addressing them when it was announced that the prince had entered the chamber. King Abbah looked up, stopping what he was writing, then leaned back on his throne as the prince came forth to speak to him.

Both were pleased to be in each other's presence. The king rose out of his seat as Kalee approached, bowing to his father and dropping to one knee. "Rise, my son," spoke the king. "I'm pleased you are back safe. I take it that all went well."

The prince responded, "We succeeded in our task but not without cost. Three of my men lost their lives in the encounter, but the creature we sought is now dead. There are more words of interest that I bear. On my return home, we encountered travelers with tales from beyond the great mountains. I'm not sure what to make of it or if I should take it seriously."

CHAPTER 25

The Tale of Giants

"TALES OF A race of giants destroying everything in their path. Not much is known beyond the mountains. They're so far away. Very few have ventured beyond their endless boundaries except traders and merchants."

"Not many of them have ever returned with any news of such things. It is not known if there are any truths to these stories or just simply fairy tales." The king paused and then said, "The Center Mountains are many miles away. And beyond them is even farther lands that are completely foreign to us.

"We do not live our lives based on fears from distant lands, nor do we move about blindly. I do consider all that I hear with the possibility that there may be truth in some words but not enough to cause concern. We shall conduct our lives as we have always done. There haven't been any threats to our borders for more than fifty years, and those who had attempted fell harshly by our swords and arrows.

"The only threat to our kingdom has been to feed the many that flood our gates to live here among us." Pausing for thought, the king then said, "I will exercise some caution in the event there are some truths in these tales. Even if that be so, there will be ample time to prepare with ample eyes patrolling our borders. I will consider our options and act accordingly."

Kalee stood quietly as he listened to his father's words, but on the inside, he was not completely settled with them. Any thoughts he had in the contrary, he held them within himself.

"Kalee, come forth, my son," Abbah then said as he reached out, placing his hand on his shoulder. "I am glad you have returned. In your absence, you were greatly missed. Your excursions into the face of danger does concern your mother when you do not have to take such risks yourself."

Kalee replied, "This is true, Father, I do not have to take the risk. But I do so because I am no better than the men that I send. They live and die just as I do. The title I hold makes my life no more valuable. Therefore, if they are asked to serve the kingdom, why shouldn't I also take such risk and serve my people?"

The king replied, "I do understand your heart, your compassion, and your dedication to the people, my son. But you are not like other men. You are heir to the throne—the future king. If you should fall, there is no other to carry the bloodline, and you are far more valuable as the leader of our kingdom alive than you would be dead, fading from memory of our people and one day gone forever.

"For this reason, many times I have been tempted to hold you back. But I know my son's heart and the burden it bears. For that reason alone, I have not restrained you from following it. With that said, the time has come that I must address the possibility of a distant threat." King Abbah paused as he looked at his son and then said, "I want you to begin to ready the men in the event that all that has been rumored, no matter how unlikely, may pose a threat to our people or our lands.

"We will not make the news public, even though I'm pretty sure the word has already spread to many parts of our lands. But we will have our soldiers begin to prepare in the event there is some truth to it. Have them ready for anything that is deemed suspicious."

"Yes, Father," Kalee replied. He then turned to one of the guards and commanded him to call his commanders to the chamber so they could convene. Bowing his head, the guard turned and left to carry out the command.

Unknown to the king and Kalee, Troguare spies had already entered the lands, hidden from sight and under the cover of darkness.

As night fell, they had quietly been surveying the lands for weeks, watching and waiting, seeking out the kingdom's vulnerabilities and weaknesses. But they were unable to infiltrate the city or the more populated lands due to their stature and beastly appearance.

It would draw attention, along with a warning, of their presence. The few who were unfortunate enough to cross their path were quickly disposed of, keeping their secret safe.

They gathered all that they needed to know before quietly leaving the land without suspicion, concealing their presence from the people of the Niejar, along with the knowledge that they were ever there.

D. R. SIMPSON

Back in the palace, the council of the Niejar generals met with the king until late evening. King Abbah decided to send forth a small contingency of soldiers along the outer boundaries in case there were any intrusions by outside forces.

Prince Kalee looked at his father and said, "I will take fifty men and explore the region out of precaution." But this time, his request was denied. His father looked at him sternly and said, "In the event there are truths in what we have heard, you will be needed here to help prepare our forces in the event of a true threat. Choose another to lead."

Though disappointed, he offered no words of resistance. He looked at his friend and one of his most trusted commanders and finest warriors. "Khalae, step forward." As commanded, Khalae silently stood before the prince. Kalee then said to him, "You will take the fifty men to patrol the northern region."

"Yes, my lord," he responded.

The king then replied, "It is done." He then ended the council and said, "You know what needs to be done. Now go." After giving his command, he sent them all on their way.

Kalee, the last to leave, made one last attempt to sway his father. "Father, hear me out." But before his son could speak another word, the king said, "You are my son, and I love you with all that is in me. In the event of war, you are my greatest leader and warrior. I cannot risk the fate of an entire kingdom on a patrol, no matter how unlikely there may be any truths to these stories. But if it is proven to be true and your life was taken, it would be a great loss to our people, especially me.

"One day you shall be king, the extension of me. Even now, the people see your strength and you give them hope and they will fight to the last for you. I am now an old man. My skills and stamina are now diminished.

"No longer do I have the strength or resolve needed to maintain in battle as I once did. I now grow weary daily. Though my mind is still strong, it is you the people will one day need, but I truly need you now. I pray that you understand the gravity of my words as we move forth, for one day I do perceive you shall be a great king."

After hearing those words, the prince nodded his head, accepting his father's words before bowing to his father. He understood the depths of his father's words and needed not to reply, only the display of obedience and the acceptance of what his father had said to him.

After leaving the chamber, he sought out his friend Khalae. Calling out to him, he said, "I will meet with you in the courtyard in an hour, and we shall discuss the particulars of what must be done." Khalae nodded to his friend, smiled, then turned and walked away.

An hour had passed. Khalae was already there when Prince Kalee arrived at the courtyard. When he arrived, they greeted each other, grasping each other's forearm, acknowledging their brotherhood as both warrior and friends.

Kalee spoke to him, saying, "I'm sure that the rumors from afar have not passed by your ears."

"Yes, I have heard the vague tales, but I don't know if I choose to believe them. Nevertheless, they have my king's attention as well as that of my friend, so I shall carry out whatever is required of me in service to my people."

Kalee smiled and then responded, "That's why I have chosen the one in whom I have the ultimate trust in. That is why I have chosen you to lead these men."

"I know, my brother," Khalae then responded. "I am somewhat curious by the news and its true origin. If there are truly truths to them, I have no doubt that we will rise to the challenge and defeat any that would attempt to destroy us."

Kalee agreed then said, "There is probably nothing to these fears, but I will sleep a little easier if certain precautions are taken to ensure that there is no threat. For peace leaves such a sweet taste on my lips. To raise a family with the comfort of knowing that no harm would come to them or the shadow of death no longer hovering over the people, I will do whatever is necessary to make that happen.

"We do what we must to protect ourselves, and you know as well what must be done to protect that ideal. The pathway to the kingdom in the north is by far the most isolated and sparsely populated as well as the most vulnerable. If any force shall enter in, it is there in which they shall come. Therefore, we must focus our efforts in that region." Nodding in agreement, Kalee and Khalae once again linked forearms, ending their meeting before Khalae left to prepare assembling his men and gathering their provisions and supplies before riding to the north.

After a week, they arrived in the region. Setting up a base camp in which they could operate, Khalae laid out the strategy for his men to follow, spending several weeks exploring the various possibilities in the event of a true invasion.

Spreading out, they covered both forests and fields. But all remained quiet, and in their minds, it was an unlikely invasion. The patrols found no evidence of movement of any kind.

With their supplies beginning to dwindle, it was time to replenish them and send back a report. Satisfied that there was little to be concerned about, Khalae relaxed, along with his men.

Looking at his men, Khalae said, "In the morning, I'll send a rider with our report, along with a request for more provisions. It is nearly a week to the closest village and not much farther than that before they reach the city."

With their food running low, along with their supplies, it was time to hunt once again. Successful with their efforts, they made camp and prepared to bed down for the night.

With fresh meat roasting over the fire, darkness began to settle in around them. As they sat eating their meal, few words were spoken as each of the men were consumed in their own thoughts, missing the comforts of their homes as they longed to return to them.

Not one of them had given any serious thought to any perceived threat, only the thoughts of their wives, families, and whatever personal endeavors that might be waiting there for them.

Shortly after settling in their tents, all was quiet. As always, two guards had been posted around the perimeter, rotating their shifts every two hours as the night proceeded.

There was an overcast sky that covered the stars, concealing the light of Tyrus's three moons that dominated the night skies. All remained still and quiet, then two muffled sounds broke the silence, but they were so low they remained unnoticed.

There was something about this night that woke Khalae out of his slumber. His sleep was restless—a question he woke without an answer. Sensing that something was wrong, he rose and grabbed his sword.

In haste, he emerged from his tent. Looking around in the darkness, he neither heard nor saw anything. The guards that were guarding their perimeters were not at their posts.

Immediately he called out to them, but there was no reply. Awakened by Khalae's calls, his men rose from their tents as they began to gather themselves to join him. "Ready your arms!" Khalae shouted.

Each with their weapons in hand, it was clear that no one knew what was happening. Each looked at the other, barely able to see their hands in front of them. The darkness revealed very little. One of the men took a torch that was burning outside of their tent, then he stepped forward about fifty feet.

It was then the answer to all their questions was revealed. Massive figures atop monstrous beasts with horns and teeth stood silently, completely surrounding them. Then the great silence ended as snarls and growls erupted.

They were facing an army that was once a rumor until this moment. None of them had ever seen a Troguare or a liborox before, only the fleeting stories of faraway lands and the tales of merchants. They now found them to be true.

They were now facing a Troguare army in the flesh, and fear flowed throughout their ranks like a running river. No one could fathom the force that stood before them.

Seeing that they had no chance to escape being impossibly outnumbered and all escape routes blocked, this would be the last images they would ever see. Khalae, with his sword already drawn, stood alongside his men as they awaited the inevitable.

Sitting atop his liborox, General Koshier, with his double-bladed ax in his hand lowered to his side, then gave a roar that shook the ground beneath them. And with that, his forces collapsed on the fifty like a sudden rush of wind. For Khalae and the men who stood beside him, the end came quickly.

The screams and cries of the men were quickly replaced by those of growling beasts.

CHAPTER 26

In the Midst of the Storm

BACK IN THE city of Umar, several weeks had passed since Khalae and his men had left. After several weeks, they had not returned or sent word of their progress at the appointed time. Walking along the hallway of the palace, Kalee anxiously awaited word from the north, but none had been forthcoming.

Beyond the gates of the city, the king's army was mildly on alert. With no evidence of a viable threat, their presence was strictly precautionary and very few of them showed any concern.

In the distance, a storm was approaching from the north, but what they didn't know was what was coming with it. This was a storm that was truly like no other that had come before or at the present.

For with it, the huge Troguare army was steadily approaching under its protective cover. The fifty men that were sent to forewarn the kingdom were dead before their task could be completed.

For decades, their borders remained safe. The sovereignty of the Niejar had been both safe and secure from all. Peace had reigned throughout the land. Beyond rumors, there was no evidence of an invading army nor was there any reason for suspicion.

That was no more than an illusion. What was unknown to them was that the Troguare army had already infiltrated the Niejar lands, hidden for weeks without anyone's knowledge, before the king had dispatched his men to the scarcely populated north.

Koshier had been watching the Niejar's movements since he arrived with his army, remaining hidden and avoiding discovery. The scouts that he had sent to the heart of the Niejar had told of a kingdom that was the richest and the most formidable of the three kingdoms that Obizar had sent his armies to destroy and conquer.

This was the reason Koshier was chosen for the task. Next to Obizar, he was the most ruthless and the most feared of Obizar's generals.

Unlike the other generals, Koshier preferred the stance of not offering any opportunity for surrender.

The screams and cries of his victims thrilled him. This satisfied his lust for the degradation and the destruction of lives while raping its land and its people, leaving them without a choice or reprieve. The butchering of his enemies, along with the sight of blood and the wailing of the people, were his driving force.

Moving along with the storm, under blowing winds and blinding rains, he reached the more populated lands of the kingdom before spreading his forces. Concealing them further, he moved within the thick forest that surrounded the sweeping fields.

Preferring to wait until nightfall while the storm raged, the element of surprise always took centerfold as the unusually violent storm provided the perfect cover. Under the pitch-black darkness, this allowed him to catch the inhabitants asleep and totally unaware of an attack.

Just before nightfall, high up on a distant hill, a lone woodsman, who was gathering the last of his bundle of timber for the night before the storm unleashed its full wrath upon them, heard one of the Troguare beast let out a shallow roar.

That caught the woodsman's attention. Looking below in the midst of the trees, at first he saw nothing, then he took a second glance and saw movement. As he focused, he saw a giant walking beside its beast, then the rest emerged from the tree line.

Startled and frightened, he stopped what he was doing, unfastened his beast from the cart, and mounted it. He knew he had to give warning to as many as he could until the news reached the ears of his king. He rode the back of his callet as fast as his beast could carry him.

It wasn't a fast- or smooth-riding beast, but he got it to gallop as fast as he could get it to go. As the last of the sunlight disappeared behind the dark horizon, Koshier gave the order to march.

This huge army flooded the fields, resembling ants pouring out of its nest. Steady and rapidly, Koshier pressed his army forward. By this time, the storm was now upon them, providing more cover as the stars and moons were now hidden behind the clouds, extinguishing the little light that they provided.

Reaching the village not far from where he first saw the Troguare army, the woodsman began to give warning of their approach. Though many had heard of these rambling tales, few paid heed to the warning, believing the man to be either drunk or crazy.

With the Troguares on the move, there was little time to prepare for their attack. With the storm now upon them, it provided the perfect cover for the Troguare forces.

Moving along in the blinding rains, they began to overtake the woodsman and the slow beast. In the midst of the storm mixed with lightning, deafening thunder, and a heavy downpour, those who had not awakened in time found themselves in the midst of the Troguare army without any hope of survival.

Too late to escape, they were slaughtered where they stood. Those who attempted to flee were overrun and killed. There were a few unlucky enough to survive. They were put in chains, while the army progressively moved forward.

Even with soldiers posted throughout the kingdom, they were still unprepared for the magnitude of the attack and were surprised. Overwhelmed by the sheer force of the attack, no one had ever faced an adversary such as these—an army of giants and giant beasts adorned in armor. The few that were able to fight threw spears and launched their arrows while trying to defend themselves, but all their efforts were ineffective, with only a few finding their mark.

Koshier, at full gallop, led the charge with his ax drawn back and swept away his opponents, splitting men in half while mowing through the lightly defended lands. From village to village, the giants laid waste to everything in their path—burning huts while slaughtering people.

Those who were not butchered were captured and quickly placed in chains that were so heavy they could barely walk while they were being harshly treated. With his eyes on the real prize—the city of Niejar—Koshier himself elected to take the bulk of his army, not taking the time to capture but to destroy everything that was in his path, moving forward and killing everyone.

With the soldiers who were posted along the perimeters destroyed without the time to give warning, Koshier's strategy was flawless. Still moving forward as time was rapidly running out, the woodsman came across a light patrol of the Niejar army.

Exhausted and not being able to press on any further, he told them all he had seen, but he didn't know how close the Troguares were as they moved in on their position.

Suddenly, they looked across the field. Both beasts and giants came into view amid the heavy downpour and lightning flashes, as only the lightning lit the fields, barely enough to allow the viewing of this massive force.

Seeing that time was fleeting, the patrol, having an extra steed, gave it to the woodsman as they rode off. They sounded the alarm, which could hardly be heard due to the heavy thunder all around.

But all this was too late as they passed, for the giants were on top of them. Many awakened out of their sleep only to find themselves being torn apart by teeth or claws or killed by a swinging ax or the end of a sword. Many were impaled as the liborox would spear them with its horns before going in for the kill.

Finally, the one with the fastest steed pulled away through the heavy downpour, making distance between himself and the army of giants. Within distance to sound the alarm, the lone soldier drew his horn and prepared to sound it. From a distance, he could hear the cries of his patrol as they were overtaken.

Placing his trump to his mouth, he began to blow it. But without his knowledge, a kill beast had been released. A kill beast was a liborox that was unmounted and trained to track and pursue.

As he blew it, he was overtaken by the beast. With its huge paws and sharp claws, it knocked the steed to the ground, pouncing on it and killing it. As the warrior gathered himself, he drew his sword. But that proved to be futile as the beast pounced on him, sinking its huge canine teeth deep within his body, killing him as the army passed by.

Hearing the warning, the soldiers moved forward, already being in position. But the Troguares were upon them. They fought furiously and bravely among all the muck and rain, stalling the attack and giving the soldiers in the flanks time to get into formation. But that wasn't enough as they were overrun by this time.

The prince was alerted as he had his archers prepared along the city walls. The king gave the order to get the queen and the royal family to safety. Grabbing his sword and donning his armor with the help of the guards, he was now prepared once more to go to war.

He turned to the queen, telling her to take herself and their daughters through the secret passage through the hidden tunnels, along with her maidens and two of the guards to protect them.

At this point, everything was in total chaos. As suddenly as the storm appeared, it ended. They proved that on this night, they were unprepared for an assault, with no word ever returning from their sentries.

The giant moons and stars broke through the cloud's cover, shedding their light. Kalee had manned the wall, along with his archers, finding spaces between their heavy armor that very few could ever find, killing them with each launch.

While many of the arrows of his men simply glanced off their armors, the Niejar warriors fought fearlessly and without reserve, but that wasn't enough.

No one among them had ever seen an army such as this; no one had ever seen Troguare giants with their massive sizes and armor so thick and beasts so powerful they seemed impossible to defeat. It wasn't long before they had overrun the Niejar army.

Like the onset of the storm that preceded them, the Troguare came without warning out of the night and rendered the Niejar's defenses useless. Their catapults and their spear-sling machines were unable to inflict enough damage.

The Troguare numbers, coupled with the fact that the Niejars were not trained in the art of fighting an army of giants, proved to be their downfall. Trapped within the city walls, all the prince could think to do was to protect as many of his people as possible, but the giants' siege machines were too massive.

They made short work of the massive gates as the Troguares flooded the city. King Abbah stood at the top of the stairs with shield and sword drawn, along with about fifty of his finest warriors at his side to protect him and the royal family.

The first wave of Troguare foot soldiers stormed the gates, killing everyone in their way. From the bridge archway connecting the inner wall to the palace, Prince Kalee picked off as many of the Troguare marauders as he could till he had but three arrows left.

From his view, he could see his father through the huge arched opening while his father was engaged in battle. Kalee displayed the skills that made him a great warrior. Along with his bow, he was equally as deadly with the sword.

He side-rolled under the first assault, slashing the back of one of the giant's legs, dropping him to his knees, before running his sword through the back of the giant's neck, killing him. He quickly turned to avoid a second blow from another Troguare opponent before driving his sword through the opening just below the enemy's armpit, also sealing his fate.

The guards that fought to protect him fought valiantly by his side despite the confined space in which to work. The massive bodies of the Troguares made movement difficult, giving the giants a great advantage. The Niejar numbers quickly diminished as they fought desperately to repel the Troguare forces, until the king was finally left standing alone.

Seeing another rapidly approaching giant behind his father, Kalee, while standing in the archway, drew his bow back, sending his arrow through the oncoming giant's eye, embedding itself within his skull.

Then he found his target once again into another between its eyes. Kalee, now out of arrows, took off his arrow sack, tossing it to the ground. He drew his sword while now facing a Troguare giant in the middle of the bridge.

Outmaneuvering him, Kalee slid between his legs, running his sword up through the giant's groin as it fell off the bridge. He then faced a second giant. He drew his dagger from his thigh, throwing it, embedding it between the giant's eye. As the giant fell forward onto his face, the time to aid his father was rapidly running out. He knew he had but a short time to reach him before his father would be overtaken.

Meanwhile, General Koshier had fought his way through another entrance of the palace. With his double-edged ax, he plowed through men, bones, and armor effortlessly. Looking up, Kalee saw the general's approach through one of the large windows. Running as fast as he could, he called out to his father, desperately trying to warn him of Koshier's approach.

His father was engaged in a fight with yet another and was unaware of the general nor could he hear his son's warnings. At that moment, the bridge shook violently as its structure began to crumble.

With fires being set from inside despite the rains, the heat from the internal flames began to dry the outward surface, burning all around. Unknown to Kalee, even the tunnels below had been set aflame as most of the structures began to crumble all around him.

Grabbing hold on whatever he could, he looked over as it was too late to help his father, the king. Koshier had reached King Abbah from behind, sinking his ax into the king's back as the bridge collapsed, sending Kalee falling to the ground through the floor until he disappeared from sight.

Kalee had ridden the crumbling structure to the ground, falling straight through into the tunnel. When he landed, he rolled into a large crevice deep within the tunnel, where he was covered by debris.

The fall had rendered him unconscious, covered, and unseen. After killing the king, Koshier searched room to room. And to his surprise, he found the queen trapped in one of the rooms.

They were cut off from their escape route. The two guards charged with protecting them had been killed, along with the maidens who were accompanying them.

The queen had found refuge there with the hope that, by some miracle, they would be saved. As the last defense of her children, she hid them in a small storage area, telling them they must remain silent.

Standing before her was a large reddish-brown figure, wide and broad. With his height, his head was nearly touching the ten-foot ceilings of the palace. Marked with three scars across his face and two large teeth protruding from his lower lip, she looked up at him.

Reaching down, she picked up a sword from a dead soldier lying near her and then held it in front of her body, pointing it directly at the giant commander. Finding this quite amusing, he turned to one of his comrades and laughed.

At that moment, she lunged forward, penetrating his unprotected side. Grimacing with pain, this enraged the giant as he struck her with the back of his massive hand, hurling her across the room and slamming her against the wall.

Dazed and bloody, when she lifted her head to see her attacker, Koshier took his battle ax and beheaded her where she sat. Satisfied with his deed, he turned to leave when he heard a faint sound.

Letting out a grunt, he turned to investigate where the sound came from. Seeing a set of double doors against the wall, he opened them. To his surprise, Olieria and Enieya were huddled together in the small space.

Reaching down to his thigh, he pulled out a small blade. With a smile, he slowly reached in and was about to slit their throats but hesitated. This would have given him great joy, for he found pleasure with the taking lives, no matter how small, but he thought the better of it.

Royal pets would be of more value alive than dead. He ordered them leashed and taken away to whereabouts that were unrevealed. After sending the children away, Koshier returned to King Abbah's body and took his head.

It was to be presented to his master, Obizar—a prize of another head of a fallen king. He then ordered that the entire city be burned to the ground. As Umar burned, the remainder of the Niejar people were carted away as slaves or scattered in the wind, fleeing from the giants' wrath.

CHAPTER 27

After the Fall of the Niejar

FOR THREE DAYS, Kalee lay unconscious under the rubble. When he awoke, his head had a stream of dried blood from his injury that had begun to heal. With his head pounding and his body aching, he found himself in a crevasse that had protected him from the heavy rubble.

The smell of burned wood and decaying flesh filled the air all around. Everything was blurry, and his vision doubled. After a few minutes, everything slowly began to focus. His last memory was watching his father die at the hands of the giant with three scars across his face.

That vision would remain fixed into his mind as long as he lived. He then thought of his mother and sisters, as well as the woman he loved. Picking up his sword that was lying next to him, he slowly and quietly climbed out of the hole that had protected him from discovery.

Not knowing what to expect, he stood ready for whatever he might have to face. When he reached the top, all was quiet and in ruins. Buildings were still smoldering, while the smell of the dead filled the air. Bodies were spread all around, bloated and ripening.

Some were torn apart. The sight of it all was almost unbearable. The people who once thrived here had either fled, were enslaved, or were dead. The invading giants had left the city in ruins and had moved on to the next.

Working his way up to the palace into the hallway where he saw his father fall, he saw his father's body lying in the hallway. He had been beheaded by the Troguare commander, and his head was kept as a trophy.

Beside him were those who fought at his side. Stricken with grief, he searched every room looking for his mother and sisters. As he searched, he saw one of the dolls lying in the hallway. It was the one he had made for Olieria.

Reaching down, he picked it up and stared at it, afraid of what his search would reveal. But he continued. Finally, he saw his mother lying there. Like his father, she, too, had been beheaded, soaking in her own blood.

Both of his sisters were missing, with the soldiers and maidens assigned to protect them spread about the chamber, dead on the floor. Kalee dropped to his knees and wept violently, then he shouted out in anger with everything he had within him.

His thoughts then turned to Tylah, the woman he loved. Hastily he turned and rushed to her home, not knowing what to expect. The question in his mind was, *Did she share the fate of my family, or did the giants take her?*

This question played over and over in his mind as he was desperate to find her. Finally reaching her home, his worst fears were realized. Her home was burned to the ground. He then followed a set of footprints where he found that her body had been dragged into the bushes.

It was apparent that she had put up a fight. A bloody sword with the hand of a giant was lying not far from her. Lying there, he rushed over and held her lifeless body.

It was evident that the giants had brutally raped her before killing her in the process. He then picked up her broken body and carried her back to the palace, placing her alongside that of his parents.

As he stood over them, he bowed his head and said a prayer before setting the bodies aflame. He then made an oath to himself that he would find his sisters and avenge the life of his family, as well as that of his people.

After a time of mourning while staring into the flames, he showed no more emotion. He bottled it all inside with these memories engraved within his mind, fueling his hatred toward these giants even more.

Knowing he could no longer stay here, he gathered whatever provision he could find to carry with him, not knowing where his journey would take him or where his destiny lay, knowing only that he would find his sisters and extract his vengeance on the Troguares with every opportunity that presented itself.

Standing alone, Kalee looked around him as he stared toward the horizon, dazed and lost in thought with tragedy of the moment

D. R. SIMPSON

engulfing him. With smoke hovering along the ground from smoldering buildings and structures, his way was now blurred by the rising black smoke that filtered his view.

Heading in the direction of the setting suns, the prince started his journey away from open ground. Across the countryside of his once great country, it had now been laid to waste.

Careful in his movements, he remained hidden as he began crossing paths with soldiers still pillaging and looting. The smell of decaying bodies was reeking in the air all around.

Bodies were scavenged by wild creatures of every sort while lying under the heat of the dual suns till they began to give way to the evening's light. Troguare soldiers were everywhere, rounding up prisoners.

He witnessed his people being loaded into caged wagons as if they were livestock. Some were forced to march in heavy chains. Those who were strong enough and able to walk on their own were fortunate ones at least for a fleeting moment.

Those who were not strong enough faced the most dire fate. Whether they were crippled, wounded, or just old and not strong enough to keep up on their own, they were either butchered or fed alive to the giants' war beasts. Despite how much he wanted to come to the aid of his countrymen, he was helpless to aid them. Alone, it would be suicide, imprisonment, or worse.

While searching for his sisters, Kalee made a vow to himself that one day he would free his people, but this wasn't the day. Finding Enieya and Olieria was his first priority.

While lying in the tall grass perfectly still, watching the events that were taking place, he felt the ground tremble, along with sounds coming up from behind him. Slowly turning to see what it was, there were two riders that were unaware of his presence a short distance away.

Their attention was focused on what was going on in front of him. Wary that he might be detected—if not by the Troguare riders then by the noses of their two beasts—he decided to crawl into a large hollow log filled with holes and openings, which was an arm's reach in front of him.

Though it wasn't totally secure, it provided some cover. Slowly he crawled into it, not making a sound, for they were now but a few feet away from him. Once he got in position, he realized his bow and arrow sack remained in view. The moment was so intense he was reluctant to breathe.

With his hand on his sword, he was sure that his scent would be picked up or his bow would be seen. Fortunately, the air was filled with the stench of the decaying bodies, which were everywhere. The Troguares neither noticed nor look in his direction as they plodded a few feet from him as they passed by to aid in the gathering of the prisoners. After they passed, Kalee reached over and pulled his bow and arrow casing close to him. Kalee remained frozen in that spot for hours. As he lay there awaiting for the suns to set, he vowed that as long as he lived, he would never stop searching for his two sisters.

Afterward, using the cover of darkness, he moved into the nearby woodlands until the next morning. Once he had awakened, he kept moving. By day, he sought refuge within the forest, avoiding the Troguare camps and newly formed strongholds. During his travels, he came across an unattended ramsteed, sleek and black and still saddled.

He surmised that its rider was either captured or dead. Carefully approaching the animal, he grabbed it gently by its bridle in a calming way, claiming it as his own. And with time, he developed a close bond with it.

CHAPTER 28

The Kingdom of the Lakes

HIGH ABOVE A hilltop on a small island surrounded by the largest lake in the kingdom, the castle stood overlooking both lake and forest around it. A long narrow bridge stretched across the lake was its only entrance by land.

Standing above on its tower, Queen Aquiline stood out on the balcony, staring out across the horizon, surveying her lands. This was known as the Kingdom of the Lakes—a land of beautiful forests, lakes, and riverways stretching as far as the eyes could see.

The queen and her people had a special gift that allowed her to psychically communicate with all the living creatures that lived within this forest, with her abilities far exceeding all others. The Kingdom of the Lakes was one of the most formidable armies of all the kingdoms.

Standing with both eyes closed, Queen Aquiline allowed the warmth of the sun to soothe her smooth caramel skin. Long black hair draped down to her back, intertwined with beautiful beads and pearls.

Her beauty was mesmerizing, and she was truly something to behold. Opening her eyes, she heard the faint sounds of footsteps approaching from behind. She turned slightly as they came closer until they reached her side.

Standing beside her was a mirror image of herself, her daughter—the beautiful young princess matching her in every way. Her name was Aquilla, her only child, had the appearance of being seductive, sultry, beautiful, and exotic. But sometimes, that could be deceiving.

She was the fiercest warrior in the kingdom and leader of the armies of the Lakes. Her skills far superseded that of her mightiest men. She was adorned in armor from head to toe, which was of a darker shade of blue and silver.

It was made of Amorian shells, which could only be found in the shallows of the Amorian Sea. It was a seafearer's gift—one who held strong allegiance to the queen and the people.

He had crafted it for her when she became of age to don it in honor of her and her family. It was soft and flexible when submerged under the sea, where they could be formed and fashioned.

Once exposed to the air, they hardened, becoming nearly impenetrable. If propelled through the air once in flight, they had special qualities that caused them to become instantly superheated (caused by the friction), allowing them to penetrate even the thickest armor.

From the bottom of her backplated armor, slightly above her waist, was a thin short cape that streamed down to the back of her ankles. She also wore her hair in locks with a helmet that partially covered her face and with three openings that allowed her hair to sprout out in three directions. One opening was toward the rear, with two openings on both sides of her helmet.

When unpinned and released, her hair fell to her waist. They were also interlaced with razor-sharp Amorian shells, able to cut through nearly any armor with relative ease. With a quick jerk of her neck, she could release the outer shells, turning them into deadly projectiles with deadly accuracy.

They had a quality about them that when hurled through the air, they instantly become superheated (caused by friction), which also allowed them to pierce through armor with little effort. Only the armor she wore, made of the same substance, was immune. All these were a part of her deadly arsenal that she held in her possession.

Away from the field of battle, she was a lady—feminine and elegant. Her charm humbled the steadiest of men, but in battle, she was fierce, known as the Savage One.

Lethal in every way, her weapon of choice was called a whippit. Its shaft was about three feet long with handguards at both ends and adjustable razor-sharp cords with spiked barbs on its end.

It could kill from both ends simultaneously, whether in close quarters or several feet away. Few had the skills to use it, but none could match her. It was said that it was better to fall on one's own sword than to face Aquilla in battle.

As mother and daughter stood, they shared this peaceful moment together. With a soft voice, the queen spoke to her and said, "Behold the beauty of all that you see. Peace," she said, pausing for a moment, then spoke again, "the tranquility of the moment, but all is never as it appears to be."

Aquilla then replied, "What meaning do your words hold, Mother?"

The queen looked over at her daughter with a smile and said, "How beautiful is this within our view. Peaceful and tranquil as it should be, but beyond our sight, all is but an illusion." Aquiline turned her head slightly, extending her arm with her palm up as the tiniest of flutterfies landed on the tip of her finger. She drew it close to her lips until it was but a whisper away. They seemed to exchange thoughts, then she extended her arm again as it fluttered away. She then spoke again to Aquilla, "Since you were a child, your gifts were with you. We are one with this land and every creature that shares it.

"We share our thoughts with everything that crawls, everything that flies, and everything that swims. We are one with our forest. They are our allies, our brothers, and our sisters connected. They speak to us of things both far and near, and they have spoken to me. Remember these words and all you have ever learned. For when the time comes, you will need their help.

"Danger roosts beyond the horizon. Peace will soon be a memory, for darkness looms just beyond our lands and once within it. Spies had already come searching for our weakness with the desire to one day destroy us but were blinded to our ways. Soon the shadow of death will come to visit us."

"I need to know more than just riddles, Mother," Aquilla replied. "Tell me all that you know, Mother."

The queen then replied, "Open your mind, and use the gifts you were born with. An army of giants shall soon come. Forces unlike any we have ever faced or known. Their eyes have already come and gone and, as we speak, are marching their massive force toward us. These giants are led by a dark and evil lord, a sorcerer, with every kingdom already fallen having tasted his wrath.

"We are the last and now stand alone. The time has now come that we will need more than our weapons or brute force or skills as warriors. When the time comes, we will need the forests, the lakes, and the lands to help us."

Aquilla then gently grabbed hold of her mother, embracing her before placing a gentle kiss on her cheek. "I shall go and prepare myself and our army for our defense." After speaking those words, she then turned to mobilize her army.

Meanwhile, many miles from the forests of the lake, the huge Troguare army was slowly advancing toward them.

Aquilla went to the garden where she trained, her mind deep in thought. She found the words of her mother troubling. She summoned two of her most skilled warriors, Barrius and Bondu, each superior fighters and both deadly. Needing to work off the trouble that filled her mind, she began to practice. Grabbing her most prized weapon, her whippit, she was prolific with her skills in using it.

The two warriors she had summoned stopped in her presence while they trained alongside her. Stopping in the middle of their motions, they stood and watched her work it back and forth.

In and out with dead-on accuracy, she struck her targets that were placed around her time and time again without missing her mark.

So focused and fluent in her movements, she was flawless. She then stopped, giving the order for the two warriors who were training beside her to prepare to spar with her.

As they began from the very beginning of their session, she easily outclassed them both. Unusually intense this morning, she then summoned three others to join the fray with the other two opponents all at once.

She ordered them to go with full intensity. Taking their position while surrounding her, they began their assault without warning. She countered their every move with a strike, which would have been deadly in real combat.

Together they could barely keep pace with her movements. Time and time again, she would avoid their attempts to strike as if their actions were predetermined within her head.

With whip kicks to her opponents, along with counter flips, she downed some as they fully extended their blows, moving forward with deadly aim. She had defeated all five opponents with relative ease. Slowly, each managed to stand on their feet, battered and bruised. Some were holding the back of their heads and others their side. Once they were all standing, she addressed them, "The news my mother shared with me was of an upcoming threat. Our brothers of the land we share have given her warning. Our world will soon be under siege.

"It has been foreseen that an army of giants are slowly approaching our position. It's uncertain when they will be upon us, but we have but a short time to prepare our people. It is time that we prepare ourselves for war. We have the security of the forest and lakes to shield us while we prepare."

Later that day, Queen Aquiline summoned her daughter as she addressed the people on the things to come. With the princess standing at her side, she began to speak, "People of the Lakes, I am giving warning for all of us to prepare. We face a dark threat that is wielded by the darkness. It is not an army of men that we face, but one commanded by a dark lord that is carried out by giants, enforcing his will. We must now call upon the power of the forest as well as our resolve to aid us.

"Only with her help can there be hope for victory or to simply survive. It has been revealed to me that we are the last of the free kingdoms to stand. All the others have already fallen to this dark entity. I pray that God will aid us with the power of the light to repel the evil that drives this army." After sharing her words, she looked over to her daughter, turning slightly with a pause before turning away into her chamber.

Aquilla looked over to the masses then said, "Prevail we must. Prevail we shall. Go and let us begin to prepare." Standing motionless, she watched the crowd disperse. Her closest comrade and friend Barrius stood behind her, then he said, "I shall prepare our archers. This will not be a battle that is won in close quarters. For the likes of giants, we must neutralize that strength from a distance."

She then faced him with a puzzled look on her face and asked, "You seem to have a history unknown to me. What do you know of giants?"

He replied, "Many years ago, I journeyed beyond the boundaries of the lakes beyond the great valley pass into unknown lands, seeking to find myself, my true place in this world. All I found was misery beyond our sanctuary. The world was being ravaged by these giants. They were led by a sorcerer king named Obizar that is said to be immortal.

"Mankind were being enslaved all over. I was warned to always stay hidden from there sight, or my freedom or my life could be forfeited. Taking heed to the warning, I knew it was time to return.

"One night while sleeping in the forest, one came up over me and abruptly awakened me, lifting me up by my locks, leaving my feet dangling high up off the ground before throwing me halfway up against a tree.

"Dazed, I was trying desperately to gain my senses. When I did, he was upon me once more. I drew my sword. With a backward thrust, I ran my sword through the closest part of his body that was in my reach." With a smile, Barrius looked at Aquilla, and he said, "He dropped to his knees with blood flowing like a waterfall, with both hands holding his most prized part.

"All he could do was moan in pain before I slipped behind him with my sword, slicing his throat, killing him. I thought the nightmare was over before I saw what emerged from the darkness, running at full gallop straight at me. All I could remember was horn, claw, and teeth of this huge snarling beast coming at me. I believed that this was my last moment until the creature was met with a host of arrows striking it everywhere. It fell flat to the ground, dead while in full stride.

"That night, I was saved by resistance fighters. They had been stalking the giants, striking at them whenever they could. They asked me to join them, but I declined and returned to where I belong—among our people.

"I am now able to share what I know. They are large and powerful. Special skills must be taught to kill them in battle. Though you may possess those skills, most of our fighters do not. Stealth will be our best defense. With their war beasts, they are nearly invincible."

Aquilla then replied, "We have the one thing the others did not have in their favor."

Barrius then replied, "What is that, my princess?"

"We can call upon our forest allies to aid us. There isn't a more formidable army on Tyrus." Barrius looked at Aquilla and laughed as she smiled back at him, with both being in agreement.

CHAPTER 29

After the Fall of the Norstar

WHILE THE THIRD of Obizar's forces, led by General Troxus, were advancing toward the Kingdom of the Lakes, four hundred miles to the north, the Kingdom of the Norstar had already fallen, along with that of the Niejar hundreds of miles to the south.

In flames and in ruins, their people were scattered, dead, or enslaved, with both of their once mighty armies destroyed. Honduro had awakened amid the smoke that had filled the air from the fires that had raged all around him. Many city structures set aflame had engulfed the city and countryside.

Set ablaze by Troguare soldiers, they torched everything in their path. The smoke was so thick it had darkened the sky and so heavy it was hard to breathe even in the open spaces.

Honduro was in chains and covered with blood, none of which was his own. It was from the giants and their beasts that were killed by his sword. Only a single stream of dried blood from an unseen blow to his head, which had rendered him unconscious, belonged to him.

Disoriented and with his vision blurred, his head was slowly beginning to clear. He could hear cries of both men and women as they filled the air around him—some in agony and others from grief. Bodies of Norstar soldiers, along with that of a few giants, were sprinkled among them. Many lay dying or wounded, which was a fate that might be worse than death.

As he began to regain himself, images as clear as crystal stood firm in his mind—seeing his king fall at the hand of a Troguare commander with a sword thrust in his back and his queen dragged away, to where he did not know.

His last memory was of himself engaged in battle, coming to their aid only a few steps away before being struck from behind by an unseen blow. He was fortunate that the blow was not fatal.

Sitting across from him in chains was the Wanderling Cyrikhan. He had been outside of the city walls while making his escape. He was caught in the middle between the Norstar soldiers seeking his arrest within the city and the advancing Troguare army whose numbers were so great it would be nearly impossible to slip past, even for one who was as skilled as himself.

Cyrikhan was faced with the choice to face the impossible, which would be the whole of the Troguare forces alone as they advanced. Left with no choice, he reluctantly had to join the ranks of the city defenders. As the battles raged, the Troguare broke through the lines of the Norstar defenders.

Though they fought valiantly, they were no match for the giants' assault. With the sheer force of the Troguare attack, coupled with their much-greater numbers, the Norstar forces were easily overrun, though there were some that had distinguished themselves during the battle— Cyrikhan being one of them.

Before being netted and bounded in chains during the battle, Cyrikhan had slain a fair amount of these giants despite their much-greater advantage of both size and strength.

His speed and skills were superior to the Troguares he faced. Most of the Norstar soldiers around him found themselves the opposite and were less fortunate, dying as they fought. They fell beside him in droves.

Wrapped and bound in Troguare nets, like a fly in a spider's web, Cyrikhan lay helpless as he witnessed the fall of many of the Norstar defenders and those who shared his fate.

While the battle raged around him, the Norstar army and the fate of their kingdom now faced the inevitable as their defensive lines were being overrun and their forces destroyed.

He had also witnessed the unseen blow that stalled the advance of his nemesis Honduro, rendering him unconscious, who, like himself, awakened only to find himself in chains.

Honduro was now a prisoner sitting across from the one he so desperately sought to throw in chains or worse. Now it was he that found himself sharing the same fate, neither knowing what the future had in store for either of them.

As they sat quietly, the captain of the guards and the Wanderling exchanged eye contact. Despite the carnage that surrounded them, one could feel the hate they shared for each other.

It was so intense that it seemed to erupt from their pores, like a lava-filled volcano. With their eyes locked and the disdain they shared for each other, the intensity was measurable as neither uttered a single word.

Honduro then broke their silence and asked, "How does it feel that an honorless thief would find himself among those who have fought and died with honor? Your face marked by the end of my sword and your life would have surely followed had it not been that my men had not interfered."

Cyrikhan then replied, "A wild boast from one that was saved by his own from the same fate that many around you have already suffered. I saw the blow that downed you. My only disappointment was that you still breathe after it was dealt. When opportunity presents itself once more, I shall see it through, so this scar that I bear across my face is a reminder to me to return the favor. Unlike yourself, I will not fail in the attempt to end your life."

Honduro then replied, "When the time comes, the settling of our dispute shall be the final one." Before another word had been spoken by either of them, a heavy growling voice shouted, "Stand to your feet, dogs!"

It was a Troguare guard that gave the command. Honduro and Cyrikhan, along with the other captives, rose slowly to their feet as their chains were tugged harshly by the Troguare guards.

Those too weak to stand fell back to the ground where they were met with the end of a whip. If they were unable or too weak to move on, they were separated from the others and placed in an open space.

There they were pounced upon and killed by the liboroxes for all the prisoners to see. Any who could not keep up were beaten. If they could not survive the beating, they share the fate of the others they had just witnessed, which was to be killed and eaten.

With the sound of bones cracking from the jaws of these creatures, along with blood splattering everywhere, the cries of the people were heard all around as they were killed by the beast or by the sword.

The women and children were rounded up and taken away to a separate place. Those who were deemed strong enough were thrown into wagons with cages to take the journey to the ore mines in faraway lands.

Whenever an army and its people were defeated, by Obizar's command, its people would be sent away from their lands to distant regions of the empire. The largest of these mines were the mines of Menoria.

The ore that was used to supply the Troguare armament was mined in that sector of the empire. Beyond the great Center Mountains through the Three-Valley Pass, Honduro and Cyrikhan, along with the others, consisting mainly of soldiers, were chosen to take the long journey ahead.

Along the way, they witnessed untold carnage and devastation of both land and its people. Nearly every town and village was in ruins— some burned to cinder and some crumbled into rubble. Bodies littered the land as they rotted in the heat of Tyrus's dual suns. The smell of decaying corpses at times was unbearable as it filled the air under the blistering heat. The two warriors were being carted off to unknown lands beyond the great Center Mountains.

CHAPTER 30

The Battle for the Lakes

S TRETCHED ACROSS THE edge of the forest were the
lands of the Lake Kingdom. One hundred and fifty thousand
Troguare giants and their war beasts waited for the command to move
forward by Obizar's most brash and overconfident commander, General
Troxus.

Of the three armies sent by Obizar into the new frontier to
conquer the last remaining kingdoms that were still standing, Troxus
commanded the largest. Despite sending scouts who had returned
with all they had seen to report, there was still very little known of the
kingdom itself.

This prompted the reasoning for Obizar to send an extra fifty
thousand soldiers as a precaution to safeguard against the unexpected.

After the fall of the Norstar and the Niejar, this was now the last
of the great kingdoms still standing and seemingly the least guarded.
Obizar was told that there would be little to no resistance.

Before advancing, Troxus gave the order for his forces to spread out
along the forest's edges to cover as much ground as possible. This was
also to conceal his numbers and to prevent surprises in the event they
were detected. After looking down the line at his commanders, he then
gave the signal to move forward using banners instead of trumpets to
prevent any unwanted ears to hear it that would jeopardize the surprise
attack he had in store for the Lake people until it was too late.

Slowly they moved into the forest where it took a couple hours
before the entire force of his army completely entered the forest.

It would take days before they would reach the Lake's fortress. Their
advance was slowed due to a combination of thick forest and density.
The only retractors were their war beasts. Liboroxes weren't the most
silent of creatures.

When agitated, they would become unruly and aggressive toward one another, which sometimes led to confrontation leading to roaring and bellowing. What Troxus didn't know was that there were eyes already on them from the moment they entered the forest and, beyond that, were aware of their every movement.

Unbeknownst to the general, the queen of the Lakes had already foreseen their coming through the psychic bond she shared with nature and all its living creatures, and they were already prepared for their arrival. The armies of the Lakes were a different kind of fighter.

Camouflage and stealth were their ways. They were people of the forest. And the ways of the forest taught them how to use its every leaf, every vine, and every piece for a cover, for they were one with it. Aquilla was also concealed, waiting patiently with her forces.

She had instructed them to remain hidden until all the Troguare army had entered deep within the forest. Aquilla knew that her army could not match their numbers, but they didn't have to. The forest was alive with their allies, and until that moment arrived for them to reveal themselves, Aquilla and her forces continued to wait. She knew that it was vital that when the time came, no giant should be allowed to escape.

The Troguares' only knowledge of the kingdom was reported by Troguare spies, whose knowledge was falsely given by the queen, allowing them to see what she wanted them to see. Once the giants were in the place they wanted them to be, Aquilla gave the command for her forces to get into position.

She commanded them to flank as many of the Troguare soldiers as possible. The giants' army was so vast it thinned the forces of the Lakes, preventing any direct assault; therefore, she had them move farther away. There was yet another strategy in effect.

While Troxus and his army were unaware of all the events that were swirling around them, they slowly pressed forward. At that moment, high up in the castle fortress in her loft miles away, overlooking the forest below, Queen Aquiline closed her eyes and began connecting psychically to all the natural inhabitants of the forest.

Every plant, every animal, and everything that crawled, she began to call upon them to defend the land. Though miles away, she could feel the presence of every creature in the forest and their movements, along with their thoughts.

D. R. SIMPSON

She could also feel the footsteps of the army of giants as they pressed forward. Suddenly, vines slowly began to sprout out from the ground in every direction seemingly from nowhere as General Troxus was beginning to become more frustrated with every step. He and his army began to become entangled by them. He began to think it was strange that all was silent and not a sound outside of his army could be heard though he, along with his army, had yet to realize what was happening.

Never one known for patience, he had his soldiers to dismount and form lines using their heavy axes to clear the way.

As they moved forward, clearing the way, the vines and scrubs seemed to begin to replace themselves when they passed. They didn't know that they were being led by the forest into a place that would prove to be a great disadvantage for them.

Finally, they stopped making little progress, and yet they seemed to be lost. The Troguares that were in the rear looked behind them as it appeared that they had never trekked these paths before.

The forest had grown back as if it was untouched as they found themselves surrounded by large strange-looking plants and vines. General Troxus began to become apprehensive and told his giants to be alert.

But before another order was given, vines equipped with poisonous barbs sprang up from the ground, entangling the soldiers and killing their giant hosts. Along with poison, the plants opened up like budding flowers, showing rows of teeth, with each plant having a ravenous appetite for flesh as they began a full assault, gorging themselves upon both giants and their beasts.

The Troguares fought ferociously until they slowly began to gain the advantage. But the Troguare nightmares had only just begun. The creatures of the forest—both large and small—joined in on the attack until they were fully engaged in battle, not by the force of an army led by men but an army waged by the land itself.

General Troxus fought furiously, witnessing his forces dwindle as winged birdlike creatures larger than the giants themselves—with talons large enough to engulf a giant's head, crushing it—swooped down from the skies upon them. The Troguares fought back, inflicting death on a great number of them, while they continued to suffer great losses.

Meanwhile, out of view, Aquilla waited with her forces hidden, surrounding the Troguare forces, before giving the command to launch her assault.

With the Troguare army now down to more than half, from her loft, Queen Aquiline began to focus her thoughts. The ground around the Troguare army began to shake. This was the final piece of the puzzle and when the slaughter truly began. She then called upon the mightiest beast in the forest—the giant island beast known as thoggs.

Each standing sixty feet tall with legs like tree trunks, they had a rocky shell resembling islands armed with a boulder-like tails. Normally peaceful, they were now being called upon to defend their home.

With a swing of their mighty tail, the Troguare army had no defense against them. They were being swatted away like gnats and stepped upon like insects. Many of the giants dispersed and fled in whatever direction they could only to be entangled by vines that helped hold them in place.

It was now time for Aquilla to give the command to begin her assault. Looking at her archers, they began their massacre, releasing their arrows on the Troguares who were entangled and were unable to escape. General Troxus managed to fight through to free himself, along with about a few hundred of his forces and commanders who were fighting alongside him.

Mounting their liboroxes, they weaved through the thickets, avoiding entanglement. Determined not to allow any to escape, Aquilla gave the order for her forces to begin a direct assault. Aquilla and her men mounted their forest gnores. They were four-eyed antelope having midlength fur with a pair of small curled horns at the top of its forehead and were both fleet of foot and agile. Faster than any ramsteed, it could maneuver through the dense, thick forest with relative ease.

Quickly they gained ground and intercepted the giants that were riding the much-slower liboroxes. It was then the battle began as warriors of the Lakes clashed with the Troguare army of giants.

As the battle began, Aquilla led the attack. With a single blow from the swipe of the liborox's claws, Aquilla's gnore was swept from under her, sending it tumbling to the ground to its death while she also fell to the ground before rolling back onto her feet as she stood ready to engage her opponent.

Seeing her standing alone while her fighters were all engaged in battle around her, one of the Troguare riders began streaking toward her on his snarling beast as she appeared to be at a disadvantage. Rotating her whippit in a looping motion from side to side, she waited as the rider and his beast were streaking toward her.

They were now nearly on top of her and only a few strides away, but before the liborox could react, she hurled herself in the air sideways, somersaulting in midair. She avoided the swipe of its claws as the blow sailed harmlessly below her head, allowing the momentum of the beast and rider to carry them passed her. She landed on her feet, and before the Troguare rider and its beast could react, in the blink of an eye, she jumped on their back.

Immediately she released the restraints on her hair, allowing them to flow fluidly and then swirling her head around in a circular motion, which allowed her razor-sharp shells that were laced within her braids to wrap around the neck of the Troguare rider.

With a quick jerk of her neck, the rider's head rolled off his shoulders as his body fell lifeless to the ground. Immediately, before the beast realized its master was dead, she drew her curved sword from her hip and thrust it through the back of the liborox's skull, killing it as well.

Quickly she moved on to the next. Now free to use her bladed locks after removing the restraints that kept them in place, she became even deadlier. With the accuracy of a knife thrower, she once again swirled her hair and then quickly jerked her neck, like a whip. She directed a portion of the shells in flight with deadly accuracy, killing three of the Troguare riders that were charging toward her, penetrating each of their skulls.

One of the liborox's met its fate after one of her shells penetrated its eye socket, lodging itself in the liborox's brain as it lay dying. Aquilla then reverted back to the use of her whippet, releasing the barbed cord from its housing while extending it. Sharp enough to separate a limb, one after the other, she used it to cripple these massive beasts as they sprawled on the ground, sprouting blood in all directions while they bellowed out an agonizing roar.

When riders rose from their fall, they would attempt to quickly engage her. With the spiked balls at the end of her cords, she used it masterfully like a whip with pinpoint accuracy, finding her mark between their eyes or in any vulnerable spot that would cripple them before she massacred them all.

Opponent after opponent, the results were the same. The size of the giants or their power had no meaning to her as she cut them down as quickly as they rose up against her. She was equally as deadly with the sword and even deadlier with her whippit, for she was, by far, more skilled than five of her greatest warriors combined in the kingdom.

She spun around like a whirlwind in battle, avoiding blades and axes that would have surely ended her life. With her skills to go along with an arsenal of weapons at her disposal despite the Troguare size and power advantages, she proved to be more than a match for any of her Troguare opponents. Her hair was her deadliest weapon. Laced with Amorian shells that were sharper and more durable than any blade, it made her deadly from head to toe.

While she fought as fluidly as a dancer, her forces had nearly completed their task with only a few Troguare giants now remaining, including their commander, General Troxus. Though the Troguares were formidable and more powerful, the Lake fighters were more agile and more skilled and now had more than tripled their numbers. The once overwhelming numbers of the Troguare army had been whittled down even further after the creatures of the forest had completed their assault.

Not far from the warrior princess, the usually boisterous and overconfident general had his confidence shattered for the first time. Neither he nor his army nor any army in the Troguare ranks had ever suffered a defeat in their lifetime.

It had been nearly a thousand years since a Troguare army had been defeated and on the brink of annihilation. It was only with the help of sorcery summoned upon by way of Obizar's magic when he called upon the help of demons to aid him that had allowed them to survive.

Only Obizar still remained alive and remembered that day and the people who defeated him. The memories of those events had long since been lost in time, only to be etched deep in the mind of Obizar himself, the immortal giant.

For the first time and out of desperation, Troxus, along with about ten of his fighter and three of his lower-ranking commanders, managed to escape the deadly gauntlet of both plants and animals as they now attempted to avoid the barrage of arrows aimed at them. Fleeing as fast as their beasts could carry them, they were desperate to get out of the forest alive.

After delivering her last deadly blow in the distance, Aquilla saw the Troguare general and the few that were with him as they began to flee while her soldiers were finishing off those giants that were lying helplessly from their wounds. Quickly she ordered one of her men to bring her a gnore. She quickly mounted it and began her pursuit of the escaping giants, along with about fifty of her warriors.

Flowing through the forest as fast as their beasts could carry them, Troxus pressed his liborox hard. Two of his riders that were with him were riddled with arrows. The hundred that had broken free in attempt to escape the first wave of the gauntlet were now less than ten after they were intercepted by the Lake warriors. Now with two more dead, their numbers were down to eight as they could see the forest opening as they rapidly approached it.

Looking at his right, he witnessed an arrow penetrate one of his warriors through the back of his neck, followed by two more to the beast as he and the beast both fell to the ground.

Just before breaching the forest into the open meadow, Troxus, along with his remaining soldiers continued to press forward as fast and as hard as they could. Curiously, one of his commanders turned to see if any were close in pursuit and didn't see the warrior princess rapidly approaching from the opposite side in which he looked. Spinning her whippit round and round like a lasso, she slung it, directing it at the commander's neck.

Finding her barbed cord wrapped around the giant's neck, with efficient velocity, she severed his head from his body as he fell to the ground, killing him instantly. As the beast turned to attack, it was riddled with arrows by the archers that were closely in pursuit behind their princess.

Despite the odds, the mighty general managed to escape the boundaries of the fortress. Despite her plans of not allowing any to escape, she decided not to pursue the general any further into the open plain.

Aquilla was wary that there might still be a greater force that was out of view and didn't want to risk the lives of the few warriors that had accompanied her to the forest's edge. As she watched what remained of the Troguare forces ride off into the distance, she, along with her fighters, retreated back into the thickets as she retrieved her whippit from around the Troguare's neck. She, along with her comrades, then returned to the rest of her army.

With his mighty army annihilated and what was once one hundred and fifty thousand strong Troguares now reduced to only six, Troxus was now left to ponder his fate, knowing he now would have to stand before Obizar and tell him the fate of his army. He knew that he may very well be put to death because of it. From there, they began their torturous journey home.

CHAPTER 31

Aquilla—a Triumph Return

I N OZARIA, MONTHS had passed since Obizar had sent forth three of his armies into the new lands. Obizar impatiently waited for word from each of his armies.

The first to report was an envoy that was sent back with the report of victory of General Zhorr, who remained to oversee the conquered kingdom for the Norstar, which was the first to fall.

Of the three generals, Koshier was the only one summoned to return and with him was his report of the fall of the Niejar. In Ozaria, there was still no word from Troxus. Obizar didn't know that that report would be more than a few months in coming and that Troxus had been defeated and his army had been destroyed. There was no one left who could deliver the message, save the commander himself and less than a handful of soldiers. For him, that journey would be long and arduous before he could reach Ozaria.

Back in the land of the Lakes, Aquilla and her forces returned home to their castle fortress. Upon their arrival, the queen sat in wait for her daughter's victorious arrival, accompanied by her soldiers. The people lined the streets by the thousands to welcome their heroes, the defenders of their home, land, and nation.

Roars echoed through the air for miles as the queen proudly awaited to address and honor the warrior princess and her forces. Queen Aquiline stood before her people with her daughter at her side, raising her arm to the sky in victory.

"God has smiled upon us this day, for the shadow of evil had fallen upon us. And with the help of the forest, our kindred spirits aided us in protecting all that God had given us to share.

"Our people stood mighty in the face of this evil and utterly vanquished it. My daughter, the loyal defender of our people and our lands, led a gallant army to victory over the likes of giants that had wanted to take away our freedom and consume our lands as if it were their own.

"For this day will always be remembered, and we shall honor all that have sworn to protect us. We shall honor them in celebration and festival, which begins now." After speaking these words, the crowd erupted in cheers once again.

People filled the streets with dance and celebration. Princess Aquilla stood there. The glow that radiated from her could be felt anywhere near her presence. Looking into her mother's eyes, though they were filled with pride, she knew her mother better than anyone. She could see beyond the smile into a still troubled soul.

She then said, "Mother, your smile is as bright as the morning suns, but your eyes tell a different tale. I sense the rumbling of an upcoming storm deep within you."

The queen looked back at her with a smile and said, "Some things are reserved for private times. This is the time for celebration. We will, at a later time, share thoughts that are far-reaching."

With those words, the queen gently reached out, holding her daughter by both arms, and leaned forward, kissing her on her cheek. Her pride ran deep within her soul and reflected through the windows of her eyes.

As she turned and walked away into the palace, she left Aquilla to join in celebration with the people who deeply loved her. Trumpeters played and singers sang, filling the streets with laughter, dance, and song.

Aquilla stood there with her most trusted friend and ally, Barrius, who showed in his eyes that his feelings ventured far beyond for his princess and his friend. He had loved her for many years, but she did not share in the sentiment.

She always respected him as a man of honor and her dearest friend, but her heart was always guarded, for the kingdom was always first. And though she always knew the feelings he had for her, she could not yield to her emotions.

But for Barrius, his desire for her had become unbearable. He could no longer keep it within himself, for if he held it any longer, it would erupt from his chest as if it was a volcano.

Looking over at her, she looked back into his eyes. Sensing the words he was about to speak, she took one finger and placed it upon his lips and smiled at him and said, before he could fully form his own words, "I know what is in your heart for me. I know the words you are about to speak. Waste them not on me but for one that will be more deserving. I've seen the way you look at me, the way you share your thoughts.

"I cannot return them or share my heart in equal terms because I am in a different place in both spirit and in mind. My love is for our people and our kingdom. I cannot allow anything to compromise that. Do I love you? Yes, I do, as a companion in arms and as my most trusted friend."

If one could look into Barrius's eyes, it was as if life itself was sucked out of them. He stood tall and strong and then said, "All that you have said to me is true. My love has expanded throughout the years for you. Though I am deeply disappointed, my love will never waver—a hope I refuse to relinquish or let go."

He then leaned forward, gently kissing her on her lips, staring into her eyes. She then responded with a smile and said, "Perhaps one day my heart will change. If that day shall ever come, I would be truly honored to be your wife. There is not a finer man in the kingdom that I'd be so honored to be with." For the rest of the celebration, they stood there sharing thoughts as they always did before this moment presented itself.

Despite all the events that were transpiring before them, the thorn that was driven into her mind by her mother's words remained. She turned toward Barrius, came over to him, and embraced him, giving him a kiss on his cheek. Then she walked back into the palace.

Once inside, she went into the chambers of her mother to satisfy that which was left unanswered in their last conversation. As she entered, she found the queen waiting as though she was expecting her. Once again she was right.

"Did you enjoy the celebration?" the queen asked.

"Yes," Aquilla replied.

The queen then said, "I know my daughter well enough to know you did not come to talk to me about the celebration or our victory. You are here because of what you have sensed in me."

"That is true, Mother. You spoke words and told another story in your eyes. Please share your thoughts with me that I may understand what it is you see."

The queen then said to Aquilla, "Come and sit here close to me that I may feel the warmth of your body close to mine as I did when you were a small child, so beautiful, so innocent. I want you close because I want you to feel the intensity of what I'm about to share with you.

"Though our victory seemed utterly final, it was far from that. The force we face is much darker and more powerful than we can imagine. They are led by a dark lord powerful enough to unleash forces that are unknown to us. He will one day return with a force not even the forest can repel. One day we will have to reach out for outside aid. I have foreseen this in my dreams, for alone we will not be able to stand against this dark force."

Aquilla then replied, "Why does he want our lands? What is it that he wants that drives him to our outer walls?"

The queen replied, "The wind has told me we are the last to survive his hand, and because he has the desire to possess it all, it drives him to our lands and our kingdom.

"He is the harbinger of death, and he will not stop until that end is met. I don't know the time or hour, just that he and his evil will one day return and stand before our gates once more. All we can do is stay ready and prepared, watch, and wait."

CHAPTER 32

A Journey into Hopelessness—
the Menorian Mines

OVER THE PAST several months, the two adversaries had been on a path that had taken them through countless towns and villages that were now replaced and occupied by Troguare conquerors. With their freedom now stripped away, they were now under the shadow of Obizar's rule. These images were now burned deep into Honduro's mind as they passed through these occupied lands.

Honduro could not help but wonder at the fate of the many unfortunates who had survived. Among the captives were only hardened men who were captured and broken by Troguares swords, and both women and children were absent from their presence. It would not be long before that question would be answered and their fate revealed.

Stopping at a large Troguare settlement while in their cages, they witnessed the fate of the women they had come across who were enslaved and what purpose they served. They were kept as items of pleasure, pawns for their amusements. They were used to satisfy the giants' most primal desires, no matter what it was. Their main purpose was mainly to satisfy the giants' sexual desires, which was accompanied with acts of untold brutality and savagery.

Many did not survive the experience, and those who did suffered greatly. Most were maimed, while others were beaten. Some were put to death—if lucky, very quickly—if they were unable to please their masters. Some faced a fate much worse—a slow death and torture. Some were prepared as meals when they were no longer deemed useful.

The children were kept and treated like abused pets until old enough. If the females were deemed pleasurable to the eyes, they were prepared as items of pleasure for their Troguare host.

If not, they were slaves to their master's will. If they were male, they were sent to slave camps or the mines. Some were placed in the custody of individual slave owners to work the fields or attend whatever was needed. Anyone that was disobedient or defiant was sent to harvest camps where they would be used as feed either for the giants or for their beasts. Anything was fitting in a Troguare's diet.

With all they had witnessed, Honduro was powerless to aid them. Between the two of them, with every passing moment, their hatred continued to grow. This was truly a time of hopelessness and despair.

Honduro made a vow within himself that one day he would find a way to escape and strike his revenge onto his Troguare host. He remembered every path and trail and every mountain and field he knew, for one day it might prove useful.

It had taken several weeks to pass through the valley pass into the land of Menoria. After entering these new lands, he noticed that one of their stops was an abandoned armory. Believed to be used by the Menoria people who had long since been vanquished, it left a mark in his mind should he ever escape.

Silent and without a show of emotion, even Cyrikhan was touched by all he had seen. Being a lone adventurer since his youth, he had been to places unseen by most. Savage lands and people, he had faced strange creatures without fear and defeated them all.

With all he had seen, this was different. He found himself touched by it, which was not known to be a trait of a Wanderling. Actually, he cared. Despite all this, his hatred remained entrenched for Honduro.

Through their journey, along with all the places they had been, he found this place had also captured his interest the most. If he was to escape, he, too, would need weapons. The Troguare's weaponry was too large or heavy to be effective. They would need smaller and lighter ones to kill more effectively.

Though they never uttered a word toward each other, both noticed that the giants' camps were spread far from one another. But even with that, their numbers were still abundant.

Three days had passed since their last stop and many months since they were captured. Finally, they reached the mines known as a the Mines of Death. Even the strongest men, if fortunate, would only last a few years. From sunup to sundown, rations were kept to a minimum.

Their purpose was to break the strongest-willed individuals who were enslaved there. It was a harsh and unforgiving place, a living hell where only the strongest could survive, if only for a few years. Rather than killing them outright, they were sent there to get the most productivity where the average man would last a few days.

Conditions were brutal. If any disobeyed the Troguare's commands, they would be beaten and tortured. If that didn't suffice, they were made to be sport for the Troguares' twisted amusement for entertainment while prisoners were forced to watch.

A menagerie of strange creatures was kept there for this purpose. One such beast was one of the most feared creatures in the forest—the giant forest groll. It had two heads with the appearance of an eagle with a horned crest on top of its head. With fur covering most of its exterior—except for its breast, head, and claws—its undercoat was protected by armor-plated scales covering its entire body.

Standing twenty feet tall, it had four arms, each equipped with four talons, including those on its feet. Those who were chosen to meet their end were placed in a pit for that purpose.

Given a sword and shield, men were thrown in to fight the beast, only to be ripped apart effortlessly. Sometimes even several men at a time were thrown in, depending on the mood of their masters. When they fell, their bones would be picked clean by the groll's sharp beak.

Another creature kept in their menagerie was the cennidon. Kept in the lower pits deep within mines, it was just as deadly. It was armed with bone-crushing mandibles and two poisonous spikes on the top of their tail.

Its body was separated in sections, each having a set of legs with a pair of pincers on each. Its speed was unmatched. Death was slow and agonizing. Its poison paralyzed its victim while it slowly fed on them while still alive.

Before the new prisoners were led away to their holding chambers, they were forced to witness such a match. Given swords and shields, two men were forced to face off against one of the horrible beasts.

As the men were thrown into the pit, there were three subterranean tunnels, each leading out into the pit. All were secured with barred gates. One slowly began to rise.

Engulfed in fear, the two men looked at each other as they awaited what was to come. Each held their shield firmly against their bodies with their swords raised and ready, not fully knowing what to expect.

They stood silent as a pair of antennae emerged from the dark tunnel, followed by the creature itself. Its body was black and shiny, and its skin, the texture of leather. The men looked at each other as they slowly began to circle.

As the cennidon began its movement out of its hiding place, its elongated body seemed to not have an end. Twitching its antennae up and down, sensing its surroundings, it appeared to be without eyes.

The two men both stood perfectly still before one took a step to the side. In an instant, with a burst toward the man who had moved, the cennidon covered a distance the length of its body, which was about thirty feet. Swinging its rear around with its spikes tilted to the side, it slashed the thigh of the second man with poison that was oozing out from it before he could react.

Its movement was a blur. Despite holding his shield in front of him, it seized both the man and his shield with its mandibles, crushing both before he could strike the creature with his sword.

All looked on in fear, except the Wanderling and the captain of the guards. Each had faced similar horrors and survived them. In their minds, this would be no different. After killing the first instantly, the cennidon focused its attention on the second man who was now paralyzed and slowly dying.

It then began feeding on him while he was still breathing until it had completely consumed him. Before retreating back into the cavern, it took hold of the prisoner it had killed first, taking his body with it to dine at its leisure.

After the tragic end of the two prisoners, there was yet another match to be made. This time, two beasts would be matched. Only this time, a wager would be made.

Two liboroxes were released into the pit after the gates to the tunnels were sealed. The giant groll had been released from its confinement, finding the two liboroxes waiting.

As it entered the arena, the two liboroxes began to circle. The groll followed each of their movements, keeping its talons ready to strike while towering above them both. With the beaks of both heads snapping at them, it was as if it was calling for them to attack.

While one of the horned beasts lowered its head, preparing to charge, the other sought to get behind it, with the groll's second head following it's movements. When the first liborox charged from the front, the groll latched on with its talons to the charging liborox's horn with another on its muzzle despite the claws of the liborox slashing at it.

The groll's armor was too strong to penetrate as the liborox's blows simply scratched the surface. With its power, it spun the liborox around, quickly placing it between itself and the other liborox before it could attack its rear.

Stabbing the liborox with one of its beaks severed its spine, killing it instantly. Attempting to do the same, the other beast shared the same fate. While one lay dead and the other dying, the groll finished it off and then began to feed on one of its choice.

The giants cheered on, ever amused by this gory sight as the arena pooled with the blood of these beasts. After witnessing this, many were shaken. Most were soldiers, but they had never seen anything like this before.

For most of them, all hope was lost, with many believing they would never leave this place. Neither Honduro nor Cyrikhan were fazed by what they had seen that day. Both only watched for weaknesses in these creatures in case the day would come that they might have to face one.

This made them even more determined to find a way of escape. Despite the disdain they had for each other, they knew they shared this one thought. From the moment they found themselves in chains, they each believed that they would not remain so.

Each believed that one day they would make an attempt to be free. Cyrikhan had lived free in the world his whole life. He was free to roam between kingdoms, paying allegiance to no one. He trekked lands and places where others would not dare. Within his thoughts, this was unbearable, and he knew he would prefer to die in the effort to escape rather than remain in bondage. From that day, both shared the very same thoughts of escape and ending each other's life whenever opportunity presented itself without sharing a single word.

At first light, everyone was led to the ore mines. As everyone began, their labor treatment was harsh and sometimes brutal. It was tiring for the hardiest of men. Days turned into weeks and weeks to months. Many who arrived at the mines did not survive, but Cyrikhan and Honduro endured on until an opportunity would one day present itself.

While the two warriors had embarked on a road toward slavery, another warrior had taken a different path. After also roaming the countryside for months throughout what was once his home, which was ruled by peace and tranquility, the young Niejar prince now found only pain and suffering.

While remaining hidden, he witnessed hundreds of his people carried off into caged carts with the rest dragged along in chains. In his journeys, he followed their trails where he observed most captive slaves consisted largely of women and children being sent back to the lands from whence the giants came—back to the other side of the Center Mountains.

The sound of cracking whips echoed through the air as flesh was being ripped with each strike. He could hear the sound of women crying as they were being separated from their children while being carted off in different directions.

D. R. SIMPSON

Alone, Kalee was helpless to aid his people. After wandering throughout, he realized all hope to do so was lost. Alone, the task would be impossible. The Troguares were complete and thorough in their conquest.

Finally, Kalee's wanderings took him to the steps of the great Center Mountains. The risk of Troguare encounters and being lost through the valley pass was too great. Kalee chose to find his own way across the mountains. Dangerous and deemed impossible, he chose to climb over the top, above their high slopes and ranges.

The odds of success were seen as impossible, a risk Kalee was more than willing to take. As he began his ascent over the treacherous slopes, looking down, his view was that of magnificence. Mountains appeared as steps leading up to the heavens. Across in the distance, he saw the Mighty Brims rolling about with their snowcapped tops, appearing as ocean waves above the clouds in all directions.

Each rising with such height, they appeared to reach the stars. Down below, he could see the heavy green forest giving way to open pastures while above him were clouds leading up to snowcapped mountains.

In between, he found an even keel that provided comfort along his course. Looking down, he could see how vast the lands were below. Between the ridges, he viewed the valleys below. There he saw what was called the Three-Valley Pass as it opened into three canyons that stretched endlessly. He could not help but think of a strategic advantage that it might hold. All had told of the passage through, but no one ever told of the view above, which he had now traveled hundreds of miles.

Before him lay new lands and vanquished cultures. As he journeyed, he would witness once great cities and civilizations now left in ruins with those of giants taking their places. Nothing was known to him beyond these mountains, which seemed to stretch endlessly.

These were of a people much like his own who dared to resist rather than to submit themselves to slavery. The cost—their lives, their homes burned to the ashes, and their people carried off, never to be seen again.

In his travels, he had learned the tragedies of Troguare slavery under Obizar's rule. Scattered resistance was in every quarter of Troguare lands that he had ventured in, mostly unorganized and unruly.

He could see hope if somehow they could all be brought together and organized. Kalee was largely restrained, and the time had not yet come for him to attempt such a feat. Crossing his path were convoys of slaves being transported to the mines and other labor camps that were more than troublesome, but it wasn't until he witnessed the true horror under Troguare rule—that of harvest camps.

It was a place where both young and old were taken out to the yards and slaughtered like farm animals. Some were screaming; others simply embraced their fate to end their daily torment.

Unable to resist, from a patch of woods in which he was hiding, he drew back his bow with deadly aim while the executioner raised his ax to slaughter yet another victim. His arrow found its mark through the giant's eye and exited through the rear of the thick skull of the giant executioner, embedding itself in the chest of yet another giant. Both fell dead in the yard while the potential victims lay confused and bewildered.

They rose to take advantage of this opportunity to escape. Though his attempt to aid was a noble one, he let arrow after arrow fly from a distance that was unfathomable. With each flight of arrow, they found their mark as both giant and beast fell dead but to no avail, for the victims were slaughtered before they could reach safety by riders guarding their human flock.

Confused as to what was happening, they finally began to figure out the direction in which the arrows had originated. The Troguares' attention was focused on Kalee's position though hidden among the trees and bushes.

This caused the giants to scramble and take up their arms, mounting their beasts as they began their pursuit, hurrying to find the source of the arrow's flight and the bowman that launched them.

Sounding the alarm with a triumph, it wasn't long before the area was filled with riders as they moved rapidly toward Kalee. Holding fast since he had not been seen, he finally saw his opportunity to escape as he slipped away in the opposite direction, pressing his ramsteed forward.

With his range and distance being longer than anyone could imagine, this allowed him time to escape. Because of the distance, by the time they reached that location, Kalee was already gone.

During his journey, every place he had gone mimicked the fate of his homeland. A sea of tears mixed with blood flowed everywhere he went. His journey now would take a different turn far beyond the grip of Obizar and his empire.

He was a world away from the place he had once called home, traveling along the outer edges of the empire where he had more freedom to roam. It seemed like yesterday since he heard the voice of his father speak, the loving praise of his mother, or the laughter of his young sisters as they played joyfully in the garden or since he held the woman he loved in his arms. All this was now gone, along with the Kingdom of Niejar, forever. It was now but a memory tearing away at his heart.

CHAPTER 33

The Land of Shadows

KALEE'S PATH HAD led him deep to what seemed to be the ends of the world—a place known as the Land of Shadows. He had now entered this dark, forested realm where shadows ultimately ruled.

He had heard many myths and legends told of this place by a few he had encountered. Those who were lucky to escape the Troguare onslaught and seeking to find their own way told of a mysterious people called the Shadowed Warriors who dwelled within these lands. It was said they were once called another name, but that name had long been lost over the centuries. Even with these claims, no one really knew if these people of legends even existed at all.

They were once the greatest warriors known before an unholy evil had driven them to obscurity nearly a thousand years ago. While Kalee ventured into the dark forest lands that were unknown to him, deep within its borders, a special ceremony was about to take place.

Torran—the son of Aczar, the ruler of the Shadowed people—heir to the throne of this unknown forest realm, the young prince, had chosen his wife. And this was the day the two were to wed. Standing six foot eight and powerfully built, it was a natural trait of his people in which he had exceeded them all.

Beloved among all the people within the Land of Shadows, he was both honorable and just, holding to the tradition that had been taught to him by his father. From his youth, he had proven himself to be an exceptionally skilled fighter. His skills and power was renowned. There was no one among them who was greater in mastering the swovel or the foreblade. His skills were legendary among a kingdom of great and powerful warriors.

The young prince had now come of age and had long since chosen his wife. They had been in love since they were children, and since that time, their hearts belonged to each other.

Her name was Tiesh. She was both tall and beautiful, with long flowing black hair that overlaid her short velvety fur, a darker shade of blue. Today was the day they had longed for, and they were about to be wed.

Early that morning, Torran came to his father, the king, sitting in his bed chambers with his mother, Queen Olivia. Adorned in his silver-blue armor, he approached them while they were still in their chamber.

"Mother, Father," he spoke as he addressed them both, "I have awaited this day since I first laid eyes upon my bride to be, but there's something I don't understand. I have faced many creatures in the forest so fierce that would cause the bravest men to falter. I have feared not one, not even for a moment. But yet now on this day, I can barely stand straight. My knees now quiver, and I can barely catch my breath. What is happening to me? This I cannot understand."

The queen looked over at her son with a smile and then stood up and walked over to him and hugged him by his waist. She then said, "There's nothing wrong, my son. It's nothing but love and anticipation. This moment has caused the mightiest men like yourself to feel the same as you do." Looking up at him, she continued to smile and said, "It's called true love."

The king laughed and then said, "A natural process, my son." He continued to chuckle. "I felt the same the day I married your mother. Love will humble the greatest of us, a fact you personally now face." The king's chuckle then erupted in laughter once more. "That's how you know it's truly love, my son."

Joining his father in laughter, Torran looked back at his mother as she continued to smile with the love for her son sparkling in her eyes. The king then stood up from his seat and said, "Walk with me, my son." As the two began their walk, the king said, "I have shared a great many things, but now it is time to share my knowledge of being a good husband. There are responsibilities that you will need to bear that transcend governing a kingdom." As the king and his son walked away, he shared the essentials of being a good husband. The queen sat and watched them walk away with her heart now filled with joy.

Unknown to the Shadowed people, many miles away, a Troguare scouting patrol had entered into their domain unseen. Nine in all, it was a large number for a patrol so far from their camps. No one entered these lands without being detected, having a set of watchful eyes being present from the Shadowed people who were sworn to guard the forest along the forest's edge. Today was an exception. No one was present, for this was a very special day. As the Troguare scouting patrol moved randomly, there was one that had detected them as he happened upon their trail. He was not one of the Shadowed people but a stranger to the lands.

The forest kingdom was preparing for this anticipated ceremony—the marriage of the prince and his bride-to-be, their next potential queen. With all eyes back at the forest city Timberu, this allowed the Troguare patrol to venture deep without resistance.

Sitting high atop their beasts, the Troguare riders had extended their view. Seeing over the low-line trees and shrubbery, they looked for signs of a long-lost people their ruler hoped no longer existed.

While they traveled deeper into the dark forest, back in the city, Torran and his bride-to-be now stood before the king and queen. It was tradition that the prince would be married by the rulers of their people. Proudly standing before them, Torran could not keep his eyes off his future bride, who was doing the same.

Their love was deep, and it was difficult for them to imagine ever being apart. The king now stood before them with both families at their side as the whole of the forest people looked on. The king then spoke the words of matrimony as all stood silently and watched. "Torran, the son of the king, and Tiesh, the daughter of the house of Laiden, the name of her father's house, you shall be bonded this day with a lifelong oath under the eyes of God. From this day, you shall be as one."

The king then gave Torran a sharpened dagger as he made an incision in his palm, drawing his own blood. He then handed it to Tiesh, who also did the same. Grasping each other's hands, holding them firmly together, they allowed their blood to mingle, forming a bond that would last for life.

Torran then looked over at Tiesh and said, "With the bonding of our blood, we shall be as one." She then repeated those words with the same sincerity with both looking over to the king as he pronounced the sealing of their bond.

She then looked into his light-gray eyes, and he looked back into hers, which was a darker shade of gray, as they kissed. The crowds began to cheer throughout the courtyard, which erupted in the streets as they began their celebration.

The talishar people held Torran with great honor and respect, for he was of the same mold of the noble warriors that came before. For hours, the Shadowed people celebrated as the king and queen looked on.

Torran and his new wife joined in the celebration as they mingled among the crowds. For hours, they engaged in song and dance until it was time for the bride and groom to turn their attention solely on themselves.

After the celebration, the Shadowed people had a tradition that dated back to their early days in the forest. The husband and his bride would go on a five-day journey to the lands they so chose.

For a month, they would remain in solitude, bonding alone with each other before they would return. Taking all that they needed for the journey, they chose four of their hardiest ramsteeds, hooking them up to an enclosed wagon that would carry them to their destination. Both were anxious to begin starting their life together.

With people lined on the streets on both sides, thousands stood by cheering, seeing them on their way. They formed a path that led out to the direction they were to travel. With her arm locked with that of her husband's, they rode off to begin their journey.

Torran and his bride looked back at the crowd, waving as they headed out beyond the confines of the city.

Shortly before nightfall, a set of eyes lay hidden under the cover of the forest canopy. They were being watched and followed, but this did not escape the notice of the young Shadowed prince. Torran knew they were being watched and trailed. For three days and nights, he and his bride continued, only stopping to make camp on the way, until moving into a small clearing.

Suddenly, Torran jumped off the wagon and shouted, "Todus! Simone!" He repeated his words again. Tiesh looked at him and asked, "Who are you calling out to?"

Crashing from the woods, two enormous bears with huge saber teeth emerged from the forest. They were one of the most powerful and feared beasts in the forest, and they were both galloping straight toward them. Both a lighter shade of brown with long black powerful legs, each ran like that of a racer. Startled but unafraid, Tiesh reached back, grabbing hold of her swovel, quickly jumping off the cart and getting into her stance.

Though they normally do not engage in battle, Shadowed women, along with men, were trained from youth in the art of weaponry. With equal training, they had proven themselves to be just as deadly.

Torran looked over at her and laughed, then he said, "Lower your weapon. They will not harm you."

Looking at him as if madness had set into his mind, she replied, "How do you know this?"

Finding it amusing, he smiled and said, "Because I raised them from the time they were both cubs."

"You raised them?" she replied, puzzled by his response. The two massive bears were now up close on Torran. Affectionately they greeted him, knocking him to the ground. One was male; the other, female. The shebear stood nearly fifteen feet tall, while her brother was nearly ten feet higher. Each looked like black-masked bandits as they took turns rubbing their muzzles up against Torran while he lay there looking at Tiesh, smiling.

"Yes, I raised them," he responded. He then lifted himself off the ground, turning to face them. Now standing face-to-face with them, he then began rubbing the sides of their muzzles. Staring at them both, he looked over to the female and said, rubbing her nose, "This is Simone. She's my personal guard. When I travel the forest alone, she never leaves my side."

Simone then lay on the ground with her belly facing upward as Torran began to gently stroke her underside with her enjoying every minute of it. He then looked over to the big male bear and said, "This is her brother. His name is Todus. I call him the king of the forest. Everything gives way to him. Sometimes he likes to go his way for days on end alone. It's his way, but he's always there when I need him. They won't harm anyone unless they feel threatened."

While he explained, she looked on silently as she listened. "Their mother was killed defending them from Troguare scouts, four riders on their beasts. When they came up on their mother, I had been trailing the giants, watching and waiting to see where their paths would lead them.

"I lay hidden from view as I watched the mighty shebear rise up. And with a swipe of her claws, she split the skull of one of the rider's liborox, killing it instantly before doing the same to its rider with a second blow.

"She then repeated her actions against a second attack that ended with the same results before she herself was killed by the hurling of Troguare spears but not before wounding another of their beasts, causing its rider to fall to the ground.

"This was the first time I had witnessed the might of these bears and decided I would not let the cubs die. I then killed the remaining giants, along with their beasts. For the last four years, I raised and trained them in the forest, away from the city and the people."

Tiesh then said, "All this time had passed, did you not trust even me to share this with?"

Torran paused and replied, "You, I trust most of all, but I didn't want you to bear my secret knowing you would also fear for my safety. There is danger involved in caring for such powerful beasts, but they've never shown me any harm.

"I knew that my father would have been against it, along with that of my mother. I did what I did having no regrets. In all my days, I have not found more loyal companions." He then looked at her with a smile. "Until now," he said, looking her in the eyes.

"The memory of that day has never left them. The scent of Troguares and their liboroxes had been ingrained in their heads, along with the hate that goes with it. That is something we all share."

Tiesh then said, looking at Todus, "I've seen bears of this kind before in the forest, but never have I seen one of his size."

Torran smiled and said, "Nor have I." He then turned toward the two bears and said, "You cannot follow me today. Go back into the forest. Go!" He roared, pointing toward the trees. Reluctantly they turned and scampered off beyond sight into the heavy foliage.

Climbing back into the wagon, Tiesh looked over at Torran, surprised by their obedience. She became silent as she was amazed. Torran then smiled and said, "They've been well trained." They then continued their journey for another day before making their camp for the nightfall.

CHAPTER 34

Blood and Vengeance—a Warrior's Wrath

FOR THREE DAYS, Torran and Tiesh had journeyed far from their home. On the fourth day, they arose from their tent. Torran looked at his wife and said, "We are but a day away from reaching our place by the lake in which we have chosen."

"I can barely wait," Tiesh replied, "for you to hold me in your arms and make me feel complete. It is a desire that constantly burns inside me, an unquenchable fire." Hearing her words, Torran smiled and then moved closer to kiss her but stopped just a whisper away from her lips.

Suddenly, a frown formed across his face. She then asked, "What's the matter?" He then looked up, then around, then back at her and said, "We're being watched." Looking back at him, she asked, "Are you sure? I don't sense anything. Maybe they're your bears."

"No," he replied. "It's a scent in the air that I'm all too familiar with." He then reached and grabbed his foreblade from the cart, snapping it to his wrist before grabbing hold of his swovel.

In that instance, the ground began to tremble. A Troguare rider then emerged from the forest across the open field about a hundred yards away in full stride. Moments later, two more followed as they raced toward them. Looking at his wife, he said, "Stay here." As they were approaching, he shouted, "Stay here while I face them!"

"No," she responded. "I shall help you." Reaching back into the cart, she took hold of her swovel. Knowing she herself was a skilled fighter, as was all the people of the Shadows, nevertheless, he didn't want to risk any harm that might come to her.

With no time to argue, Torran quickly freed one of the ramsteeds from their cart and mounted it, then he chased off the others, preventing her from following him. Grabbing hold of his bridle, he looked back at her and shouted, "I will protect you!" He rode off to intercept them.

With his ramsteed in full gallop, he was fueled with the full fury of a true Shadowed Warrior. Twirling his swovel in his hand, his intent was deadly. With the riders driving their beasts toward him equally hard, each held their axes high over their heads, mirroring Torran's intent.

With one rider leading the way, he was well ahead of the others, pressing his beast. The Troguare was determined to be the one to bring the head of a Furrier to his masters in a sack, proving their existence in the hope that he would receive a reward for it.

Now only moments apart from each other, Torran extended his swovel outwardly to the side while he leaned forward, pressing his ramsteed even harder. As the two got closer, the rider's beast displayed its deadly arsenal of weapons—horns, teeth, and claws—a sight that would cause the bravest men to turn and flee.

The Shadowed prince was not fazed by any of this and was now but a few strides away before clashing. With the Troguare holding his ax, preparing to deliver his blow, Torran quickly jumped up in a standing-crouch position on his steed's back, showing unfathomable balance in full stride over uneven terrain.

Timing his jump mere moments from his adversary, Torran leaped from the back of his steed, taking flight with his momentum, carrying him toward his opponent as his steed drifted off, avoiding the claws and teeth of the Troguare beast. While in midair, he then grasped his swovel with both hands, arching his back as if it was a bow.

With both blades churning like a windmill, he swung it like an ax while in flight, slicing off the giants head as he passed by him. It was like a blur; it all happened before the giant could react. Landing on the ground in a tumble, Torran was quickly back on his feet. As the momentum continued to carry it forward, he was now at the rear of the liborox, as its rider fell from its back without his head being attached. Without hesitation or wasting a single thought, before the beast could turn and attack, Torran, with catlike agility and speed, ran and leaped on the back of the liborox before its momentum had ceased.

With the blades of his swovel spinning and with a twist of his wrist, he used its swirling blades, slicing the beast in the same spot twice with each blade, severing both bone and muscles in the back of its neck, leaving its head dangling, bloody, and with only a strip of flesh barely keeping it attached. Its blood continued pumping, resembling a fountain, before falling to the ground, joining its master's fate. The last two riders were now upon him.

Now on foot, Torran easily outmaneuvered both giants and their beasts, sliding under one of the beast and avoiding its deadly swing. Using his right arm, he thrust it upward, gutting it in return with his foreblade, causing its rider to fall.

Torran then quickly killed its rider before he could recover while the last of the rider circled, attempting to get in position to strike. Recklessly, the Troguare charged with Torran outmaneuvering the cumbersome beast as he had done with the others easily, avoiding its blows, along with the swing of its master's ax blades.

Quickly finding an opening, Torran immediately took advantage of it. Casting his swovel aside, he leaped high into the air, driving his foreblade deep into the liborox's forehead while avoiding its bite before the giant could place himself in position to swing his ax again. The momentum of the liborox falling forward also caused the giant to lose balance and lean forward over the top of its horn casing atop its skull, leaving the Troguare's head and neck exposed. In one motion, Torran spun and, with a powerful blow, separated the giant's head from its body as he had done to one of the riders before it.

Looking in the distance, seeing that Tiesh was safe, calm quickly came over him until six more riders emerged from the opposite side of the field, streaking toward him. They had yet to see Tiesh on the far side of the field. Their focus was on Torran, seeing their fallen comrades and their beasts scattered around him.

After seeing Tiesh was still safe, he braced himself for another attack. He took his stance—crouched with his left leg extended forward while also holding his swovel in front of him with his left hand and with the other having his foreblade reared back with its pointed tip directed toward the oncoming attackers.

The rider leading the charge was but a few strides away, but before he could engage Torran, two arrows streaked through the air seemingly from nowhere, finding their mark. They were but a few strides away when he and his beast tumbled and fell dead before reaching him.

Torran was confused as to what had just happened until he saw arrows embedded in both rider and his war beast. He didn't have time to think of where his help was coming or from what direction the arrows flew. All he knew was instead of facing six, there was one less to fight. Just as he was about to engage them, a hooded archer emerged from the forest on a black ramsteed streaking toward them. Immediately, the giants split their force—with two continuing their frontal assault on Torran, while the remaining three rode toward Kalee. There was a sudden gust of wind that blew the rider's hood backward, revealing Kalee's face with his locks blowing in the wind. He had been tracking the Troguare patrol since he came across their tracks, not long after he arrived in these lands.

Kalee himself had now become a wandering nomad without a home since the fall of his kingdom with the intent of killing any Troguare that crossed his path. He had been following this patrol with the intent of killing them all the moment the opportunity had arrived.

With a silver armored armguard glistening under the sun, he used this to lock his arm in place while holding a double-stringed bow. As the riders split to surround the archer, Kalee released another arrow into the eye of the oncoming beast of the rider leading the frontal charge directly in front of him.

As it fell, it threw its rider to the ground, making him hit his head on a stone and stunning him. His accuracy brought out a fear in them, causing the remaining two to become distracted and confused. At that moment, they spotted Tiesh by the tree, believing she would be an easier target.

Watching the events unfolding from a distance, she held her swovel ready, seeing that the two riders had altered their attack. Not seeing the woman in the distance, Kalee focused on the fallen giant who was attempting to gather himself after his fall.

Now on the attack, Kalee rode toward the giant to finish the task. With his back to where Tiesh was waiting for the assault on her, Kalee was still unaware of her presence and had yet to see her. Torran saw them both riding toward her but was unable to aid her as he had already engaged the Troguares who were before him. He furiously went on the attack. Being too fast and fluid, they were too slow for the agile warrior. Despite their size advantage, they couldn't match his strength. Physically, he was both stronger and faster.

Even their liborox were too slow to find their target. He needed to quickly end this. Quickly he killed one of the riders while crippling his liborox, all while avoiding the blows from the other rider and his liborox. Looking over, he saw the two riders gaining ground on where Tiesh was waiting. This had distracted him long enough to cause him to take a glancing blow from the paw of the liborox, knocking him to the ground, stunning him.

Meanwhile, Kalee was now up on the dazed rider who had just gotten to his feet in time for Kalee to ride past him with his sword drawn, slicing the giant's throat before he could raise his sword to protect himself.

Lying on the ground, Torran was still dazed as the beast rose up with its claws extended and its fang and tusk visible, ready to make the kill. When Kalee reached back, he pulled a slayer headed arrow from his sack in one motion, aimed, and released in what would equal a blink of an eye.

The arrow passed through the heart of the liborox and continued through it until embedding itself in the rider's heart as well. Both were dead before the liborox fell backward on top of its rider. While Kalee headed toward Torran, he was beginning to gather himself.

When Kalee arrived, he dismounted his steed and hurried to him. Before he arrived, Torran pointed to where his bride was standing. Kalee then quickly drew three of his arrows from his sack, spreading them apart and quickly aiming and releasing them.

With the arrows in flight, all three found their mark as the arrows struck nearly simultaneously. The first arrow dropped the beast of the first rider, sending it to the ground just before it arrived to where Tiesh was standing in wait while the other two arrows struck both the other rider and his liborox.

The arrow had wounded the rider instead of killing him. He had moved his body slightly by chance. The arrow had a slayer head attached that would've surely killed him, penetrating his thick armor and severing his spine. But it struck the back of his shoulder instead, easily penetrating the thick armor.

The third arrow struck the top of the shoulder of the beast he was riding as it bellowed out in pain. Fearful that the next arrow may very well find its mark, he broke off his attack and headed for the thick forest a distance away. Both were injured, but the rider's injury was far worse.

Looking back, seeing his beast lying still on the ground, with an arrow buried deep in the back of its neck, the rider that was with it had now left it and fled. He then turned his attention toward the woman.

Seeing that she was alone and unprotected, he thought of her as being easy for the taking. To his dismay, he found that even a woman of the Shadowed people was more than a formidable opponent.

Standing before her, the giant laughed and then said to her, "Before your mate can come to your aid, you will be dead." In the distance, Kalee had reached for another arrow, but he didn't have a clean shot. His view was hampered by the hanging tree branches and leaves that were around them.

Torran had finally gathered himself as both mounted Kalee's steed and hurried to aid her. In the distance, they could see the fleeing rider slumped forward on the back of his beast as it ran with a noticeable limp.

Meanwhile, the Troguare and Tiesh was standing face-to-face with each other as the giant took a step forward. Tiesh took her stance, with her leg back and her swovel slightly to the side, with its blades churning.

The giant found her to be amusing. He cast his ax to the side and removed his sword from his belt and held it to his side and then continued to move forward. Towering over her, he believed he would simply overpower and kill her.

She allowed him to get close before she leaped forward. Using her swovel, she drew first blood, taking off an ear, causing him to grimace in pain. He placed his hand where there was once an ear, with blood pouring down the side of his face. His reflexes barely saved him from a swift death as he moved slightly away from a blow that would have split his skull.

Now enraged, the giant swung his sword mightily, missing her badly. She rolled up under his sword, avoiding his blow that would have surely put her life to an end. Though his first attempt failed, her counterstrike did not. Spinning completely around with her swovel, she sliced him at the knees, causing him to drop down on all fours.

With her second move, she finished his struggle, twirling her swovel with both hands before extending it outward. And with an upward swing, using her left hand with its blades rotating, she cut his throat, causing him to fall forward onto his face. The battle ended so quickly Torran and Kalee had yet to arrive.

She was so focused on her opponent she was unaware that his liborox was not dead but badly wounded. Kalee's arrow caused it to temporarily go into shock, but it had just enough strength to come out of it and rise for one last kill. She was being stalked from behind by the ten-foot beast.

Furiously, Kalee and Torran raced toward her with Torran shouting her name repeatedly, trying to warn her. "Behind you!" he shouted. Kalee now in position, drew back and then released his arrow. Like Torran's warning, Kalee's arrow came too late. As she turned, the liborox was behind her as it delivered its blow, burying its claws deep within her, knocking her several feet backward before it succumbed to its injuries. Torran rushed to be by her side; his pain was apparent. If his face was a tablet, it would have been written all over his face. Torran reached down, lifting her into his arms while looking her in her eyes and calling out her name. Looking up at him, she was too weak to move. Kalee dismounted his steed and then walked over and stood behind them while looking around and making sure all was clear.

Bleeding badly, Tiesh looked into his eyes as she attempted to smile. With what remained within her, she lifted her arm. And with the palm of her hand, she placed it on the side of Torran's face, attempting to speak. Her eyes filled with tears. Torran gently lifted her, caressing her closely as life slowly began to fade.

Whispering into her ear, he told her how much he loved her with words that were barely a whisper. She replied, "I love you more, my husband." With her face grimacing in pain, along with blood streaming from the side of her mouth, she then said, "If only we could have had more time to share . . ." She paused to take another breath. She attempted to continue, but before she could finish her words, life had slipped away from her.

He called out her name, repeating it several times. But this time, there was no reply, for she was gone. Clutching her lifeless body close and tight, the fury in his heart began to mount, but he spoke no more words.

Torran roared and then turned his head as he watched the lone scout attempting to flee in the distance. It would've seemed impossible to strike the wounded scout with any weapons from that distance, but Kalee was no ordinary bowman. There was no other who was better. This time, it wasn't important to kill the liborox, only its rider. Placing the single arrow on his bow, one that was specially designed to kill giants, he drew it back with its double lines as far as he could stretch them.

Locking his armored armguard in place to give him stability, with the winds starting to pick up pushed by an approaching storm, a shot from that distance would be impossible even for him.

More than four hundred yards away with the target steadily moving farther and farther away from where he was standing, Kalee began to judge both wind and distance. Kalee took aim high into the sky and far to the left of his fleeing target. With great concentration, he released his arrows into its flight.

Torran looked on in amazement from a distance that was unimaginable. The arrow rode the wind as if guided by an unknown force before finding its target with dead-on accuracy, embedding this time in the center of the giant's back, just missing the spine by less than a hair. Already wounded, the giant slumped over even more before falling to the ground.

Now at the edge of the open grassland, his beast continued without its master. Just before it entered, Todus, the male bear, emerged from the forest's edge, intercepting it with a display of veracity.

Todus's attention was on the wounded liborox. Despite its injury, it had turned to face him. Lowering its horns, it attempted to charge the bear, but it was no match. Wounded or healthy, the results would still be the same, for the power of the huge saber bear was unmatched.

Rising to his feet, the twenty-foot behemoth attacked with a single downward blow to the top of the liborox's head, crushing its thick skull, causing its horns to buckle and snapping it like a twig.

Miraculously, the Troguare rider slowly rose to his feet despite having two of Kalee's arrows buried in his back. Painstakingly he reached down to pick up his ax that was lying on the ground where he had fallen.

With the male bear distracted, hovering over the liborox, making sure it was dead, the giant struggled to reach it to deliver one last blow for killing his companion. At that moment, Simone the shebear emerged from the woods. Hearing her snarl, the Troguare turned to see what was behind him, but he was too late.

With a single swipe, she knocked him to the ground as he dropped his ax and then took hold of him as she sank her teeth in him, ending his life.

Afterward, Kalee once again walked over to Torran and his wife, who had just died in his arms. In the distance, he could hear the thumping sounds of footsteps as the two bears galloped toward them.

Seeing the two bears approaching them, he quickly reached and grabbed two more arrows and quickly prepared to take aim. Torran gently laid Tiesh on the ground and then reached out and grabbed the end of the arrow, lowering Kalee's aim toward the ground just before he could release his arrows. Torran then said to him, "They are mine and shall not harm you. Stranger, I thank you for your aid. Who are you?"

Still with his eyes on the approaching bears, Kalee replied, "I am Kalee, prince and son of Abbah, king of the fallen Kingdom of Niejar—a land laid waste by these giants." Kalee then asked the furred warrior the same question.

Torran replied, "I am Torran, son of Aczar, the king of the Shadowed people. These woods are our home. Until this day, no one has ever journeyed this deeply within them. A day I shall never forget."

"Was this your wife?" Kalee asked.

Looking down at her lifeless body, Torran replied as he held back his emotions, "Yes, we had loved each other since we were children. She's was my first and only love. We had married only a few days ago, but our union only lasted four days. We were traveling to our place that we had chosen to consummate our marriage. That was the way of our people."

Staring down at her with unexplainable hurt etched in his eyes, he said, "Even though our time has been cut short, I shall continue our journey we set out to complete. There I will bury her by the lake, the place we once had journeyed when we were young. This was a place she so loved and made me promise that when we became of age, we would return to this place." Torran paused and then said, "Once I have laid my bride to rest, then I shall strike vengeance upon every giant I face with every breath I take. They will indeed feel my wrath."

Kalee then replied, "We both share the same sentiments. During the cover of night and heavy rains, they attacked and were at our doorsteps before a warning could be sounded.

"During the battle, my love, Tylah, was lost, along with most of my people. Those who survived were placed into bondage. They have taken everything from me, all that I had and all I have ever known. My land, my people, my kindred, all gone. And I was unable to protect them.

"While I fought, I watched my father fall, and I was helpless to aid him. The structure beneath me had collapsed, sending me tumbling to the ground where I awaken days later, buried under the rubble.

"When I freed myself, I found my parents dead, both my young sisters taken, my country destroyed. The woman I was to marry had been raped and murdered. With everything now gone, I left my lands behind to search for the only family I had left—that of my two sisters."

Torran then asked, "What brought you to this place, a land remote and wild?"

Kalee then replied, "In my quest to find them, my journeys have taken me to places I never knew existed—lands that were both wild and strange. I sought to find out if there were others that still knew the taste of freedom, which also brought me to this place. There is rumored to be only one such place, the kingdom of the lakes but it's a thousand miles from here.

"It wasn't until now through you that I find there is yet another. I had been tracking this Troguare patrol, awaiting nightfall to kill them all while they slept, starting with their war beasts. They kept on the move. It wasn't until now that I found out why. They must have picked up your trail and had begun tracking you. They had split up to extend their search. This is why their attack was staggered and not in a single force.

"My only regret was that I wasn't able to complete that task before this tragedy happened. I have witnessed much carnage and pain caused by these monsters, and I will kill as many of them as I can.

"I've tracked and killed many Troguare patrols. This was the largest I've seen to be so far away from their established lands." Kalee then looked at Torran and said, "I do not believe our paths have crossed by chance but by fate."

Seeing the rage in his eyes, Kalee looked at him and said, "Your anger is building in you. I know this because I have carried that same feeling in my heart since the fall of my people. The things I've seen are more than I can bear. My purpose has grown beyond that of my personal feelings or revenge, but one that is much broader.

"I've made an oath to myself that no longer shall I stay in the shadows, hiding, picking, and choosing where I'll extract my vengeance without my enemy even knowing that I exist. This is an oath I am determined to fulfill."

Torran looked at him and asked, "What would that be?"

Looking the Furrier in his eyes, Kalee responded, "Freeing the bonds of man and all those enslaved by the Troguare giants. Uniting them all is now my purpose while seeking to find my two sisters. Creating an army of one people with one mind trained in the art of killing giants, ending the reign of Obizar, turning his empire into ruins.

"In my travels, I have witnessed the harsh treatment and cruelty under his reign—women raped to death, children broken and discarded by their brutish owners, but worst of all, the consumption of human flesh. Their cities and village reek with the stench of it. These things must end, for I can bear it no longer."

CHAPTER 35

A Tale of Woe in the Shadow of Truth

TORRAN LOOKED AT Kalee and said, "The story of Obizar I know well. It has been taught to us from generation to generation." Kalee listened with interest in what Torran had to say.

"We, too, were once a great kingdom of the Central Plains at the edge of the Wasteland Desert a thousand years ago. From beyond the wastelands, they came. Their origins to this day are still unknown, arriving onto our borders with the intent of conquering our people and taking our lands, a mistake that had been made a few times before to the dismay of all who tried.

"Obizar believed that we could easily be defeated but learned that he was mistaken. He believed his attack would be one of surprise, but to his surprise, he found our armies already prepared to greet him, led by our greatest king that they so named Norval the Great.

"He was the last of the true kings that ruled under the name Talishar. He and his army brought Obizar and his forces to the brink of defeat, driving them back into the great wastelands from which they came.

"It was said that Obizar's forces were so great in number that it stretched across the horizon. With Norval's forces only a fracture of his numbers, he reduced the giants' army to a little more than a third.

"Only a sparse number of our warriors lost as Norval slaughtered the Troguares in droves. Rather than accepting defeat, it was then that we learned the true nature of the evil warlord, as well as the power he possessed. The dark wizard called down the power of the darkness onto our people, summoning a three-faced demon named Kreel, along with its winged hordes of flesh eaters, to fall upon my people.

"Not of this world, their power was too great to overcome. No weapons could stop them nor could they be killed. There was nothing our people could do but fight to the very last.

"Facing our inevitable end, it had been taught to us that something strange then happened. No one knew the answer as to why, but for reasons unknown, the demon ceased his attack and returned from whence it came.

"In their wake, Norval lay dying and our people nearly wiped from existence. Cyris, the son of Norval, who fought by his side, miraculously survived when his father died in his arms.

"Gathering what remained of our people, he led them to these lands far away from our home and away from the Troguare's advance, making a decree that has lasted to this day in which our people would never again fall subject to such evil. We then retreated deep within the Shadowed Forest, never to be seen by any other again. We now stand as a forgotten people.

"In the aftermath, it was believed the Talishar was no more, but Obizar was not satisfied. It was that day the Troguare king learned the meaning of fear and was determined to put that fear to rest.

"He sought evidence that my people still exist, though to this day, we remain hidden and unseen. You are the first outsider to see a Shadowed people face-to-face. Despite this, he continues his search for our existence throughout centuries. We were the only people to have defeated him before the darkness came and drove us away."

Kalee then said, "During my travels, I learned that Obizar has been around longer than anyone can remember, an answerless riddle that no one knows the answer to but Obizar himself. What is the secret of his immortality? Was he born as such?"

Torran looked at him and said, "Maybe the answer lies within his sorcery, or maybe it does not. Only he knows his secret."

Kalee then looked at Torran and said, "That may be an answer that no one will ever know. That no longer holds any value, but what does is that he will not live forever. It is his end that I shall see that I will make come to fruition."

Torran then asked, "Will you join me in burying my wife?"

Kalee looked back at him and replied as he extended his hand, "It would be my honor." Torran then reached over as they grasped each other's forearms as they shook firmly.

This began a bond of brotherhood between both warriors. Torran then said, "After I have buried my wife, I will go to my father and ask him to break the oath that has been kept through the centuries.

"We have lived in the shadows like rodents in the night, bearing the fears of our fathers, for far too long. It is time that we walk into the light once more, turning our rage into war against our longtime foe." He then turned to Kalee and said, "You are welcome to return to my home with me. No one has ever seen our forest kingdom." The two warriors were now bonded together like brothers, both sharing the same hatred for the wizard king as well as his Troguare empire.

The two warriors journeyed to the lake where they buried Torran's bride while traveling alongside them were the two bears. Torran shared with Kalee how he had raised them from cubs and that they were now his faithful companions.

The two were like spirits, both suffering deep wounds. Upon arrival at to the forest city, Torran was determined to ask his father to end the ancient vow and aid in the struggle against Obizar and the Troguare Empire.

It had now been twelve days since Torran and his wife had left for their destined journey. He had now returned to the city with his wife absent and unexpectedly along with an unknown stranger. This had broken an unwritten law that had been in place since they had made this forest their home. As they entered the city, the Shadowed people looked on, pondering his early return without his wife, along with being accompanied by a stranger.

It was an unspoken law that the Shadowed people remain to all as a myth. Upon their arrival, a messenger had already informed the king that his son had arrived and was without his wife. He also informed him that he was not alone and was accompanied by a stranger.

As the king came out to meet him, Torran bowed in respect to his father, as did Kalee out of respect for his title as ruler. Approaching them both, the king looked at his son and then at Kalee and said, "My son, why have you returned so quickly, and where is Tiesh, your wife?" The king then looked at Kalee and asked, "Who is this, and why did you bring a stranger among us? It is the most ancient of our unwritten laws forbidding anyone that is not of our people to be brought among us. You have been taught this from the days of your youth."

"Father, may I speak?" Torran replied.

The king then replied, "You may."

"On the fourth day of our journey, we were ambushed by Troguare scouts deep within our lands. They entered the forest during the ceremony when all eyes had returned to witness it.

"On the way to our wedding place of consummation, we were ambushed by their scouting patrol. During the battle, Tiesh was killed though she killed one of their riders during the encounter."

Looking at Kalee, Torran then said, "This man came to our aid but was too late to help save her. He fought along with me with the skills of an archer I had never seen before, finding his target from distances one would deem impossible to find."

The king grew silent and then looked at Kalee and asked, "Stranger, who are you?"

Kalee stepped forward proudly and said, "I am Kalee, prince of the Niejar, son of King Abbah and Queen Aniyah, my mother." He spoke with great pride.

The king then replied, "The Niejar, yes, but now it has fallen. Before the giants came, it wasthe kingdom beyond the great Center Mountains."

"Yes," Kalee replied. "You've heard of it being that it's so far away."

Aczar replied, "If you keep your ear to the ground, there are many things in this world one can learn."

Torran then stepped to his father and said, "For generations without end, the Troguares have searched the lands seeking our presence so that they may once again seek to wipe us from existence. Like deer hiding in the woods, we flee and scamper whenever they come looking. Occasionally, we wipe them away so that we can hide once again safely for another day. Now they came once again, but this time, they found us, killing my wife before meeting their end.

"My heart has now been shattered, and now the only thing I see is rivers of Troguare blood flowing across the land by the rotating blades of my swovel. My wife is now dead. The next time it may be our entire people.

"I've grown weary hiding in the forest, hoping not to be discovered. The time has come to face them. Therefore, I come to you, Father, asking that you break our ancient vow. The rule of a madman has lasted for centuries and must not be allowed to go on. How many lives have been lost because of his hunger for power and his ruthlessness to obtain it?"

Speaking passionately, he continued, "While we sit here in hiding, how many more shall have to suffer, be tormented, and be tortured under his rule?"

King Aczar then stepped forward, looking into his son's eyes, then said, "We have not concealed ourselves because of fear of any man or giant. There isn't a sword or an army on this planet that can withstand our might. We face an evil that is determined to destroy us—one that we cannot fight.

"Obizar has the power to summon a foe that cannot be killed or stopped. We came to this place to preserve our race. The evil sorcerer released the hounds of darkness upon us once and will not hesitate to do so again if faced with defeat.

"He will never relinquish his power even if it means the destruction of an entire world. So I say to you, my son, that it does grieve me, the loss of your bride. The tragedy that has befallen you, along with that of our people, under the dark lord's rule brings an unmeasurable rage in my heart.

"The very thought vexes me without words, as does the fate of all the lives that he has affected. But I will not risk our existence on revenge or a futile attempt to restore order based on the power of our swords.

"The defeat of Obizar without being able to balance the evil that will follow, all we know or ever will know will be lost forever. For this cause, the answer must be no."

The disappointment fermented firmly on Torran's face. The Shadowed prince then looked over at Kalee as he held back his words. Kalee then said to him, "I have received all that was said by your father. Though being both noble and wise, I have to disagree within my heart. Your father has spoken with the breath, as well as the strength of your people, but the one who could speak to me, life has already been taken from him. This leaves me to make my decision unaided." Kalee looked into the eyes of king Aczar and said, "It is better not to exist at all in my world than to be under the constant suffering under the rule of a giant whose heart is as black as night. I am, therefore, compelled to do what I must. I will stay for the night if you so allow and leave these lands without memory of it."

The king then replied, "For aiding my son, you have my deepest gratitude, and you are welcome to make our land your home if you so wish."

Kalee then replied, "Your hospitality is most gracious and welcomed. Your offer is almost too tempting to resist, but I will have to decline the latter. My destiny lies beyond these lands, not to be hidden among you or waiting within the shadows of this forest.

"With respect and gratitude, great king, I must follow my own path. I have made a promise that runs deep within me—to defeat the evil that is Obizar and find my two sisters." Kalee then paused, looking the king in the eyes, and said, "Or die in the wake of it. I will have to refuse your gracious and generous offer. My word is my bond, and my honor is in my name. Your secret will always be safe, and the words we have shared today will never be spoken again."

Looking at Torran, he said, "Goodbye, my friend, I will stay the night and leave at the first sunrise." He then looked at Aczar and said, "Farewell, great king of the Shadows." He bowed his head before turning and walking away.

Torran then said boldly to Kalee, "No, wait!" Kalee paused. Torran then turned back to his father, greatly disappointed, and said, "I, too, shall depart in the morning along with my friend. I share his thoughts and, with them, the destruction of the Troguare Empire. In my heart, we have remained hidden much too long, and I must follow my heart, which leads me away from these lands and my people in whom I truly love." With those words, he, too, bowed and walked away as the king stood silent, contemplating every word that was spoken.

As promised, at the rise of the first sun, Kalee mounted his ramsteed, along with Torran at his side. They began their journey away from the Land of Shadows. Beyond the security of the Shadowed Forest, the world was like an open doorway leading to a vast and hostile world. The two warrior princes each had separate beginnings, but they both shared the same fury in their hearts and the same goal—the destruction of the Troguare Empire and putting an end to Obizar's reign forever while setting the people free. They headed west into the unknown.

To be continued.

INDEX

M

mal-lace, 10, 12–14, 90–91, 106–8
Mautaur Valley, 61, 68–70, 72, 78
Menoria, 225, 242
Mighty Brims, 3, 248
Mines of Death, 243

N

Northern Mountains, 30–31, 33, 69, 79, 96
Norval the Great (Talishar king), 24, 35–38, 47–54, 57–59, 61–64, 66–67, 69, 72–84, 95, 99, 101–2, 104–6, 108, 110–23

O

Obizar (Troguare king), 10–20, 25, 28–29, 84–85, 87–93, 101, 103–9, 111–19, 121–22, 126–33, 135–40, 142, 201–2, 209, 222, 225, 227, 233, 235–36, 241, 248, 250, 269, 273, 277
Odarr (Westland king), 5–7, 9–13
Olieria (Kalee's sister), 193, 208, 211, 213
Olivia (Shadowed queen), 252
Orchard (Norstar king), 174, 179, 181
orophyx, 147, 154, 166
Orthimar (leader of the mercenaries), 143–46, 152

P

Pricillica (Talishar queen), 35, 47–52, 61–62, 64–65, 82, 97, 117, 124

R

realms
Darkness, 3, 18
Living Light, 2–3
Rexthor (Norstar general), 175, 179, 181
Rolo (Troguare commander), 20, 85, 93, 126–27

S

Sanulites, 30, 32, 34–37, 39–41, 53–63, 65, 68–75, 78, 80–81, 96
scepter of the light, 3
Shadowed Forest, 123, 125, 127, 277
Shadowed Warriors, 127, 251, 259
shape-shifters, 30, 32, 68, 72
Simone (shebear), 256, 267
Slyth (Sanulite commander), 32–34, 40, 42–43, 45, 70–71, 74–75
Soya (Sanulite king), 30, 32–33, 39–45, 53, 68, 70–72, 74–75, 78
Stoned Forest, 34, 36, 38, 45
meeting at, 39
swovel, 26, 30–31, 54, 56, 65–66, 75–78, 81–82, 96, 106, 108, 119–21, 251, 255, 258–62, 264, 275

T

Talishar, 25–26, 29–34, 38, 42–43, 45–47, 53, 61–62, 64, 66–75, 77–78, 80–82, 93–94, 96, 98, 100–102, 104–7, 109–16, 122, 126–28, 271–72
Theor (Talishar commander), 36–38, 51, 53–55, 57–60, 63–64, 67–68, 74–76, 78–80, 82

thoggs, 230

Three-Valley Pass, 130–31, 142, 174, 189, 225, 248

Tiesh (Torran's wife), 252, 254–55, 257–58, 260–65, 267

Todus (bear), 257, 266

Torrad (Talishar king), 30, 32, 54

Torran (Aczar's son), 251–69, 271–77

Triclores, 144, 146–54

Troguares, 10, 17, 22, 104, 106, 112, 114, 116, 118, 126–30, 175, 181–82, 203–6, 213, 223, 228–30, 233, 235, 243, 247, 260, 262, 271–72, 275

Troxus (Troguare general), 133, 174, 222, 227–30, 233–36

Tybrus (Pricillica's father), 50–53

Tylah (Kalee's lover), 190–91, 211

Tyrus, 2–3, 15, 45, 60, 122, 130, 199, 221, 226

U

Ultur (Westland general), 5–7, 9, 11

W

Wanderlings, 147, 154–57, 160, 242

wantu, 187

Wasteland Desert, 16, 18, 30–33, 51

Western Brims, 10, 15, 18

whippit, 217–18, 231–32, 234

Z

Zhorr (Troguare general), 133, 174, 177, 179, 236

Zorrax (Talishar commander), 69